THE SHADOW RYANA

By

C. R. Daems

The Shadow Ryana
Copyright © 2012 by C. R. Daems

Version 1 of *The Shadow Ryana* was published in June 2012
Version 2 of *The Shadow Ryana* was revised in November 2013
Version 3 of *The Shadow Ryana* was revised in July 2014

ISBN-13: 9781481057882

Check out all our novels at:
Talonnovels.com

TABLE OF CONTENTS

MAP of HESLAND

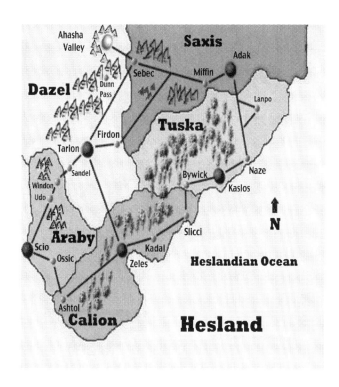

CHAPTER ONE

Dunn Pass—Dazel Province

I crouched on the gray, rock-laden ground, chickens squawking and my head throbbing with pain. My father stared down at me. His face twisted in anger, fist clenched inches from my face and nostrils flared as he sucked air to yell again. He was a small, thin man with leathery skin from long days in the sun, brown, scraggly hair, and a haggard face.

In my short life, he had taught me terror. It infested every fiber of my puny body. I wanted to run but lacked the strength. Besides, where would I run? No one in the village would help me. My father was an elder.

The area around Dunn Pass was rocky and the soil poor. The land fought the crops and barely supported the village goats. They would protect the goats but not me.

"Curse you, Ryana. That food is for the chickens, not to be wasted on a girl-child. We can't eat you. Work and you can have the scraps, otherwise leave." His chest expanded as he sucked in air to yell again. I tried to scramble backward to avoid another blow but collapsed after a few feet—tired, hungry, and weak. As he turned and stalked away, mumbling, the chickens returned to me. I could feel their hunger.

No one cared what I did so long as I took care of my chores. My father and brother were gone all day, tending the village herd of goats. In the mornings I swept the floors clean of yesterday's dirt and droppings, fetched water from the village well, fed our few chickens, and collected their eggs. Afterward, I was free until my mother began preparing the evening meal.

I carefully made my way around the village to a rocky area of shrubs and small trees, nourished by a shallow stream that appeared after a rain, and settled down near a clump of shrubs so I couldn't be seen. I had just sat when I sensed a rabbit near and felt its hunger. I picked a few small leaves from above my head and mentally coaxed it to me.

It came willingly and nibbled the leaves, grateful for even this small meal. If I had been my brother, I would have killed the rabbit for the dinner table. My father thought him a good son. He thought me worthless. If he knew I hadn't tried to catch the rabbit, he would have beaten me bloody. I was starving, but I couldn't kill an animal that had done nothing to me.

A shadow crept over me. Whoever it was had approached as silently as a feather on the wind. The rabbit ran. I shut my eyes and sat trembling, arms around my thin legs and head down, awaiting the first blow.

"What's your name, child?" a woman's soft voice asked.

Terrified, I squeezed my eyes partially open and looked up. A scream stuck in my throat. Her head and face were covered in black so that only her gray-green eyes were visible. They pinned me to the ground. A tall and thin woman, compared to the village women, she was dressed in black.

A dead ancestor had come to punish me for not thinking of my family.

I tried to scramble backward but a bush stopped me. Its thorns dug into my back and neck. Although it felt like a thousand needles had pierced my skin through the thin rags I wore, I made no sound. She didn't move.

"Can you call the rabbit back to you?"

I could but wouldn't. No matter what she did to me, I wouldn't hurt it. Feeling no anger from her, I breathed a small sigh of relief. She turned to her horse and got something out of a saddlebag. Reaching down, she handed me a piece of bread.

"I'll not hurt you or the rabbit. The food is for you to share. A reward for humoring me. The rabbit's very hungry."

Looking at the bread, my mouth watered. I broke off a piece for the rabbit and held the other piece toward her, unsure how much she would let me have. I was hungry, too.

"Yes," she said. Her voice gentle, but her eyes sad. I mentally searched for the rabbit. When I found it, I coaxed it to me with the promise of food. Trusting me, it came and nibbled the bread from my hand.

"Eat, child," she said. I stuffed my mouth full and gulped the bread down.

The woman reached down, pulled me to my feet, and hand-in-hand walked me back to the village. I didn't know what to expect, but I knew I was in trouble. It seemed to be my destiny. For the thousandth time, I wished I had been born a boy-child. As we entered the village, the people scrambled away or disappeared into their huts.

They were afraid!

"Which is your house?"

I pointed to my father's small mud and stone house. To my amazement, the men had left the herd and were returning to the village. They maintained a cautious distance from her.

They were afraid of a woman!

"Who owns this girl-child?" Her voice rang loud and clear. She showed no fear.

My father shuffled forward a few feet, keeping his distance and looking ready to run. His posture mimicked mine when I thought him angry and a beating sure to follow.

The woman was a God!

"I…I do, Mistress."

"Do you intend to sell her at the market next cycle?"

"Yes, Mistress." A small smile touched his lips. "Do you want her, Mistress?"

The woman stared at him without saying a word. He shuffled back, head down, and eyes fixed on the ground.

"You'll only get a few coppers. She's scrawny and weak and will require extra food to make her worth anything. I'd be doing you a favor to take her. You should pay me."

He nodded agreement but said nothing. I felt sorry for him being embarrassed in front of the whole village. He was a harsh man, but I was only a girl-child. It sent shivers through me knowing I would be sold to this woman or at the market next summer.

Why had I been born a girl-child?

"How much?"

"Four coppers?" He continued to look toward the ground, his voice a whisper. The God said nothing as she dropped four coppers from her hand. A cloud of dirt and dust rose as each coin hit the ground. She remained silent, but I felt her calling something. Everyone scrambled to get out of the way as a silver-gray wolf entered the village followed by a black stallion. When the two reached the woman, the horse stopped, and the wolf sat. I sensed its readiness to defend the God.

I stared at the horse, thinking it would bolt any minute with the wolf so close and no one holding its reins. But it remained calm.

A hush hung over the village as she lifted me easily and placed me on the horse. I sat still and held my breath; afraid I might fall off or spook the horse. If I did, it would run off to only the gods knew where. She placed a foot in the stirrup and swung up behind me. As we left the village, my heart pounded. I had heard whispered stories of what happened to girls who had been sold at the market. I wanted to cry but feared she would beat me. I wished I were dead.

CHAPTER TWO

Ahasha Valley—Dazel Province

The woman took me to where the gods lived. I had my own room, a straw sleeping mat, two sets of clothes, and warm blankets. Best of all, I had plenty to eat. The gods wore head wraps that covered their faces and left only their eyes showing. Even their bodies were hidden in their long-sleeved shirts and baggy pants.

We were being taught to read and write, but the lines meant nothing to me. They looked like chicken scratches in the dirt—all the same but different. I had been here two seasons—twelve sixdays—and had only memorized the meaning of a few scratches and frequently got those mixed up. The other five girls were well ahead of me. I knew I would be rejected if I couldn't learn their meanings. In desperation, I worked well into each night. Then, too exhausted to continue, I fell into bed and cried until dawn. Although the youngest, I knew that wouldn't matter.

"Ryana, what's this symbol?" The god Alica asked.

"A hut," I said, hoping I had guessed right.

"It represents a tree." She was a small woman compared to the other gods. Dressed in the traditional clothing of the gods, only her light-colored skin, friendly blue eyes, and thin brown eyebrows showed, which were more prominent when she frowned—like now.

"It doesn't look like one." I sobbed in frustration. I had failed and would be made to leave. A tear slid down my cheek. She sighed.

"What should it look like?"

I brushed my sandbox smooth and carefully drew a tree with branches and added a couple of leaves. "Like that, Mistress."

"Yes, that's a nice tree. In the long ago past, people drew their trees like that. But it took too long to draw so they trimmed it like this." She drew what sort of looked like my tree but did not. "Because that was still too slow to draw, they trimmed it more and then more, until it looked like the symbol you see." Each time, the new symbol had fewer lines.

I looked hard at the scratches. As I stared, they unraveled into a beautiful tree. Then I imagined shrinking the tree back into the symbol before me. Mistress Alica watched me for a long time. When I said nothing, she shook her head.

"Yes, the tree you drew was nice. I'll assume its leaves are green. Now draw me a tree in the fall when the leaves are turning yellow and red."

"I've no colors," I shouted in frustration.

"Now you see the problem. We must use symbols to describe the world around us. This is the symbol for red and this for yellow." Her stick cut the sand into two symbols. I stared at them. As I did, they began to glow—one red and the other yellow. Like the tree, I saw what it represented—not the scratches. I smiled as she left to help another girl.

Each night, I used the light from my candle to study and draw the symbols the god Alica had introduced that day. As I drew each symbol, I could envision it expanding into the thing it represented, and a new and wonderful world opened to me. I could draw the symbol for a tree and then turn the leaves red, green, or yellow. Best of all, I could see the tree changing colors.

Late one night, my candle went out, and there was too little left to light. I shivered in fear. My father had told me often how everything cost more than I was worth. I stayed awake all night, worrying what would happen in the morning. I rose at dawn and carried what remained to the god Alica.

"I'm sorry, Mistress," I said. My hand trembled as I held out what was left of the candle. I deserved a beating.

"Did you forget to blow it out?"

"No, Mistress…I…used it at night…to study," I stammered. She turned and walked back to one of the huts. I stood there shaking, not knowing what to expect. Had she gone to get the senior god? To my astonishment, she returned with a large candle.

"Here, Ryana. Don't work too late into the night. You need your rest; otherwise, you'll be too tired to pay attention in the day." I cringed as her hand moved toward my head to pat it—a reflexive reaction from my many beatings. Her eyes looked sad, but she said nothing.

One morning, four seasons—a half-cycle—later, the god Alica came with several pieces of dried animal skin, a bowl with a black liquid, and a brush. She drew a beautiful symbol on the skin, which I recognized as a tree. She then dipped the skin in water and the symbol disappeared. When the skin dried, she drew another symbol on it—more magic from the gods.

I struggled to copy each symbol perfectly, going over each line several times to get the shape to look like hers. She made it look so simple.

"No, Ryana." She took my hand in hers and twisted it to make the lines flow and change shape like hers. Several strokes and it was done. Night after night, I practiced until my symbols looked something like the ones I had learned that day. It was slow work because I had to wait for the skin to dry after each symbol disappeared in the water. Frustrated, I made the symbols smaller so that I could squeeze more onto my small piece of skin. It took a lot of practice to get them smaller but was worth it. A cycle later, I could draw ten symbols before I had to wash them away. I began to make up short stories—a hawk flying high in the clouds, a wolf running through trees… Now that I could see what the symbols represented; the stories came alive.

When I had been there two cycles of seasons, Mistress Alica approached us with several large pieces of skin. "Today I want you to make up a short story about a hawk that left Ahasha Valley and flew to one of the five provinces. You're to write the story on your skin. You must finish today." She handed one large skin to each of us and walked away.

Mistress Alica returned as the sun began to set. When I looked up, the blue sky and puffy white clouds of the morning were now streaked with brilliant shades of orange and shadows stretched across the valley floor. I sat holding my breath as she scanned each of our skins.

"Leila, you finished, and your symbols are adequate."

"Ana, you failed to finish and your symbols illegible. We'll place you with a family who will teach you a profession."

"Zaria, you finished, and your symbols are very good."

"Jelena, you finished, but your symbols need work."

"Maja, you finished but many of your symbols are wrong. Like Ana, you'll be placed with a family to learn a profession."

The meaning was clear—you cannot stay here. A cold shiver passed through me. It had been a test. If I failed...I would have to leave.

"Ryana," She stopped and scanned my skin for a long time. "You failed to finish on time."

I couldn't stop shaking and bile rose in my throat. I had failed and would be sent away.

"Tomorrow I want you to finish the story." She handed Ana's skin to me. She looked at my skin again before handing it back. I had heard her say that Ana had failed to finish and would have to leave. I returned to my room in turmoil. I washed Ana's skin clean, determined to finish tonight. Maybe the god Alica would consider that when she judged me tomorrow. It took several tries before my hand stopped shaking enough to draw a decent symbol. Toward dawn, I went back to the class area and sat, waiting for her to return.

Much later in the morning, she appeared. She took my skin and spent a long time examining it.

"You spent all night doing this, didn't you?" She stared down at me, shaking her head slowly. My response stuck in my throat, but before I could answer, she continued. "Stop shaking, child. You passed. Next time I say in the morning, I mean in the morning. I want you to go to bed and sleep until you're rested. Then return to me. I mean it—to bed." She turned and walked away. I wanted to dance and sing, but the god Alica had told me to go to bed, so I did.

* * *

Shortly after I entered the teaching yard later that day, the god Alica and the senior god, Morag, approached. She walked without making a sound or leaving a mark on the ground. From what I could see of her face, she had smooth, cream-colored skin like I imagined the nobility. Her green eyes scanned the area as she walked toward me. I began to tremble. The senior

10

god never met with the younger children, but she was coming to talk to me.

"How did you do it, Ryana?" Morag asked. "Sister Alica told me that you were the slowest student in her class. She felt certain you wouldn't pass the test. Yet, this story is beautiful and your symbols adequate. For their small size, they are more than adequate."

"Mistress Alica showed me the secret," I said, feeling less afraid now that she said she liked what I had done.

"I did?" Alica said and shook her head like she didn't believe me.

"Yes, Mistress. You showed me how to unfold the symbols into beautiful pictures."

"What do you mean?" Morag asked.

"When I see the symbols, they become the things they are. When I look at the symbol for a tree, it becomes a beautiful green tree. When I see the symbols for a red tree, I see the leaves change from green to red. The symbols come alive."

"The wonders of youth," Morag said. "You're doing well, child."

* * *

The next day, the god Alica introduced us to the god Sanda. She was taller and looked thinner than god Alica. Her eyes were almond shaped, and the skin around them had a pale-yellow tint. Before she spoke, her brown eyes inspected each of us in turn. I shivered as her eyes fell on me. I didn't know what to expect.

Would she consider me worth keeping? My father sold me because he thought me not worth feeding.

"Girls, you've completed the first phase of your training—reading and writing. During this phase, you'll study the people, customs, major trade items, and leaders of the five provinces of Hesland. You'll learn to cook, recognize edible and poisonous plants, and be given a sixday free each season to find an animal friend."

It sounded like each of us had an animal friend, somewhere. Our job was to find it. Although I didn't understand, I enjoyed the free time to wander the valley.

The gods' village lay in a dead-end canyon, surrounded by rugged mountains. The entrance to the village ran through a narrow valley rich in grasses, bushes, and trees fed by small streams from the surrounding mountains. The cycle-long runoff produced a river that ran through the center of the valley and supported a large variety of wildlife. In addition to the ever-present population of small animals, birds of prey, wildcats, and wolves roamed the valley. Many made it their home while others strayed in from the open plains beyond.

On my free sixday, I walked the entire valley, climbed into the lower regions of the mountains, and explored the river. Although I could sense the feeling of many of the animals and birds, none seemed inclined to be my friend. They visited only for the tidbits I carried and out of curiosity. I was always sorry to see each sixday end.

A half-cycle passed, and I still didn't understand what I was supposed to accomplish. The gods expected something—another test. Eventually, I worked up enough courage to ask the god Sanda.

"Mistress, I don't understand what I'm supposed to do. I know I'm not given free time each season to have fun," I said, hoping she wouldn't punish me for… The gods had never punished me, but my past made me uncertain and fearful of everything.

"Finding an animal familiar," she said as if that explained everything. She didn't feel mad, but she didn't explain. As I stood there confused and not knowing what to say, a hawk glided down and landed on her outstretched arm. She lifted it to her shoulder and smiled.

"Thank you, Mistress." I now understood. I was looking for a life companion, like the god Sanda's hawk. I understood, but that didn't help me to find one.

Four more seasons passed without success. If I failed this test, it would end my stay with the gods. On my next free period, I felt too sad to search. I made my way up a small trail into the crags, where I sat, expecting nothing but hoping for a miracle. As the sun went down, hundreds of bats exploded out of a nearby cave. I couldn't resist looking inside. The cave's entrance was small and narrow, but once inside, the dim light revealed a huge, eerie cavern bathed in shadows. The stone floor swam in bat droppings, and the pungent air stung my nose, made my eyes water, and sent my head spinning. It took several minutes before my eyes adjusted to the dim light. When they did, I saw that a few bats remained in the crags of the walls and on the ceiling.

Maybe, like me, they were too depressed to look for food.

My world looked to be ending. The only question—when?

Turning to leave, I nearly stepped on two tiny bats squirming in the droppings. I picked them up. They stank and I almost dropped them. I didn't want to see them die, but…how could I nurse a baby bat, and should I? I had heard the Ahasha bats fed on blood and had a poison that could paralyze and kill. Handling them could be dangerous, but I couldn't bring myself to leave them to die.

I held them under a trickle of water running down one of the cracks to wash off the dirt. I had nothing with me to feed them, so I put them inside my shirt and walked back to the compound. At dinner, I saved a few drops of milk. Back in my room, I pricked my finger with a thorn for some blood to mix with the milk. With a thin spine of a thistle plant, I fed them a drop at a time, hoping I was doing the right thing. For the next several days, I spent my free time nursing them. They didn't die, which made me happy!

Unfortunately, I had no place else to keep them but my room, which I scrubbed daily trying to keep the pungent odor down. I failed.

"Ryana, what's that smell coming from your room? You're supposed to clean your room and clothes daily. We won't tolerate filth." The god Sanda opened my door and stepped back, scanning the room from the doorway. Everything was spotless—except for the latest droppings.

"Bats?"

"Yes, Mistress. I found them on my last free sixday. If I hadn't nursed them, they would've died. I'll let them go as soon as they are able to fly. Please. Or else they'll die." I could tolerate the smell if it meant they would live. I was torn apart. I didn't want to be asked to leave, but I didn't want the bats to die. The god Sanda stared at me for a long time.

"What do you feed them?" she asked, her forehead furrowed in a frown.

"I've been feeding them a little milk and blood," I said, while looking at the floor. She appeared to be waiting for me to say more. I feared what was to come next, but the gods hated lies. "Sometimes I get blood from a goat and sometimes they feed on me."

She knelt and held me by my shoulders. "Ryana, you're the only person in this village who would nurse Ahasha bats, and worse, let them feed off you. Child, they are dangerous."

"Please, Mistress. I don't want them to die."

14

She rose. "Until they can fly, sleep in the barn. Perhaps the animals can tolerate the smell. Besides, they need blood—preferably not yours."

I moved to the shed, which everyone seemed to avoid. The god Sanda gave me the chore of feeding, cleaning, and caring for the goats. Over the next few days, the bats took short flights around the shed and fed off the animals. But unlike regular bats, they slept on me—in my hair, inside my shirt, or in the crook of my arm.

To my great relief, none of the animals appeared harmed by the bats' feedings. One night several sixdays later, they flew out of the shed and off into the night. Relieved, I began moving my belongings back to my room, only to find they had returned during the night. I stayed in my room that night. I was sure they would leave for good—soon. It would break my heart, but it would please everyone else. I couldn't help feeling that I would be asked to leave if I couldn't make them go and spent sleepless nights trying to solve my dilemma. Several days later, the god Morag entered the shed while I was cleaning the floor.

"Well, Ryana, you've again bewildered us. First by the beautiful story you wrote, when Sister Alica thought you would fail, and now by adopting bats. Something no one else would dare do." She looked at the bats, which were hanging from my shirt. So did the aging hawk sitting on her shoulder. A tear rolled down my cheek. I had worked night and day to stay, and now I would be asked to leave because I saved two bats. But I couldn't have done anything different. I felt like dying. "You need to learn the skills the other children are learning if you're to stay with us. We'll find a way for you to take part in the classes and keep your bats. Only the gods know why an animal chooses to stay with us. Who am I to argue with them?"

I stood there in shock. What gods? They were gods.

The god Morag looked hard at me, then laughed. "No, child, we aren't gods. We're women like you'll be someday. We are called Shadow Sisters by those who hire us." She turned and walked away shaking her head.

CHAPTER THREE

Ahasha Valley—Dazel Province

To my relief, my bats learned or sensed they should leave their droppings outside, and life returned to normal. I rejoined the class and did well. Learning about Hesland and its five provinces opened a fascinating new world for me.

Mistress Morag paid me an unexpected visit after the bats remained with me a second season. "Ryana, follow me." She walked away from the compound. I followed as she strode in silence up a narrow mountain trail, which I had never seen. The steep trail took us higher into the crags. My nervousness increased when she entered a large cave. Mistresses Alica and Sanda waited inside.

"Release your bats, Ryana," Morag said.

I wanted to scream. She meant forever. I looked for somewhere to run or hide, but the three women surrounded me. Tears ran down my face and my body trembled at the thought of losing them.

"Ryana, do you love those bats?"

"Yes…Yes, Mistress Morag," I whispered.

"Would you tie their wings, so they couldn't fly away?"

"No, Mistress. I'd never hurt them." I sobbed. The thought of losing them hurt too much for my ten-cycle-old heart to bear. I reached into the harness that I had made to carry them during the day and removed one and then the other. It required all my will to extend my hands toward Morag and open them. When I did, the bats flew deeper into the cave. It felt like my heart had been ripped from my chest.

With tears streaking my face, I stood frozen, staring into the dark cavern after them. As time passed and nothing happened, my hope faded. No one moved. Then out of the black two bats appeared, circled, and landed on my shoulder. I stood paralyzed with fear and hope, resisting the overwhelming urge to reach for them. Then as Mistresses Morag, Alica, and Sanda began chanting, a gray mist arose around me. While they chanted, one of the bats launched itself into the air, circled once, and landed on my outstretched hand.

"We name you Kasi."

The other bat launched, circled twice, and landed on my other hand.

"We name you Anil."

"We name you Ryana," they chanted. I screeched and could hear the echoes. I could smell the blood that flowed through the women's veins. I felt my fingers elongate into the skin that stretched from the side of my body, and my thumbs change into claws. When the mist cleared, I stood holding the bats—in normal hands.

"By their own free will, Kasi and Anil are bonded to you and you to them," Morag said. I fainted.

Over the following seasons, I began to see and hear through Kasi and Anil. Slowly, I learned to interpret their echoes, and they began to sense my wishes.

* * *

At the end of two cycles, Leila and Zaria were asked to leave. They had failed to find a familiar. Now I understood—another phase, another test, and another thing to fear. I hoped I would prove worthy.

Jelena and I were introduced to Mistress Hajna, our instructor for our weapons training phase. She had black hawk-like eyes, which froze me, light-brown skin, was taller than Mistress Sanda, and moved like a cat—quiet and deadly. Her weapons blurred in her hands as she spun from an upright stance to a low, coiled, snake-like position. Jelena and I began our training with wooden weapons. They couldn't kill, but they did leave nasty bruises and sometimes cuts. We learned each Shadow Sister was required to be competent in five weapons: sword, staff, bow and arrow, knife, and the natural weapons of the body—and expert in two. After the first cycle of the seasons passed, I proved good at defending myself but poor at offense. I could sense when my opponent was unbalanced and vulnerable yet remained reluctant to attack.

"Ryana, you must learn to attack. You're good at defending yourself, but you don't go for the kill. In a fight, you would lose. Learn from Jelena; she has the aggressiveness you need." Hajna shook her head. Without warning, she attacked. I avoided her for three strokes but not the fourth. She had been intentionally slow. Then she attacked Jelena. On the third stroke, Jelena countered and attacked. She managed to survive for several seconds. "There, Ryana. Do you see the difference? Jelena defended herself by attacking, so she had a chance of winning and surviving."

I understood, but it wasn't in my nature. Growing up, I had learned to defend myself but never dared to fight back. From then on, I forced myself to attack and improved somewhat. But it would never come naturally.

I headed for the river and its cold water after each workout. It helped to reduce the swelling of my bruises. I didn't like attacking or hurting Jelena or anyone. And while she didn't intend to hurt me, Jelena lost herself in the fury of the fight and always felt sorry afterward.

Today, I submerged, using a hollow reed to breathe. The icy-cold water felt wonderful and helped dull my aches and pains. I must have dozed off for a few seconds because I woke fighting for air. I sputtered up the water I had sucked into my lungs. When the coughing stopped, I wiped my eyes and blew into my reed to clear it. Weeds and water shot out, landing on the shore. Fascinated, I spent the rest of the day loading it with tiny pebbles and blowing them out. In the days that followed, I amused myself by making tubes of wood and shooting pebbles, assessing the accuracy and distance of each. Then I made sticks with feathers—like arrows. Over the next two seasons, my darts, accuracy, and distance improved. What had begun for amusement had become an obsession.

Mistress Morag found me one day at the river practicing. I feared she would be mad at me for playing when I should be studying.

You worry about everything. All your teachers accuse you of working too hard. She should be happy to see you relaxing, I chastised myself, but I still worried. Working hard had saved me from being made to leave.

"Well, Ryana, I finally found you relaxing, or are you? What do you have there?" Morag asked as she neared and sat.

"I've been…playing with this tube," I said after I recovered from the shock of her sitting down next to me.

"What are you doing with it?" She seemed interested, so I relaxed—cautiously.

"I'm trying to shoot darts from it. I've sent one five paces."

Morag took the tube from me and inspected it. Then she picked up the dart, turning it around in her hand to examine the feathers.

"Show me."

I loaded the feathered dart into the tube and prepared to blow when she pointed to a log some six paces away. I took a deep breath and blew. The dart wobbled as it went and fell short by a hand's width. I tried not to let my disappointment show.

"You've never been conventional, Ryana, so I guess that I can't expect it now. I've heard of such a device but never seen one. I think you'll have to smooth out the tube and redesign your feathers." She paused and studied the dart. "If you wish, I'll help you play with your dart weapon."

"Yes, Mistress. Please." I felt shocked. Ecstatic. Excited. Then it hit me—weapon!

"Meet me here each day after your lessons with Sister Hajna, and we'll work on it. Don't neglect your other weapons."

* * *

For the next six seasons, Mistress Morag and I labored over refining the weapon. We smoothed the inside of the tube, experimented with different lengths, and tested a variety of feather arrangements. I could now blow a dart some twenty paces with a fair degree of accuracy.

One day she took me partway up the side of the mountain and pointed to a small flowering vine growing out of the side of a rock face.

"Those black berries are called rockberry. They are poisonous and quickly paralyze." She continued climbing until she found a beautiful blue-tailed lizard. "That is a rock lizard. Their skins contain a deadly poison called rocktail." She went on to explain how each could be made into a poison—one to paralyze and one to kill. Then, to my delight, she blessed the weapon and informed Mistress Hajna that it should be part of my training.

I practiced during class and spent hours on my own. Five seasons later, I could blow a dart from twenty paces into a two-inch circle every time. It be-came my weapon of choice.

"Well, Ryana, I'll accept the blowtube as your weapon of choice. Dipped in rocktail or rockberry, it would be an effective weapon. But you need a second one," Hajna said, turning the tube over in her hand as she did when evaluating a weapon's quality. I had stained it black, which made it difficult to see at night and almost invisible against our black clothes. As spies, a Shadow Sister wore clothing appropriate to the profession or person she impersonated. But for formal meetings with buyers of her services, she wore black shoes, pants, shirt, and a head wrap, which left only her eyes exposed, precluding easy identification.

"Two, Mistress. A blowtube and…" I reached down to my ankle and pulled out two sticks from a sheath I had made. Made from hardwood, they were a hand's width long, finger thin, and sharp at one end. "Needles. One I coated with rockberry and another with rocktail." Hajna nodded her approval.

Another cycle passed. I had improved my blowtube and its accuracy. My knife throwing also proved better than normal and my knife and needle fighting excellent. Knives and needles required me to get in close. They were effective against long weapons. I could step inside the weapon's arc, making a long weapon ineffective, and deliver a killing or paralyzing strike. Against short weapons, the blowtube was effec-tive. This phase came to an end, and we were tested to judge our competency. I had been so consumed with my blowtube weapon, I never thought about failing this phase—until now. I wasn't sure if I would be com-peting against Jelena or some other undisclosed criteria of Mistress Hajna.

It went as expected. Jelena was far better than me at every weapon except the knife and my special weapons—blowtube and needles. It didn't matter to me. I wanted to be a Spy, which only required me to be expert in two. Jelena intended to be an Assassin, which required her to be expert in the standard five.

"Ryana, tonight you and I will try an experiment. My weapons will be the bow and my wolf. Your weapons the blowtube and your bats," Hajna said to my horror. I wasn't qualified or interested in being an Assassin. I would have been excited at the chance to prove the blowtube a serious weapon—against anyone other than Mistress Hajna. She was an Assassin with many cycles of experience and could put an arrow in any target at any distance. "I'll enter the valley at dusk. You'll follow when the sun sets."

"Yes, Mistress." My mind raced with possibilities and fears.

* * *

I stood ten minutes away from the compound where the valley narrowed, the traditional starting line for tests. I waited as Kasi and Anil scouted ahead. I soon knew Mistress Hajna waited five hundred paces ahead with her wolf, Yafa, fifty paces off to her right.

Yafa will be a distraction, which Hajna will use to get me in a position to kill, I mused as I trotted across the starting line.

We had agreed that I wouldn't use my bats to attack her or her wolf since this exercise was intended to test the effectiveness of the blowtube as a weapon.

As I neared her position, I slowed, knowing Yafa would warn her long before she could see me. Keeping shrubs and trees between her and me, I inched closer until I was within the range of my longer blowtube. Although I had been well within her bow range for some time, she hadn't taken a shot. She might be giving me a chance to even the odds or didn't have a clear shot. Now that I was within range, I maneuvered myself behind a large tree and stopped to consider my options. While I considered them, Anil warned me that Yafa approached from behind and to my left. Kasi alerted me Mistress Hajna knelt thirty paces in line with my tree.

To shoot the wolf, I would have to step to the left, exposing myself to her. She wouldn't miss. If I moved to the right to shoot at her, one of them would get me before I could aim and shoot.

Yes, she was the professional, I lamented.

Having no good options, I waited. Yafa continued to close, while Mistress Hajna stood ready. The wolf would force the issue.

With a burst of speed, Yafa attacked. I braced myself against the tree, my needle poised. When Yafa landed on me, I had my needle against its belly. Yafa dropped to the ground as if it had really been poisoned with rocktail. I spun left, hoping Hajna would expect me to go right. I aimed and blew hard, sending the dart in her direction. Before I could twist back behind the tree, her padded arrow slammed into my chest, driving me to the ground with a wind-shattering thud. I didn't have time to see what happened to my dart. As I lay there trying to catch my breath, Mistress Hajna walked up.

"I didn't think I had put Yafa in danger. You fooled me twice. First by taking on Yafa and second by jumping left. Since I had been expecting you to spin to the right, it caused me a second's delay. You killed me," she said, pointing to the dart in her arm, and laughed as she helped me up. "I'll have to revise my opinion of the blowtube. I had thought it a novelty of limited value. I was wrong."

Three more cycles had come and gone.

* * *

Since Jelena and I hadn't been asked to leave, we had passed the weapons phase. That meant another phase and another test—something new to worry about.

"Sister Rong," said Mistress Hajna. "This is Jelena and Ryana. They are adequate with weapons and are now yours." She nodded to us. "This will be the final phase of your training. Sister Rong will teach you the art of being a Shadow Sister and prepare you for your final test."

Mistress Rong looked us over in much the same manner as Mistress Hajna evaluated a weapon. She was a petite woman, even smaller than Mistress Alica. Her brown eyes crinkled in the corners as though she was laughing. I liked her.

"With me, you'll play games for many cycles. These games will teach you the secrets of the Shadow Sisters. You'll learn to walk as silent as a shadow, leaving nothing in your wake, to be anyone you wish from a washer woman to a princess, and to lie on a second's notice so well even you'll believe it."

Mistress Rong had a mind like a fox. Every day brought a new challenge. By the end of three cycles, I could sneak up on a rabbit without it moving, run a mile through any terrain without leaving a trace of my passing, act the part of a hundred people, and without the slightest hesitation make up a lie to fit any situation. I had learned the secrets of the Shadow Sisters. All that remained was to meet with Mistress Morag and select the test that would determine my position in the Sisterhood—given, of course, that I passed. She met with us the next day. I had been with the Shadow Sisters for ten cycles—eighty seasons—four hundred and eighty sixdays.

* * *

"I've met with Sister Rong. Jelena, she finds you a bit too aggressive. You've trouble being the humble servant or lower-class worker, and you've a tendency to act too quickly." Morag looked from Jelena to me. "Ryana, you've good instincts but are too cautious. Do either of you wish to comment?"

"No, Mistress," we said in unison. As far as I was concerned, Mistress Rong's evaluation was correct. It was hard for me to shake loose the fears of my childhood. I had never been sure what I had to do to avoid another beating. Even here, I worried. I had never been sure what I had to do to avoid being asked to leave. I worried too much to trust my instincts.

"Jelena, I assume you wish to qualify for the rank of Assassin."

"Yes, Mistress," Jelena said. A smile lit her face.

"You'll take the Assassin's test tomorrow night. If you succeed, which you should, you'll leave with Sister Sanda two days later. She and you are being assigned to Araby Province, under the direction of Sister Fayza."

I wondered why Assassins were ranked lower than Spies. The Shadow Sisters' chain of authority in the field went: student Assassin, student Spy, senior Assassin, senior Spy, student Spy/Assassin—one who had passed both tests—and senior Spy/Assassin. Mistress Morag waved to Jelena to go and held up a hand for me to stay.

Stop worrying. They have prepared you well for your upcoming test. True, but...

"Sister Rong told me that you continue to be unorthodox. We teach our students to use logic to defeat their opponent. You reverse our teaching and use your opponent's logic to defeat him. She said you do poorly using logic because you tend to be too cautious.

But when you use your intuition, you excel at every problem." Morag sat quietly looking at me for a long time. Even the hawk on her shoulder seemed to be assessing me. I began to wonder if she was waiting for me to say something.

"Two days from now you'll take a special test. Eight mercenaries will be waiting for you. I want you to Kill—disable—four and determine the belt colors of the other four. You'll wear a red and white belt."

Now I can worry. This wasn't the standard Spy's test, which had four mercenaries and required no Kills.

"Any questions, Ryana?"

"No, Mistress." I lied. I had a million questions: why eight? Has anyone taken a test like this? Is it possible? Why me…? I felt dizzy from the questions bombarding my mind. After a moment, I steadied myself. *Mistress Morag has told me what she wanted. I'll do the best that I can to meet her wishes. There was no need to question her. If she wanted me to understand, she would have told me.* I left worried but determined.

CHAPTER FOUR

Ahasha—Dazel Province

Two days later, I lay by the river enjoying the warm sun, the whispering sound of the water flowing by, and the soft feel of the grass. Kasi and Anil slept inside my shirt. Mistress Hajna had stressed many times that a relaxed person fought better than a tense one. "To fight your best, you must be devoid of feeling, thoughts of yesterday or tomorrow, living or dying, winning or losing, hating or loving—only the moment." It had taken me awhile to forget about the test and its consequences, but I had. I lay enjoying the moment. I could feel the mist from the water bubbling over the rocks, see caterpillars munching on the leaves in the tree over my head, smell the flowers on the bushes, and hear the squirrels running up and down the trees.

I lay at peace with myself. The tension had dissolved—no past, no future, only the moment. I was determined to capture this experience during the upcoming test. I could neither change the rules nor predict the outcome, but I could enjoy each moment and not let fear control me, which it had for so many cycles. Tonight, I would put my trust in Mistresses Hajna and Rong.

Toward dusk, I walked back to my room, where I dressed in the traditional Shadow Sisters' black outfit and wrapped the red and white belt around my waist. I stood for a long time admiring those clothes. Tonight, I would be a student, tomorrow—I vowed—a Shadow Sister.

I strapped my longer blowtube to the outside of one leg and a set of sticks to the other. The shorter blowtube, along with ten darts, I tucked in my belt. All were dipped in a solution of rockberry, which would paralyze and count as a Kill. With Kasi and Anil hanging from my shirt, I walked to the starting line and launched them into the night.

I closed my eyes and watched as they zigzagged across the valley in search of the mercenaries. As soon as they found their locations, I crossed the line and a horn blew, signaling the start of the test. The mercenaries had positioned four men on the west and four on the east side of the river that ran down the valley. Panic reared its ugly head before I had gone fifty paces. I stood frozen, not knowing what to do. Then Kasi landed on my shoulder and I relaxed with her touch. Remembering how I had felt by the river earlier, I reached for the moment. There no logic existed, only the intuition that had served me well during Mistress Rong's games.

What would the mercenaries expect me to do?

I couldn't help but smile as I picked up a good-sized rock and threw it arching through the air. It produced a rustling sound as it sailed through the brush and thudded to the ground.

"Dirk, move more to the east, and we'll shift more to the west. She's being cute throwing rocks to convince us that she's near the river," someone on the west side shouted.

Thank you.

I moved forward into the gap they had thoughtfully provided. After I had passed their line, I turned east behind the four on that side of the river. I ghosted along using the trees and shrubbery as cover while noting the color of each man's belt: green/blue, gray/black, blue/gray, and maroon/green.

"Plan Red," the same sounding voice hollered. Clever. Directions would tell me what they were planning. The bad news: they were retreating south in my direction. A good move on their part. The moon was full and the visibility good, especially in areas with an abundance of wild grasses and few trees. They would expect me to run, but if I did, they might be able to identify my red-and-white belt. And I would fail the test. So, I found a good-size bush and lay face up in its shadow and waited. A minute later, I could hear them coming. They sounded like a herd of hogs. Gray/black was heading toward where I lay. Any moment now he would see me if he didn't trip over me first. As he neared, I put a dart in his side. He staggered a few steps before falling near me.

What would they do now? I asked myself. Soon they would know I had to be in front of them and on the east side of the river. These were the types of games I had played with Jelena for many seasons and won, until she realized I used her expectations against her.

They would expect me to move east or west, so I pulled gray/black into the shadows with me and waited.

"This is Adler. Roll call," a voice boomed into the silence.

"Dirk... Egon..." came from the side I was on. "Gotz... Lenz... Cabe... Owen," came from across the river.

"Abe's missing, plan color emerald." Adler shouted.

I didn't need Kasi. I could hear the three on my side trashing through the brush toward me. Anil showed two of the men on the west side crossing the river and moving toward the advancing three. The other two on the west side stayed guarding the river. I assumed color emerald, stood for converge east. I waited. The three heading back to the north passed thirty paces to either side of me. They didn't expect me to stay around Abe's position in the line. After they passed, I headed west and crossed the river. I then worked my way toward where the two stood, watching for me to try crossing the river to escape the two lines converging on the east side. The mercenaries thought they had me boxed in—between the three moving north, the two moving south, the two at the river on the west, and the cliffs on the east. A good plan if I had tried to avoid them by running rather than staying put. Their logic had allowed me to slip by. I was now on the west side, near the two watching the river. I silently worked my way through the undergrowth until I could see one of the men. Kasi indicated the other one waited another fifty paces north. I darted the nearest one. He staggered and collapsed as he reached for the dart in his neck. Again, Adler shouted.

"Roll call."

"Dirk… Egon… Gotz… Lenz… Cabe…"

"Owen is down. We've an Assassin, and she is on the west side now. She has her two Kills and will head for the finish line. Since Dirk, Egon, and I are the furthest south, we'll cross over and try to beat her there. Cabe, join Lenz and Gotz on the east side and race for the finish line in case she crosses back over."

As Cabe began to cross the river, I darted him. *The moment, intuition*, I reminded myself. I crossed back over the river and lay down behind a clump of riverside brushes and waited. Soon two men ran by. One wore a black/yellow and the other a green/gray belt. Now that I had everyone's colors, I only needed to Kill one more. I followed behind the two, who hurried toward the finish line. They were too close to Kill one without the other one seeing me. Anil showed the three on the other side were almost at the finish line waiting.

I was one Kill short. Resigned, I decided to cross the finish line. I had failed.

Mistress Morag waited at the finish line. When she saw me, she paid the mercenary leader eight gold toras, one gold for each man who had taken part in the hunt. If they had caught me, they each would have received an additional tora. Those were the contracted conditions for each hunt. When he left to collect his men, Morag mounted her horse and gestured for me to mount the other. We rode in silence for a while, until I could bear it no longer.

"I failed, Mistress. I only Killed three." My words mixed with bile. I wanted to die.

"Did they see you?"

"No." Why did it matter?

"The colors of those you didn't Kill?"

"Green/blue, blue/gray, maroon/green, black/yellow, and green/gray." One too many.

I hated myself and wondered what my decision not to Kill one of the five remaining mercenaries would cost me.

"Why did you fail to Kill the fourth?"

"At the end, they bunched up. If I had tried to Kill one, the other one would have seen me and my belt."

"You could have used Kasi or Anil."

"Yes, either bat could have Killed one of the mercenaries, but their poison could have killed, not just paralyzed him. For revenge, they might have murdered the next student they caught. Besides, a mercenary didn't deserve to die so that I could pass a test. I'm sorry, Mistress. I couldn't follow your orders."

"Sister Ryana, I'll give you your assignment tomorrow. Be ready to travel at sunrise." She dismounted, tossing me her horse's reins before walking away. Sister? It must be a mistake. I failed the test. How could I be going on an assignment? Who would want to go on an assignment with a student who failed? Exhausted, I dropped into bed and fell asleep.

* * *

In the morning, I finished packing in preparation for my coming assignment, still confused. I didn't understand how I had become a Sister or my rank, since I took neither the Spy nor the Assassin test. I had been tired and upset last night. Maybe I misunderstood. The thought that Mistress could be sending me away brought tears to my eyes. I left my packed bag on the floor and headed for Mistress Morag's cottage. Her door stood open.

"Come in, Ryana, and sit," she said, while shuffling through several sheets of thin paper. I sat rigid on the edge of the chair, waiting for her to talk.

Finally, she looked up. "You've a question, Ryana?"

"Yes, Mistress. I don't understand why you called me Sister last night. I failed your test." I studied the flower design on the rug under my feet, dreading the answer.

"My child, you must stop worrying. You've achieved your long-desired goal. The Shadows Sisters have taken you into the Sisterhood." She smiled. "Tell me the rules for the Spy test."

That was the test I had hoped to take, instead of...

"The Shadow Sisters hire four mercenaries for the test, who are paid to locate the student by identifying the color of the belt she's wearing. To pass, the student must be able to describe the belt colors of at least two mercenaries without her belt colors being discovered."

"That's correct. The test you hoped to take," she said. I nodded agreement. "Now describe the Assassin's test."

"Four mercenaries are paid to capture the student. They usually capture the student by disabling her, using a weapon with a mixture of rockberry or by physically disabling her. They are paid nothing if the student is crippled or killed. To pass, the student must Kill at least two mercenaries before reaching the finish."

"Correct. That's the test you weren't interested in taking."

I nodded agreement, unsure of why she was asking questions every student knew.

"How many belts did you identify last night?"

"Five."

"Did any of the five identify your belt?"

"No."

"How many mercenaries did you disable?"

"Three."

"It appears you took the Spy and Assassin test and exceeded the minimum requirements for each test. You failed to do the impossible because you refused to possibly kill a man and jeopardize future students' lives so you could pass a test. Would the Shadow Sisters want a student who did?"

If I hadn't been sick with worry, it would have made sense last night. I still didn't understand, but I let out a breath I hadn't known I was holding. My dream had come true. I had a family where I was wanted. I rose when Mistress…Sister Morag did.

"Give me your hand, Ryana."

I reached out my hand, and she grasped it. I could feel her power. Only the senior Sister had the power to make a student a Shadow Sister and to imprint her rank. It was burned deep in the palm where no one could see it. But any Shadow Sister could feel it when the two joined hands. I felt it as it was being burned into my flesh. First, she drew a circle. Afterward, a straight line was drawn near the top and a parallel line at the bottom—the mark of an apprentice Spy. The rank I had longed for. While I reveled in the thought, she drew two more lines to form a box—the mark of a senior Spy. That confused me. She continued, drawing a diagonal line through the box—the sign for an apprentice Assassin, which I hadn't been interested in. Finally, she drew another diagonal line forming an "X" within the box, designating a senior Assassin/Spy—the highest Shadow Sister rank. My head spun. I didn't understand. I didn't want rank, only to belong.

"What I'm going to tell you now is for you alone. You're not to repeat it to anyone." She paused and waited for me to nod. "Five of our Sisters have been murdered over the last two seasons. An Assassin/Spy and a Spy employed by Lord se'Dubben in Calion Province; a Spy with Lady wu'Lichak in Araby Province; and an Assassin/Spy and a Spy with Lord zo'Stanko in Tuska Province. Our Sisters in Saxis and Dazel Provinces remain alive as well as three Spies and one Assassin on training excursions with their apprentices. I'll tell you their names and locations before we leave."

My head whirled with conflicting thoughts. As far as I knew that information was never disclosed. If a Shadow Sister was captured and tortured, she couldn't disclose what she didn't know. I'd know far too much. I'd want Kasi and Anil to kill me before I could divulge anything of value, but it was probable I was immune to their poison. I'd have to think of another method before I left Ahasha Valley.

"I'm afraid to contact them since I don't know who's to blame for our Sisters' deaths. I would hate to think it a Sister, but it's possible." She paused.

Why was Mistress…Sister Morag telling me about the deaths?

Although I was willing to be the bait to attract the killers, I would know too much to risk capture.

"I should send a senior Assassin/Spy with extensive experience, but I fear a senior Sister might be too easy to recognize. Whoever's responsible has some knowledge of the Sisterhood and will be waiting for an older, experienced Shadow to investigate. You, on the other hand, will be difficult to identify. You're too young to be considered a Shadow and not well known among the Sisters. On the other hand, you've no experience."

Morag was right. I lacked experience and would be facing killers, not mercenaries with toys. My mind raced with questions, doubts, and excitement. It would be an opportunity to prove myself, to help…my Sisters—or to fail.

"The only way I could make that decision would be to test you and the effectiveness of your unorthodox approach, familiars, and weapons." Morag reached up and ran her finger across her hawk's feathers. I hadn't realized I was being untraditional—good thing—I suspect I would have failed if I had tried being traditional.

"I decided to combine the Spy and the Assassin tests. The combination made the test four times more difficult and came closer to approximating the stress and decision making you might encounter in the field. Telling you that I wanted four killed and four identified increased the difficulty of the task, added stress, and restricted your approach. A terrible thing to do but better you fail here than in the field."

36

I almost didn't hear her last words. They were but a whisper. The enormity of Morag's dilemma became clear. A wrong decision could place the Sisterhood in jeopardy.

Maybe it would have been better if I had failed.

"The unpredictable circumstances surrounding your fourth Kill answered a serious concern I had about you. You've fanatically followed the Sisters' instructions. You never deviated. I worried you would take my parting advice as orders, not suggestions: find the information, return safely, and try not to kill anyone. If you survive, that will be a bonus. Getting the information is the assignment. If you need to kill to do that, you must. You can't run back to me for advice. You must be willing and capable of making your own decisions. Only you'll be there and only you can decide what should be done. By not disabling the fourth mercenary, you demonstrated you're capable of making independent decisions." Morag paused. I laughed.

"Did I say something funny?"

"... I've worried myself sick for the past ten cycles desperately wanting to belong but never sure what I must do to stay. Today, I desperately want to help my Sisters but again I'm not sure what I must do to succeed. I succeeded before because I didn't know what was traditional; therefore, I guess its best I don't try to understand what I should do," I said. Morag laughed.

"I've decided to send you, Ryana. I know I'm throwing you to the wolves, hoping you can somehow learn to outrun them, before..." Her glaze softened, and she lapsed into silence for several minutes. "I wish I didn't believe you had the best chance, although slim."

I took a deep breath before venturing a comment. "I'm honored. The Sisterhood's my family. I'll gladly give my life if dying can save it." *No more worrying*, I promised. *I'll do my best. It's all I can do.*

"Give me your hand Ryana." Morag reached toward me.

Now what? A secret I had never been told?

As she grasped my hand, I felt a searing pain and almost collapsed. When I could think again, I had Sister Morag's sigil burned into my palm.

"Why?" I stuttered.

"I suggest you trust no one, including your Sisters. Of course, the decision will be yours. If you do, you'll need the authority I've given you. You've my authority to give any Sister orders. I don't need some well-meaning Sister telling you what you should or shouldn't do. This assignment is your sole responsibility. As for the Assassin/Spy rank, if you fulfill this assignment, you'll have earned it. If not, it won't matter. You'll be dead."

I smiled mentally. This was another phase and another test. The difference was that before, I fought to belong. This time I belonged and fought for my family.

"Get your things, Sister Ryana. We leave within the hour."

CHAPTER FIVE

Sebec—Saxis Province

As we rode away from Ahasha Valley, I tried to memorize every bush, tree, and bend in the river. I couldn't know when or even if I would see it again. Soon I would be alone. My education had given me extensive knowledge of the people and cities. I had learned how to fit into any environment and play any part but knowing and doing weren't the same. Morag broke into my thoughts just in time. I had been ready to turn around and race back to Ahasha.

"Within the next few days, a gypsy caravan will visit the city of Sebec, a three-day ride southeast of here. They perform there every two cycles currently. You and I will meet them there. The clan leader, Marku, is a friend of mine. He will let you accompany them. You'll pretend that you've been asked to leave because you weren't suitable for the Sisterhood. Marku will claim he's providing you transportation to the city of Scio in Araby Province, where your parents live. Over the next cycle, Marku and his clan will perform in each of the provinces. Traveling with them, you'll have an opportunity to visit every major city in Hesland. In addition, it'll give you a cover you wouldn't have traveling alone," Morag said.

"Am I to avenge them?" I asked. Although I had been trained in weapons and knew how, I hadn't been groomed to be an Assassin. Those who planned to be Assassins trained longer and were required to be expert in all weapons. Those who planned to be Spies, like me, were required to be expert in only two. But now, I found myself both Spy and Assassin.

I pondered my recent test. What if my darts had been dipped in rocktail or my rockberry hadn't been diluted? The three mercenaries would have been dead not sedated. I felt sympathy for them. Although to capture me, they would have beaten me into submission. But could I kill someone who wasn't trying to harm me even though they had killed my Sisters? I realized that I didn't know and wouldn't until the situation arose.

"Your task is to find those who are killing our Sisters, the reason they were killed, and get that information back to me," Morag said. "We must stop the killing. Everything else is secondary. Having said that, you must decide how to achieve that goal. You're not to sacrifice your life to avenge our Sisters. Get the information back to me, and together we'll avenge them."

I had too many unknowns to even ask an intelligent question. Ironically, when I knew the question, it would be too late to ask.

As if Morag had been listening to my thoughts, she added, "The only advice I can give you, although I'm loath to say it, is to trust no one. Place your trust in your intuition and don't linger on things you can't change. Stay focused. Don't look backward. What you should have or could have done can't be changed. You can affect the future not the past."

I felt overwhelmed. I had been taught to obey any Sister without question. And as an apprentice, I should trust and obey any Sister my senior. Morag's words were an antithesis—trust no one, take orders from no one.

"I've sent a message by swift-wing Kite to our Intermediary in Adak, informing her that I'm sending a Shadow to investigate the murders and to notify Shadow Karsa, our Spy there. I'm hoping that will get to the killers and spur them into action. It's a dangerous gambit but necessary if you're to have any chance of discovering who they are."

* * *

Enough of this doubt. Sister Rong would be ashamed of me. She has taught me well and declared me ready.

I shifted in my saddle and ran my eyes over the pack mule loaded with gear. On top was my kit, looking like a typical cloth carrying case with wood handles. It held my everyday clothes and a false bottom, which could only be opened by twisting the small, wooden rests in the right direction. Under the false bottom lay my blacks, blow tubes, darts, drug compounds, and face scarf with the rune, Perthro, which declared me a Shadow Sister. Perthro suited the Shadows well. Its sign stood for mystery, occult abilities, fellowship, knowledge of one's destiny, and things feminine. Most saw the sign as something dangerous—rightfully so.

I nodded to myself. My gear was prepared. So, must I be.

I'm Ryana, a girl who was unsuitable for the Shadow Sisters and has been told to leave. I had been accepted because I had an affinity with animals. I only agreed because I wanted the prestige of being a Shadow. I made it through phase one because my father had me tutored on how to read and write. I faked my way through the second phase by appearing to have found a familiar—although that would be impossible. In the third phase, I did poorly. About halfway through phase three, they discovered my animal wasn't a familiar. I would have failed anyway, because of my poor performance with weapons. Except for the embarrassment, I wasn't upset with having to leave. It was too much work. Besides, no one would know I was a Shadow, as they kept their identity secret.

If I had really failed, I would have died. Not of embarrassment but of a deep, burning loss. There must be two Ryanas, the one everyone saw and her shadow—the real me. The visual Ryana must be independent of her shadow.

"Mistress Morag, it isn't right that you're asking me to leave. I'm not good at weapons, but it wouldn't matter. I want to be a Spy," I said.

"Now Ryana, you know you aren't suited for the Shadow Sisters. You'll be much happier with your father."

"Why did I need a familiar? I wanted to be a Spy. How much of a secret would it be with a dumb bird sitting on my shoulder? Some disguise I'm going to have with bird crap all over my clothes." I glared at Morag. Her lip twitched and her eyes sparkled. I kept my eyes narrow and lips tight. A smile or small twitch would be uncharacteristic for someone whining. "I'll be the laughingstock of Scio."

"Your father will be delighted to have you home. You know he didn't like the idea of you leaving."

"I have to leave here because the Shadow Sisters are jealous. They can't be beautiful like me if they hide behind masks."

"That's right, Ryana. You deserve to be seen, not hidden behind a mask."

The exchange went on for three days, day and night. Morag helped me refine the visual Ryana with her answers: your wealthy father, the boy who wants to marry you, your love of clothes…

On the way, I was discovering a new world. We had exited the valley onto a large plateau. At first, it appeared to be flat lowland; however, the occasional steep drop-offs revealed we were still high in the mountains. This was all new, and I couldn't help shifting in my saddle to capture it all. As the days wore on, we descended into leagues of rolling hills. For two days, Morag led us along dirt trails that seemed to go on forever with little change in the landscape. I was sure that I could never find my way home again. So far, the trails had been little more than animal paths.

Morag had casually pointed out the Whitedox Mountains on our left and the Blackdox Mountains on the right, which led to Sebec. As we neared the outskirts of Sebec on the fourth day, the land flattened, and small farms began to appear. The town's primary income came from exporting cattle, wheat, corn, and a variety of vegetables.

By the time we reached Sebec, the new Ryana had been born, weaned, and grown into a young woman.

Morag wore the traditional garb for a Shadow on public display: pants, shirt, and sash made of black cotton, soft black leather boots, weapons, and a head scarf, which covered her entire head and face except for the eyes. The Shadow's Rune, a red Perthro, appeared on the scarf. Morag's hawk rode her shoulder. I wore clothing appropriate for a girl of moderate means: a rough cream-cotton shirt, brown pants, leather boots, and a dark brown wool jacket.

Just before entering Sebec, we encountered a large market with twenty or more tables loaded with meats, fruit, and vegetables, surrounded by crowds of shoppers. The scene fascinated me. For the past ten cycles, my life had been devoted to training to be a Shadow Sister. In Ahasha, I had no social life or exposure to the outside world. I had learned about the world but had never experienced it. Normally, it wouldn't have mattered. I would have been assigned a senior Sister to guide me for my first cycle or two. Without a mentor, it was going to be a difficult adjustment.

I would have loved to stop and wander through the stalls and watch the people, who were staring at us. Morag appeared not to notice and continued though the market into the town. The roads were packed dirt and the buildings old and spread out, making the town appear much larger than it was. The local businesses catered to the nearby farms, selling feed, seeds, clothes, work animals, and farm equipment. There were three inns with attached taverns. Morag stopped at a two-story one with a large frothy mug carved into a piece of rough wood and "Happy Mug Inn" painted in white at the bottom. Inside the inn, a few customers sat with large steins at sturdy wooden tables. Morag paid for a room with two beds, a small table with a bowl and pitcher, and one stool. The room was sparse but clean. I thought it no better than my room at Ahasha. Each bed had one sheet made of a rough cloth and a blanket of coarse wool. I didn't want to break character, but...

"Sister Morag," I said, still uncomfortable with the idea of her being only my senior Sister. She had been Mistress for too many cycles. "How much did this cost?" I needed to understand what things cost because I would soon be on my own. I knew money and how to do sums but not what I should pay for food, lodging, and personal needs. A gold tora equaled twenty silvers, a silver equaled twenty coppers, and a copper four bits—so what?

"Eight coppers. The innkeeper is afraid of cheating a Shadow or her feeling cheated; otherwise, he would have charged ten or twelve. He gave us a double room with an evening and a morning meal tomorrow."

"Do the Shadows generally get money to live on when they are on assignment?" I had many questions and too little time. But I was Shadow trained and would survive.

"Normally, no. Those who hire us pay very well for the information we give. They know not to cheat us." Morag smiled. Clearly, she thought the idea funny. "Yes, I find the idea amusing. The Shadow Sisters started with one young woman, who had been abused and left homeless to fend for herself. She lived in the streets and survived by doing menial jobs. By luck or chance, one day she subdued a thief who had tried to steal the few coppers she had earned cleaning floors and collected a reward for his capture. She came to realize that she could earn more money hunting thieves than cleaning floors and washing clothes. She became so good at it the city guard began using her to find people. Over time, other women joined her and together they perfected the art of spying, which has made the Shadows sought after by the wealthy and influential. Most don't know how or why we were formed, but they know we can be helpful and dangerous."

"Do you think someone is seeking revenge?"

"Or power."

"Why power?"

"I believe one of our Sisters discovered something that threatens a group or organization. Rightly or wrongly, they feel that the Shadows can or will discover their secret and use it against them. They're trying to eliminate the threat. I say again, trust no one." Morag opened the door, and we went downstairs to the main room.

When we arrived downstairs, all eyes turned to her. The tavern was a large open space with three small tables, which sat four or five, and six long tables, which could accommodate ten to twelve. The barmaid, a thin girl of no more than fourteen cycles, led us to one of the small tables. It remained empty, although the room was crowded. I suspect the barkeep had kept it free for Morag. Our meal consisted of a watery stew of meat and vegetables, which I found tasty. The Sisters ate little meat and used few spices. Halfway through the meal, a tall man dressed in colorful mismatched clothes approached. Men and colorful clothes were new experiences. Men weren't allowed at Ahasha, and the Sisters wore traditional clothing tailored for action not show. This man wore clothing made for show: an orange bandana, yellow silk shirt, purple pants tucked into snakeskin boots, and a large curved knife tucked inside a red sash. Although fascinated, I avoided staring. I continued to glare at Morag, maintaining my image of a girl sulking.

"Mistress Morag, what a delight it is to see you again. To what do I owe this pleasure?" the man said in a melodious voice and made a small bow.

"You're as spectacular as usual, Marku," Morag said. "Please join us for a meal or a drink."

"Thank you. Who's your young companion?"

"This is Ryana. Ryana, this is Marku, the leader of the Dorian clan. They are the greatest show on Hesland."

I turned to look at Marku. "She's getting rid of me," I said.

"It's disappointing, Ryana, but it should be obvious to you that you don't fit in. It's better to leave now than to be asked to leave a cycle or two from now. Your parents will be glad to have you home, and you'll be well provided for. They never wanted you to join the Shadow Sisters." Morag patted my hand. She was good. For a minute, I became so caught up in the story, I believed it.

"Marku, I'll pay for her passage to Scio."

He looked at me for several seconds before answering. "Ryana, if you travel with us, you'll have to do your share of the work."

I ignored him, continuing to glare at Morag, although deep down it hurt to do so.

"Why me?" Marku sat down and signaled the barmaid for a stein of ale.

"I need some way to transport her back to her parents, and I've no one available. I'm willing to pay you to take her. You don't have to worry. Ryana isn't lazy."

"Well, Ryana, are you willing to do your share of the work?"

"If you'll give me some training. I don't want just to clean, fetch, and carry," I said. "I learn quickly, although they won't admit it."

"How much, Marku?" Morag asked.

"Seven toras."

"Four."

"Six."

"Five, or I'll find another way to get her to Araby Province."

"Done." Marku shook his head but smiled. "You're a hard woman. I'm glad none of my clan saw you take advantage of me. It would be embarrassing."

"Come to my room and I'll pay you."

He followed Morag up the creaky stairs. I stomped up behind them while continuing to glare at Morag, Marku, and anyone else who made eye contact with me. Pretending to hate her was painful. I consoled myself by rationalizing it was the visible Ryana, not her shadow. I didn't relax even after we had entered the room and the door closed.

Morag reached inside her shirt, produced a bag, and counted out twenty gold toras, which she handed to Marku.

"Mistress, what's going on?" Marku asked, looking from Morag to me. I glared back. I needed the practice and would stay in character until Morag indicated otherwise. Besides, I was beginning to enjoy the deception. "You know I won't take money from you. You saved my clan from disgrace and exile. We owe you more than we can ever pay." Marku pushed Morag's hand away.

"The money's for Ryana, but you should keep it for her. She's a Shadow, Marku. Five of our Sisters have been killed in just the past three months. I'm sending Ryana to investigate."

"She isn't old enough to be a Shadow." He shuddered and shook his head before turning back to Morag. His suntanned face had turned ashen. "And I've seen her face!"

"I'm sending her because she does look too young to be a Shadow. As for you and everyone else seeing her face, it's an unavoidable risk. If Ryana does her job right, only you'll ever know her identity. I'm trusting you with her life." Morag nodded to me. Marku turned toward me to find me smiling. Marku shook his head and gave me a weak smile.

"You fooled me, Ryana, and I make a living being able to read people. I know the Shadows impersonate people when they are seeking information but thought it would be easy for a person like me to identify them. I change my pitch to earn coppers, but I'm still Marku. If I had your training, I'd be rich." This time he gave a hearty laugh. "We need to fit you into the clan so that no one's suspicious. You must continue the ruse that you were rejected by the Shadow Sisters and are being returned home to Scio. The clan will know I'm doing it as a personal favor for Mistress Morag. Even so, they'll expect you to do your share of the work. They will give you no special treatment."

I nodded agreement. "I'll need to keep your weapons and anything else that would betray you."

48

I stood silent for several minutes thinking. He was right to be concerned, but I had concerns of my own.

"My kit must be kept in a place I can access day or night and without your help." I may not need unimpeded access but…

"Agreed. We must consider what kind of work you can do. You could clean, cook, or be part of the show. That could include juggling, tumbling, knife throwing, running our games of chance, or fortunetelling. Of course, it would be good if you could do more than one thing." His eyes sparkled and he wore a wide grin.

"I prefer activities that won't focus too much attention on me. I could learn to help with the games of chance and maybe do some tumbling. I don't mind cleaning. But you don't want me cooking." I smiled at the thought. The best you could say for my cooking was that it wouldn't kill you.

"Come and watch the performance tonight. After the show, I'll introduce you and get you settled."

After Marku left Morag turned to me.

"Ryana, your assignment's important to us. Even so, we ask no more than that you do your best." Morag held my shoulders and looked into my eyes. "You've worked long and hard to become a Shadow Sister, but now you must pretend to have failed."

"Kasi and Anil will be constant reminders that I'm blessed. You've nurtured me for many cycles and have prepared me to assume the duties of a Shadow. It's now my turn to repay you."

After a leisurely meal, Morag and I left to watch the performance. By the time we arrived, a large crowd had gathered. Most looked to be commoners or merchants and in a festive mood.

The clan's wagons were made of wood and looked like small houses on wheels. The sides of the wagons were decorated with bright paintings of landscapes, animals, and people. The wagon facing the audience had a large makeshift platform. People were milling about several colorful tents off to the side. Although closed, the painting on the tents indicated they were for games of chance. A black tent stood off to the side with a picture of a woman with a hood looking at a crystal ball.

Morag had been right; the acts were outstanding, and the audience enthralled. After the performance, the tents were opened, and the games began. Most of the people seemed willing to spend a copper or two at the games. Mostly women visited the fortuneteller tent.

"There you are, Mistress," Marku said as he neared us. "I'll take Ryana now."

"Thank you, Marku. I appreciate you agreeing to take Ryana home for me." Morag nodded to Marku, turned, and departed. I felt a lump in my throat, watching her walk away without so much as a goodbye. The visible Ryana glared at her back before turning back to Marku.

CHAPTER SIX

Sebec—Saxis Province

"Ryana, come with me back to the wagons, and I'll get you settled." Marku led me into the circle of picturesque wagons. I had never seen so much color, not only on the wagons but also on the clan's clothing. It drove home the difference between Ahasha and the outside world, between theory and reality. We headed in the direction of a middle-aged woman sitting on the steps of a large wagon. Her auburn hair was tied with red, yellow, and green ribbons, and she wore a yellow silk blouse and a wide, flared skirt with a colorful floral pattern.

"Stela, this is Ryana. The girl I told you about earlier. She will be traveling with us until Araby."

"Morag made me leave. She claims I didn't fit in." I whined and curled my bottom lip. It wasn't hard to sulk. I had just left everything I loved.

"Well, Ryana, perhaps it's for the best. A Shadow's life isn't for everyone, just as gypsy life isn't, although we love it. You're young. In time you'll find what suits you best," Stela said. "Everyone has something they do better than anyone else. Maybe staying with us will help you find your special talent."

When I didn't respond, Stela took me around to meet some of the others who were not occupied. There were twenty-one members of the Dorian clan, including five children. Eleven wagons comprised the clan's homes, including one dedicated for supplies and one for equipment, which also acted as a backdrop for the makeshift stage. Marku decided I could sleep and keep my kit in the one that stored the gear for their shows. It was cramped but met my needs perfectly. It provided privacy and would be the least disruptive to the clan's current arrangements. Besides, I could come and go without disturbing anyone and have easy access to my kit.

The clan stayed in Sebec five days. I watched each performance, trying to decide where I would best fit without attracting unnecessary attention—like a servant—present but ignored as an individual. While I decided, I helped with cleaning and preparations for each performance. Late each night, I crept out and let Kasi and Anil loose. During the day, they slept in the wagon safe behind some unused stage props.

* * *

We left Sebec five days later. The travel to Miffin would take two sixdays. Each night when we stopped, I worked with two girls, Alida and Ilka, to learn how to work the games of chance. In concept, it appeared easy. A huckster, the person selling and operating the game, tried to entice the people milling around after the performance to bet a copper for the opportunity to win a half-silver, ten coppers. Each game had its own tent.

In one tent, the game involved darts. The player—a mark to the clan—had three tries to stick a dart into one of five wooden balls hanging by strings. Luring the customers and taking their money was the easy part. Learning to stick a dart into one of the balls was the hard part. The hawker needed to be able to demonstrate that it wasn't only possible but easy. It helped knowing that the bull's-eye painted on the ball was slightly off center. Unless you hit the ball in the real center, the ball twisted, and the dart fell off.

The second game involved throwing a ball into vases with narrow necks. To get the ball into the vase, you had to have the right arc and speed. Otherwise, the ball hit the rim and bounced off. Again, the hawker had to be able to show she could do it. I spent every night practicing. The darts were easy, but I made it appear harder than it was. The ball and the jars seemed impossible at first, but I kept at it as I had with every task, I had been given at Ahasha. I also decided I could take part in the tumbling act. Most of the act centered on a teeter-totter-like contraption. One or two people stood on a high platform while another stood on the teeter-totter. On signal, the person or people on the platform would jump off, landing on the vacant, raised side. The impact propelled the other person high into the air. The individual in the air performed flips and turns, sometimes landing on someone's shoulders. Other times, he or she landed on a second teeter-totter, propelling another person into the air. One act had a person walking on a tightrope strung between two wagons while performing acts of balance. Other acts included juggling, knife throwing, a puppet show, magic, tumbling, and acrobatic horse riding.

With a little practice, I became one of the platform jumpers and took part in the team tumbling acts. I enjoyed learning the routines. My flexibility made it easy. As a bonus, it kept me limber and in good shape.

I was enjoying myself. I learned quickly, loved challenges, and found the clan easygoing and friendly. It was in stark contrast to the Shadow Sisters, who tended to be serious most of the time, especially around students. At night, the clan told stories, danced, played music, and sang songs from faraway places. Trained in the art of deception, I continued to maintain my pretense of having been rejected by the Shadow Sisters—a comment made now and then or just sitting quietly pretending to sulk. Not enough to be shunned by the clan, but enough to maintain the illusion. It helped that I cheerfully undertook every task.

Two days out of Sebec, Yoan, one of the two unmarried men, sat down next to me. A knife thrower, he was a popular attraction each night. He was young, lean, muscular, and handsome, and he knew it.

"You've taken to the clan's ways very quickly." He smiled. Yoan had been flirting with me for several days, much to Ilka's annoyance. I wasn't sure if he was getting interested in me, flirted with any woman, or was trying to make Ilka jealous. If the latter, he had succeeded. I, on the other hand, found the flirting fun, stimulating, and good practice for later, but I didn't want to antagonize anyone in the clan. I may need their help and cooperation in the future and didn't need enemies.

"I've been enjoying myself, but I'm looking forward to getting home. Hopefully, my father's young assistant hasn't forgotten his true love." That quieted Yoan and put a smile on Ilka's face.

"I'm sure he would be a fool to have forgotten you, Ryana," Ilka said. She smiled and sat down next to me. The only way to describe Ilka was voluptuous. She had long black hair, a round face, a straight nose, and a dazzling smile.

"I'm true to him, and he better be true to me. The Shadows kicked me out, but not before I learned a few things he wouldn't like." An evil smile crossed my lips. I noticed that Ilka was giving Yoan the same evil smile. My response had achieved the intended results. I had diverted Yoan's advances, made a friend of Ilka, and discouraged further advances by pretending I had a serious boyfriend. Hopefully, no one noticed the discrepancy—students left home too young to have boyfriends waiting for them.

Late that night, as I did every night, I wandered outside the circle of wagons and released Kasi and Anil. Because of my training, I didn't need more than five to six hours' sleep. Besides, the clan was slow to rise in the morning, so I could sleep an extra hour or two if necessary. I strolled, enjoying the gentle breeze against my face, the smell of the pines, and the echoes from my darlings. Finding an old fallen tree, I sat, content to listen to Kasi and Anil hunting food. The horses were a frequent target.

My thoughts wandered to Adak, the capital of Saxis. This assignment was unique. Normally, only the senior Sister in a province knew who was in her area and their assignment. Morag had broken that convention by telling me every Sister's assignment and their rank. If I were caught, I hoped Kasi and Anil could kill me—if they would.

Morag had said to trust no one. That extended to Sister Karsa, a Spy in Adak, and to Dotino, the Sisters' Intermediate, who provided the interface between potential employers and the Shadow Sisters. I had to take her warning seriously, but lacking experience, I would have to succeed or fail based on my instincts—not logic. I had proved poor at using logic. Thinking of Morag, my shadow-self felt an ache in her chest—I missed her so much.

A sudden change in Kasi's echoes caught my attention, wrenching me out of my misery. Kasi had detected three individuals heading in the direction of the horses. They were coming out of the forest, not from the road. The hour was late, and the clan had retired to their wagons, although maybe they were not yet asleep. I could disable the three men, but how would I explain it? I decided to wake Marku and let him handle the situation. I didn't shout for fear of alerting the approaching men. Instead, I ran to his wagon and opened the door without knocking. The dim light from Setebos, one of Hesland's two moons, produced a murky interior. As Marku jumped out of bed, moonlight reflected off the knife in his hand. A second later Stela jerked awake, reaching for something I couldn't see in the shadows.

"What the –" I put a single finger to my lips, held up three fingers, and pointed in the direction of the horses.

"What is it Mar–" Marku put his hand over his wife's mouth. He rose and headed for the door.

"How far?"

"About thirty paces," I said after listening to Anil's echoes.

"Wake Yoan and his brother. Tell them to meet me at the horses. You can do whatever you think best," Marku said, already moving in the direction of the horses. I dashed to Yoan's wagon and yanked open the door. Yoan jerked awake, knife in hand. His brother, Vali, tried to jump out of bed but got tangled in his blanket and landed face down on the floor.

"Ryana, you shouldn't –"

"Hush. Marku wants you at the horses. There's trouble." I didn't wait for an answer. While Kasi and Anil kept track of the intruders, I entered the forest far away from the threesome and circled around behind them. Where the clan had camped, the trees were small but the bushes numerous and dense. Although I didn't have my blow tubes, I never went unarmed. I knew how to defend myself without weapons, but it was my last line of defense, as most opponents had the advantage of weight and reach. Consequently, I always carried several small needles strapped to my leg. I kept some dipped in rockberry and some in rocktail. For more serious and unexpected encounters, I had my deadly bats. Tonight, I couldn't use the bats if I wanted to maintain my deception, so I stopped and removed one of the rockberry needles before proceeding.

56

A few minutes later, I could see the thieves. Anil's echoes showed Marku and the two brothers off to the right of the horses. When the thieves reached the horses, Marku, Yoan, and Vali charged. The numbers were equal but not the weapons. The clan had knives. The thieves had swords. Not wanting to interfere unless I had to, I stood watching from behind a cluster of bushes. Yoan threw his knife when he saw his attacker's sword. It sank into the man's chest. Vali danced around his opponent, dodging sword thrusts. Yoan, now without a weapon, threw a rock into the man's back. He dodged when the man turned on him. For the moment, it was a standoff. Their opponent couldn't attack one without opening himself to the other.

Marku had more of a problem. His opponent had him up against a wagon. Trapped, he had nowhere to go. As his opponent moved in for the kill, I landed on his back and jabbed a rockberry-dipped needle into his neck. He staggered a few steps, like a drunk, and then crumpled to his knees. I scooped up a rock, slammed it into his head, and tossed the bloody rock a few feet away.

By that time, the camp had come to life, and the third thief took off running with Yoan and Vali chasing him.

"Thank you, Ryana. Is he dead?" Marku asked, leaned close to me, panting and sweating. Blood trickled from a shallow cut on his arm.

"No, just drugged. He'll recover in a couple of hours."

"How did you know…no, forget I asked. Can you make up a plausible story?"

"Two or three if you like." I smiled.

Marku shook his head and began walking with me back to the wagons.

"What happened?" several asked at the same time as we entered the circled wagons.

"Ryana alerted me to the trouble, so I sent her to wake Yoan and Vali. Yoan killed one, Ryana hit one from behind, and Yoan, Vali, and others are chasing the third one."

I had always enjoyed the classes where you were given a situation and had to make up a plausible story. A good Spy had to be not only inventive but spontaneous. Everyone looked toward me.

"I couldn't sleep, and it was a beautiful night, so I decided to take a walk. I never saw them, but I heard one swear when he tripped. They obviously weren't up to anything good, so I went to Marku's wagon and woke him."

"What did you hit one with?" Ilka asked, looking at me with real interest.

"With a rock. I jumped on his back and hit him in the head. He'll probably have a terrible headache when he wakes and a lump the size of a goose egg." I laughed, held my head, and wrinkled my face in mock pain.

"The Shadows may have made a mistake when they let you go, Ryana," Ilka said, looking serious.

"I'm still mad at Morag, but I've to admit there's more to being a Shadow than hitting someone in the head with a rock."

The camp was awake now and everyone sat around the fire talking about the thieves. By then, the third one had been captured and the two lay tied to one of the wagon wheels. The clan bombarded me with questions. I stayed with my original story, embellishing it only slightly. Someone started a fire and drinks and food magically appeared. Soon the camp came alive with songs and dancing. I wasn't used to the chaos the clan took so naturally but forced myself to join in. The gathering broke up as dawn brightened the landscape with gold- and orange-streaked clouds. While the clan went about their morning chores, Marku walked me back to my wagon.

"I love Morag, but I have to admit I found it hard to believe her. Thank you, again. The loss of the horses would have been very costly in so many ways."

Marku had been obscure on purpose, and I appreciated his caution. The Sisters had been adamant about the need for caution. An overheard word could mean your death.

"If I helped the clan, it's the least I can do. You've treated me like family." I left him and walked back into the brush, needing to collect my darlings before the clan was prepared to move.

CHAPTER SEVEN

Miffin—Saxis Province

I lounged on the wagon seat, enjoying the feel of the early-morning chill and the serenity of the open prairie with its gentle rolling hills. It provided a stark contrast to Ahasha Valley's steep canyon walls, rocky terrain, and thick vegetation. Vali had taught me to drive the storage wagon, which I now considered my home. I felt comfortable in my new role. In the past three sixdays, I had become part of the tumbling act, albeit a small part, learned to operate the tent games and drive my wagon. My cycles of training had made me flexible. Even so, the workouts with the tumbling group had improved my agility, a useful skill for my current assignment.

My musing ceased when I saw Marku approach on his beautiful Vanner stallion. Mostly midnight black with a few white spots and streaks of white through its mane, it was a magnificent animal. When I realized he wanted to talk, I slowed the wagon. He nimbly stepped from his horse onto the wagon, leaving the stallion to trot alongside.

"I've heard a rumor that a Shadow in Adak has been killed. They didn't know her name." His face furrowed with concern.

"Karsa." My thoughts collided in chaos. My assignment was no longer just another exercise. I found myself alone in a labyrinth of killers. With Karsa's death, my anxiety over killing another human had been resolved. Those who killed Sister Karsa and…the others must be held accountable. If I tried to succeed as a

Spy, I would be prey. I knew now why Morag had given me the rank of Assassin/Spy.

"Did you know her?" Marku asked, breaking into my thoughts.

"No. I'm afraid this changes my plans."

"How so?"

"Whoever killed Karsa knows far too much about the Shadow Sisters. That knowledge could put you and your clan in danger. I intend to leave your troop as soon as possible." I would miss them.

"It isn't for me to tell you what you should do, but it would please me if you stayed. I promised Mistress Morag safe haven for you as a small repayment. The clan owes her that."

"But the clan doesn't understand the risk," I said while weighing my options. I would be safer traveling with the clan, but they would be more vulnerable. Alone, only I would be in danger. Staying, I put everyone in danger. These people didn't deserve the risk I presented.

"If I could tell them, they would feel the same way I do. Not knowing, they are less likely to make a mistake that might expose you and them. At least stay for a while. You can always leave if you need to."

"For a while."

* * *

That evening after the meal, Marku guided me over to where Alida and Ilka were sitting. "Alida, Ilka, I would like you to pierce Ryana's ear and give her one of our clan earrings."

The women looked to me and back to Marku.

"Is she joining the clan?" Alida asked.

"I thought we would make her an honorary member. She's helping with the acts and games. Besides, she kept us from losing our horses. I'm afraid for her safety."

"From whom?" Ilka asked.

"You heard the rumor that another Shadow was killed," Marku said, more as a statement than a question. When the women nodded, he continued. "If the killers find out Ryana studied with the Shadows, they could decide to kill her, too."

"But she failed…asked to leave," Ilka revised.

"She's obviously too young," Alida added.

"They might not see the difference or care," Marku replied. "It will make her less conspicuous in our acts."

Looking around, I realized all the clan had earrings. Of course, I had seen the gold rings, but the significance never registered until now. Without one, I would stand out as an outsider. I had thought wearing similar clothes and being part of the acts would be the perfect cover. I shook my head at my own inexperience and arrogance. Thank the gods Marku recognized the flaw in my thinking. Still lost in my thoughts, I allowed them to lead me to the campfire.

"Clan!" Alida waved her arms. "Today Ryana's to become an honorary member of the Dorian clan. Why, you ask?"

"Because she's part of the acts?" someone shouted.

"Because she saved our horses?" another shouted.

"Because she saved Marku from being embarrassed," Yoan shouted to everyone's amusement and laughter.

"Yes, yes, and yes. And because someone's attacking Shadows. We promised Mistress Morag that we would see her safely home," Alida said more softly this time. "Does anyone object?"

Looking around the assembled circle, I saw no dissent. I hadn't realized how much a part of this small clan I had become, and my growing attachment to them. Those thoughts were interrupted by a burning sensation in my left ear. Training kept me from screaming, until I realized that wouldn't be the normal response.

"Ouch!" The pain receded when Ilka rubbed some ointment on the ear, and Alida held a mirror for me to see. A gold ring hung from my earlobe. I smiled. I quite liked the look and honor the clan had bestowed upon me.

Where did acting a part end and becoming the part begin?

I hadn't realized they could meld into one. Although I had no choice but to pretend to be something I was not, there was no reason not to enjoy the experience.

"Thank you, everyone. I'll wear it with honor." The next several hours were filled with singing, dancing, and feasting.

* * *

One day short of Miffin, a group of eight men stopped us. They looked and acted like veteran soldiers. They had good horses and were well armed with swords, knives, and bows, but they weren't wearing uniforms. As they neared, the clan subtly began preparing to fight, as hands discretely moved within reach of weapons.

"We want no trouble, gypsies. We're looking for a woman wanted by Lord qi'Jochen," A broad-shouldered man said while his men began drifting along the wagons, scrutinizing each of us. I stared back when a thin, scarred-face man stared at me. He smiled. I did not. I had to look clan and knew they wouldn't be hiding their faces or smiling.

"What did she do?" Marku asked. I prayed he wouldn't fight to protect me. If he did, I would have to decide whether to stay to help or fade into the trees and disappear. The Dorian clan had become my friends, yet my assignment could determine the future of the Shadow Sisters.

Damn, life was complicated.

"We're all clan," Marku said. His horse stood a few paces from the leader. The two sat staring at each other for several minutes.

"Then you won't mind if we check for ourselves?" the raider said, clearly meant as an ultimatum, not a question.

"Two men, accompanied by one of mine. If finding this woman's your sole intent, two should be enough." Marku waved to Yoan, who jumped down from his wagon. In turn, the leader pointed to two of his men, who dismounted. They walked back to the last wagon. One entered the wagon while the other looked at Stela, who sat in the driver's seat. The search took close to an hour. They entered each wagon and scrutinized every person.

Morag had let the Shadow's Intermediate know she had sent a Shadow but not what she looked like or how she traveled. Morag had been right. I would be considered too young to be a Shadow. They would expect an older, experienced woman; therefore, it didn't surprise me when the mercenaries gave me only a cursory look. I doubted the clan's earring made any difference, but Marku had been smart to realize it may, if not today, then someday. It would be a long trip to Scio.

"You're free to go. Keep in mind there's a reward for this woman should you run across her. Twenty toras."

"She's definitely worth finding. How will I know this woman from any other?"

"She will be older. In her thirties and traveling alone or with someone she has just met. She will have clothing she's stolen from a Shadow she killed. Be careful, gypsy, she's dangerous."

"How will I find you if I do?"

"I'll be at your performance tomorrow." He turned his horse, and he and his men rode off. Afterward, I realized that my part had become real to me. I had remained in character, acting like any other clan member. And like the rest of the clan, I had been ready to fight. I had alerted Kasi and Anil and had palmed one of my rocktail-laced needles. I had come to realize the clan and the Sisterhood's interest lay on the same path.

* * *

Most of Miffin's population worked the iron mines or made swords and knives renowned for their high quality. I had practiced martial dances with a Miffin sword. It had felt like it possessed magic of its own.

As we entered the town, Marku rode in his most colorful outfit, which was in sharp contrast to his midnight-black horse.

"My good citizens of Miffin, come join us tonight for acts of skill and games to make you rich. We begin at sunset at the east edge of town," he shouted as we moved through the streets. When we reached a vacant strip of land just outside the town, we circled the wagons and a mad rush began to set up for the night's performance. I carried planks for the stage, hauled on ropes to set up the tents for after the show, and fed and watered the horses. We had barely finished when the first people began to stream in. Stela stood at the makeshift entrance collecting a copper each. There were always a few who avoided paying, but it wasn't worth the trouble or ill feelings it would cause to catch them. A copper was a modest amount. The gypsies made most of their money on games of chance, fortunetelling, and selling items they bought in the other provinces.

The leader of the men who had stopped us on the road and a few of his men were scattered among the crowd. I doubted he attended to watch the performance. They were hunting a Shadow. Little did they realize they were staring at her. I scanned the crowd looking for the Sisters Morag had indicated were in Miffin—a Spy and her apprentice. It would be an older woman accompanied by a young woman. If the mercenaries knew about them, they sought three, not one.

Before I could get a good look at the audience, Marku announced the tumbling act. We entered with a coordinated set of jumps, rolls, and spins. Next, each of us performed a separate acrobatic sequence followed by two- and three-man acts. The teeter-totter act was the highlight of the performance. It looked and was dangerous but beautiful to watch. During Yoan's knife-throwing act, I stood to the side observing the crowd. How good were my Sisters' disguises? As far as I could tell, there were six mother–daughter pairs unaccompanied by men. That would be a mistake if the mercenaries knew a team was operating in Miffin. Keeping separated would have been wiser. I began eliminating the pairs. Two of the younger women were my age or younger. If that were a disguise, it was perfect. Two of the older women were older than I would expect the senior Spy to be. Of course, a Spy could pull that off. If that was an act, it too was perfect. The other two were hard to eliminate. Finally, I had them. One pair was excited by the acts, while the other pair's excitement was stilted. It looked more like they were evaluating the acts. I would bet they were the Shadow Sisters.

Concerned for my Sisters, I watched the mercenaries wandering the crowd. They had their attention on the audience not the acts. They appeared to be searching for a middle-aged woman rather than a pair, although they didn't ignore pairs. Since the mercenaries were on the lookout, one misstep could put one or both in jeopardy.

Soon the acts ended, and my time came to work the dart-throwing game. Since it would go late into the night, I instructed Kasi to watch the pair that I had identified. The two had left early, reinforcing my guess. By the end of the night, I had paid out one silver and made a profit of five. When the night's activities ended, the clan cooked a meal and sat around talking.

Afterward, I went back to my wagon and considered my dilemma. Morag had told me to trust no one, which sounded like good advice, but should I do that at my Sisters' peril? Yes, if it endangered my assignment. I laughed at the irony. I dressed in a Shadow's traditional garb and strapped on my blow tubes and needles. With my head wrap stuffed in my shirt, I then covered everything with the clothes I had used to travel to Sebec. When everyone had gone to bed, I slipped out of the wagon, making sure I avoided the step that squeaked, and wandered casually into the small forest behind the wagons. Once out of the trees, I wove in and out of the streets toward the place where they had rented a room. In the shadows behind the inn, I slipped down my pants and then pulled them up again over my skirt. I removed my shirt and stuffed it into my chest harness to make it looked like I had mature breasts. Mine were almost boy-like. I had tried this when I had been alone and decided it filled me out around the hips and breast, changing my figure and age.

Watching through Anil, I had determined their room and present profession. Although bats never use their eyes at night, they have good eyesight as well as hearing. Over the cycles, I had learned to see and hear through them. They didn't understand what they heard or saw, but I did. I scaled the wall to their second-story room and slipped through the window. The room was small with two narrow cots, table, chamber pot, and pitcher for washing. The room probably was provided as part of their wages—a tavern wench serving food and drinks, and a cook.

I slipped the small blowtube with a dart, dipped in rocktail, along my left forearm, and a needle, dipped in rockberry, in my left hand. Then I lay down on one cot and waited. Two hours later the door opened, and the young apprentice walked in followed by the Spy, who closed the door. The young one walked to the table and lit a candle.

"Very sloppy, Sisters," I said just above a whisper. The Spy reached for her knife immediately, while the younger one was slow to get hers out from her shirt. "Don't. If I wanted to harm you, it would already be too late."

The Spy had her knife ready to throw but did not. Nor did she lower it. "Who are you?" she asked, keeping her voice low. To me, it felt like a cat-and-mouse game with them the mice. I instinctively knew I would win. Her essence, her life revolved around being a Spy. They knew weapons but would be a fraction slower. I lay on the cot relaxed but prepared to put the young one between the Spy and me. The apprentice would go first.

"You're ordered back to Ahasha. There are mercenaries and others hunting the Shadow who Sister Morag sent to investigate our Sisters' murders. Although they look for her, they are scrutinizing everyone. One followed you here tonight."

"How did you find us?" the Spy asked. Her body was as tense as a fiddle's string.

I lay there considering her question. "You were acting the part rather than being the part."

After a minute, she nodded agreement.

"What does she mean?" her apprentice said.

"She means we were evaluating the performance rather than enjoying it like everyone else—a dangerous mistake. I should know better. Thank you, Sister."

"Hold out your hand." I stayed on the cot and held out my hand toward her.

"I'm Zeta and this is Salma." Carefully, Salma reached for my hand. I could feel her one line indicating an apprentice Spy.

"She's an Assassin/Spy," Salma's hand jerked away from me like it burned. Zeta lowered her knife and smiled.

"I should have known. We'll leave tonight."

"Eight men have a roadblock about an hour out of town. Be careful. May the shadow of our Sisters be with you." I rose from the cot and backed toward the window. I hated to be cautious around my Sisters, but I couldn't afford trust. "I'm sorry, Sisters. I don't want to see you again."

"What does she mean?" Salma asked.

"She means she'll kill us if we aren't gone by tomorrow." Zeta nodded. "I acknowledge your right."

I took a few steps backward, sat down on the windowsill, tucked my knees to my chest, and rolled backward. My knees took the shock as I hit the ground. Working with the gypsies had improved my confidence and balance. I found myself trembling as I faded into the shadows. Had I been intuitive or arrogant tonight? Intuition could save my life. Arrogance could get me killed. Had lying on the cot avoided a confrontation or put me at risk? Was I right ordering the Sisters home? What would Morag think? Did I enjoy ordering people around? I was but a novice Spy by choice and never wanted to be an Assassin. But I felt like an Assassin/Spy. I had found the Shadows and knew I could've disabled them. I had much to think about. Many lives could depend upon the answers.

With Kasi and Anil scouting ahead, I ghosted through the town. Few people were out this late, but it wouldn't have mattered. The shadows provided all the cover I needed. I could've slid by anyone only a few paces away. The Sisters had taught me well.

When I was within a hundred paces of the wagons, I changed back to my dress and shirt. On the fringe of the trees, I saw Alida sitting on a fallen tree stump. I could've avoided her, but there was no reason.

"Evening, Alida," I said. She jumped up and whirled around while reaching for her knife. I felt sorry for the gypsies. They led a difficult life. Everyone enjoyed the entertainment they gave. Most didn't trust them, and some wished them harm.

"Don't do that!" Her eyes were wide and her face pale. "You scared me to death. We're going to have to put bells on you."

"Sorry. You didn't hear me because you were deep in thought. Want to share?"

"I want a husband and children. How do I get one when there are no eligible men around?"

"How do the others? What about Yoan?" I asked. I knew little about the gypsies and their lives. I knew little about life outside of Ahasha.

"Yoan and I are related. We are second cousins. Besides we aren't interested in each other that way. The other gypsy clans have eligible men, but we don't see them often and then only for a few days. We meet men as we travel, but very few want the life of a gypsy, and few of us want to leave our family and friends." Alida's eyes misted. I hadn't thought about

70

husbands and children. I had spent the entire ten cycles at Ahasha worried about being a Sister. Still, I could understand her dilemma.

"Find one you like, and I'll kidnap him for you," I offered. She giggled.

"It may come down to that. Thank you. I needed someone's shoulder to cry on. How come you're up so late?"

"The Shadows don't believe students need sleep. Eventually, you get used to it. I guess I haven't adjusted yet. Until I do, I find the night relaxing."

"And you keep the horse thieves away." She had a soft, melodious laugh. I thought she would make a good wife and mother. Back in the wagon, I put my clothes away, waited in the doorway until my darlings fluttered inside, and settled down under the covers to sleep.

CHAPTER EIGHT

Miffin—Saxis Province

The last night in Miffin, I saw a woman wearing a long robe watching the performance. Her robe was black with red flame-like trim on her sleeves and hem—a Fire Wizard. I had learned about the four types of Wizards during our weapons training: fire, water, wind, and earth. A Fire Wizard could conjure fireballs that were deadly at twenty paces and dangerous at forty. In addition, they could surround themselves with a firewall that incinerated anything entering it, including arrows and knives. We had been told to avoid confrontations with them because we couldn't hope to survive the encounter. Wizards belonged to guilds, as did the thieves, assassins, and religious cults. Their policies and alliances varied by province. I wondered whom the Fire Wizards of Saxis supported. I couldn't go up to her and ask, but it would be good to know because they might be players in the deaths of my Sisters.

Traveling with the gypsies, I was learning a lot about the outside world—far more than I would have traveling on my own. It would have taken cycles to learn about the real people behind the masks they wore. For some reason, people let their guards down at performances, and I got a glimpse. Fortunetelling gave the most insight. Alida had been teaching me the tricks of the trade: how to read palms and tea leaves and use a crystal ball. If the fortuneteller listened, most people revealed what they wanted to know. For some reason, they thought the gypsies knew how to conjure the secrets of the future and were willing to pay good money to hear it.

The games catered to human greed. People were willing to risk money they could ill afford in the hope of winning a lot. Ironically, the more they lost the more they spent trying to win it back.

It would be easy to forget why I was here. No matter what happened in the future, I would always cherish my time with the Dorian clan.

* * *

Adak—Saxis Province

The trip to Adak took three days. The roads through the rolling plains were well traveled, which made the ride easy. The weather stayed clear except for a welcome thundershower on the second day, which helped settle the dust. On the third day, we again saw the mercenaries. This time they merely watched as we passed. I suspect they assumed that the Shadow had somehow eluded their roadblock into Miffin, or that she had gone around the town. They probably left Miffin after scrutinizing the audience at our first performance.

"Mind if I join you, Ryana?" Yoan asked. He was riding a small gray horse with a black saddle and silver-trimmed tack. He had dressed conservatively today: a red vest with a yellow vine design, white ruffled shirt, and black pants.

"Hop aboard," I said with a smile. He looked the typical gypsy and filled with youthful energy. He swung up, leaving his horse to follow. I marveled at the training that went into their horses. Most would have wandered off when the rider left it.

"You seem to have gotten over leaving the Shadows," he said with a devilish smile.

"I was mad at being embarrassed, but the truth is Morag was right. I wouldn't make a good Shadow. If she hadn't asked me to leave, I would have left anyway. I learned a lot, but it was no life for me," I lied easily. My Shadow-self laughed at the absurdity of the statement. I wanted no other life. "I quite like the gypsy way, although I'd imagine the constant traveling would get tiring after the second or third time around Hesland."

"Traveling would get tiring if it weren't for family and clan. Not to mention creating new acts and meeting new and exciting people…like you." He bowed his head. He was a rascal, flirt, and amusing. I think he liked me. He had been working with me for two sixdays, teaching me knife throwing. Because I hadn't wanted to be an Assassin, I hadn't been required to be expert in multiple weapons. Ironically, Sister Hajna had considered my knife throwing adequate—a considerable compliment from her. It meant I came close to matching Yoan's skill. He would be considered an expert even by Hajna's standards. Yoan thought I had improved over the past season, although I was still far from his definition of good. That meant I could hit the small black circle in the center of the target about half the time. Of course, I could hit it ninety-five percent of the time if I wanted. I couldn't let him know without raising too many questions, so I cheated by intentionally missing the circle frequently. I guessed teaching me was a subtle way of trying to get to know me and my feelings about gypsy life. Like Alida had said, it was difficult to find a mate. If I hadn't been a Shadow, I might have liked Yoan and the life.

"I'm enjoying my time here. You and your clan are wonderful people, and I've learned a lot thanks to you." It was the truth.

"The feeling is mutual, or you wouldn't be wearing that ring." He touched my ear lightly. "I'll see you later for practice. Who knows when you might have to fill in for me?" He laughed but looked far too serious.

I had better continue to miss often enough for everyone to conclude that would be an awfully bad idea.

* * *

When we reached Adak, it was too late to set up for a performance, and besides, everyone was tired. We found the campsite for gypsy caravans, which passed every season or two. It was a large open area a league out of town, bordering a forest and small river. I decided to send Anil off to the Intermediate's house and kept Kasi near me. Maybe I was becoming paranoid, but the gypsies seemed to attract more than their share of trouble. Probably the reason everyone carried a knife, and they appeared so quickly. I'd bet the five children each carried one and knew how to use it. Doing Morag a favor might work to the clan's advantage, as I was prepared to do whatever I could to repay the friendship they had shown me.

I trained with Yoan for several hours after a leisurely meal and the traditional pre-performance discussions to determine assignments, the order of the acts, and the hundreds of housekeeping chores required to get ready for each performance. The practice went well until I forgot myself and began hitting the black circle more often than I should have.

"That was great, Ryana. You hit the target seven out of ten times. Marku will be pleased. We can always use another knife-throwing act." He looked serious.

Damn, my visual Ryana went to sleep.

"Beginner's luck. I've substantially improved thanks to you, but I don't think I could do that again." I vowed the visual Ryana would be more vigilant in the future. I had been able to identify Zeta and Salma because they had let the Shadow take control—a deadly mistake.

The evening performance went well, and the tent amusements collected several toras. I had been working the darts tent and paid three successful men. Ironically, that had attracted more customers, and I netted ten silvers, half a tora. The next night, I worked the fortuneteller tent.

After the evening meal, I grew restless feeling I should be doing something—but what? I wasn't here to hide, just not to be discovered. I decided to visit our Intermediate's house and pulled on what had become my dual-purpose clothing, which matched the visual and shadow Ryana I had become.

I reached the house close to midnight. Slipping through a side window, I crept to her bedroom. The room looked murky, lit only by the rays of the moon Setebos. Pressing my hand over her mouth, I laid a knife blade across her throat. At best, she might be able to make out I was a Shadow. She jerked awake but my hand held her down.

"I want you to send a message to Ahasha," I whispered in a rasping voice.

"Yesss," she stuttered. I guess she wasn't used to being woken up at night with a knife at her throat. She relaxed. "I'll leave it on the table. Send it tonight. It would be safer after I leave." My message was simple:

NOTHING IN ADAK, LEAVING FOR NAZE TONIGHT.

That would get some action. If she were involved, it could throw suspicion away from the gypsies and me, because we wouldn't be leaving for a sixday. Otherwise, I'd know she was loyal to the Shadows.

Halfway back to the gypsy camp, Kasi saw a swift-wing hawk leave in the direction of Ahasha. Five minutes later, another hawk left in the direction of Naze.

"Kill it," my thoughts went out to Anil. Anil overtook the hawk and killed it with its poison. I hurried back to where the hawk lay. The message read:

TELL SIR HARIS AND LORD G.

ASSASSIN SHADOW ELUDED US IN ADAK.

HEADED TOWARD NAZE TONIGHT.

So, they think the Shadow Sisters sent an Assassin. That could mean they think they know who needs killing. Interesting.

I returned to the camp, leaving Kasi to keep watch at the Intermediate's house.

Two hours later, the leader of the mercenaries appeared at the Intermediate's house. He stayed a few minutes and left. Kasi tracked him through the town to Lord qi'Jochen's castle. When he exited a few hours later, Kasi followed him out of town into woods where his men were camped. This time Kasi found a position near enough to hear.

"I talked to the noble who's paying us and informed him that the Shadow they sent to investigate is an Assassin. She plans to leave Adak today. He's sending a messenger to Kaslos informing them that she's going by way of Tuska on her way to Naze. He believes she's hunting a specific person or persons the Shadows want killed. We're to block the road to Naze past the crossroad from Lanpo to be on the safe side. The Fire Wizards would try to find out if anyone tipped her off to the roadblock to Adak, and they'll let the assassins' guild in Lanpo know to be on the lookout for her. We leave in one hour. The Lords are going to be very unhappy if we let her get past us again." He stood banging his fist into the trunk of a nearby tree. "Damn that woman. I'll flay her alive when I catch her. She will tell me every secret she knows."

I shuddered. The thought of being under that man's control made me break out in a fevered sweat. My mind ran wild with terrifying images of a mangled body. Feeling overwhelmed, my childhood memories came crashing back, and I wanted to find a safe place to hide. But like then, there was no place to hide, even temporarily. I refused to contemplate the future. The present was all that mattered.

I'm a Shadow. They are just ordinary men.

I had proved that today. I had discovered that our Intermediate in Adak was in league with the killers. One or more of Lord qi'Jochen's nobles were in on the conspiracy, and the cabal extended into Tuska. In addition, the Fire Wizards' guild in Saxis, the assassins' guild in Tuska, and mercenaries supported the instigators. And I had them chasing ghosts. The bad news: this conspiracy was far larger than Morag had imagined. She had sent one apprentice to do battle with an army.

* * *

"Ryana, can I talk to you for a minute?" Marku said. I had seen a lot of him over the past week, but we had little chance to talk.

"Of course."

"Yoan tells me your knife throwing has improved, since he's been teaching you. Is that true?" I wasn't sure why he frowned as he waited for an answer.

"Yes. He's a good teacher." Neither he nor Yoan knew it was my weapon of choice after the blowtube. Even so, Yoan had helped me hone my throwing distance and accuracy.

"He would like to include you in a new act. I'll tell him no if you would rather not. I know you didn't want to draw too much attention to yourself."

"So long as it's a minor part, I don't mind."

"I hope you're enjoying your time with us, and it's going well," he said. I was impressed. That question was as obscure as he could get—is your assignment going well?

"I love your clan, and yes, things are going well thanks to you." I doubted anyone could decipher this exchange. He smiled, so I assumed it had been clear to him.

"I'll let Yoan know."

* * *

As I sat by the fire that evening, Yoan strolled over to me.

"Marku tells me that you'll take part in the act. Do you have any ideas?"

"I think so. What if we do something funny rather than serious? It could precede your act, going from funny to serious." I guessed he had something serious in mind. If so, that might focus unneeded attention on me. Comedy was unlikely to, because of the funny dress and makeup.

"I had thought something more serious, but I like that idea." He laughed. "Come, let's see what we can make up." We spent the next two days working on various skits. We kept parts and disregarded others until we arrived at one we both liked. After practicing for several days, we decided to try it out in front of the clan after the evening meal. When everyone had relaxed with something to drink, Yoan began.

"Ladies and gentlemen, you too, Vali. For the first time performed anywhere on Hesland, I give you 'The Thief and the Lady.'" Yoan left the stage. When I entered and lay down on the bed, the candles went out, dimming the stage. Yoan crept onto the stage dressed in dark clothes. When he picked up a bag, which clinked like money, I jumped out of bed and the mayhem began. He backed against the wall. I shouted at him and threw a knife, pinning a hand to the wall. Everyone jumped up to help, until they realized it was a fake. I chased him around the stage, either missing him as he jumped and howled, hitting some fake part of him, or tumbling around with Yoan getting the worst of it. The skit ended with me tossing him headfirst out the door.

We got a good round of applause, and the clan pronounced it ready for the public. Yoan and I agreed to wait until we reached Lanpo, a small town and a good place to test a new act. Besides, it would give us more time to practice. Although a skit, I threw sharp knives.

* * *

At the next performance, I saw a Fire Wizard in the crowd. Not too hard to recognize with his distinctive robe and the clear space around him. No one seemed willing to stand too close. After the tumbling act, he walked up onto the stage.

"This caravan would be a good way to sneak a Shadow into town. One sent to kill Lord qi'Jochen." He pointed to Ilka. "Come with me, girl. I believe you can tell me what I want to know." As he spoke, the crowd backed away. "Any objections?"

"Yes," I shouted, waving at him. "Take me, I'm smarter than her."

"Why would I want some skinny kid like you?" he said, looking at me. He again pointed at Ilka. "It will be easier if you come with me and tell me what I want to know, or I can burn your clan's wagons now and save time. Which is it to be?" He grabbed her wrist.

80

"We've done nothing, Wizard. We were searched before entering town." Marku's face turned red as he approached the Wizard. He looked to Ilka and to the clan, who stood scattered around. Each had a weapon of some kind.

Unfortunately, Marku could do nothing without risking the entire clan. The Wizard could destroy the wagons and everyone in the clan. Although it would take him five to twenty beats of his heart to generate each fireball, he could construct a firewall to protect himself while he created one. I backed away and slipped into my wagon, changed, grabbed my throwing knives, and slipped out as the Wizard stalked away, dragging a struggling Ilka behind him.

While the clan huddled in a knot around Marku, softly debating what to do, I slid into the darkness, watching the Wizard through Anil and Kasi's eyes. My chances were nonexistent against him, but I couldn't bring myself to abandon Ilka or the clan.

Ilka planted her feet in the dirt, and when he jerked her after him, she kicked and tried to bite. He turned into a dark, narrow street, managing to pull her with him. I raced in behind him and threw one of the knives. Before it reached him, a ring of fire, almost blinding me it was so bright, went up around him. My knife dropped to the ground, molten metal. The ring dropped and a fireball headed for me. I hurled myself to the right into a small doorway, which hid only half my body. A heartbeat later, the fireball flashed pass. I blanked out the pain, focusing my mind on the battle—nothing else existed. The wall next to the door began to crackle and pop with flames. I stepped out and threw another knife. It was useless, but an alternative escaped me. The firewall went up and my second knife melted into a puddle. I dashed across the alley and dove into another doorway. A fireball spattered flames where I'd been standing, and the flames shot into the air. Windows shattered. I pitied the residents—and me. I had three knives left, and they would be of little use—except as a distraction.

Never do what your opponent assumes logical.

I stepped out and threw a knife, and again it melted in the fire ring. I waited for a moment and then darted back into the same doorway and loaded my blowtube with a rockberry dart. The Wizards threw his next fireball to the opposite side of the alley, anticipating that I would dash across as I had before. It hit the building and exploded in flames. I stepped out and threw a knife as the firewall went up. I started counting. Ten…Nine…I blew the dart high. If I was right, the dart would drop into the ring from above…five…I sprinted toward the ring…four…three…I blew a dart at the ring and dived at the ground, sliding toward the fire ring as it dropped. Lying with my last knife clutched in my hand, it felt like the world around me had stopped. The Wizard stood frozen, and Ilka stared glassy eyed at nothing. Then everything seemed to come back to life. The Wizard collapsed to his knees and then onto his face—a dart in his neck and another in his shoulder.

I took a deep, shuddering breath as the pain in my arm and side hit me. I staggered up, grabbed Ilka by the shoulders, and turned her away from me.

"Walk, don't run, to the end of the street. If a crowd develops, join them. If not, make your way back to the wagons. Go." I gave her a shove, and she began walking stiff legged as if in a trance.

The Wizard lay unconscious, unless two doses of rockberry had killed him. I couldn't take any chances. I jabbed two rocktail-dipped needle sticks through his scorched, burnt-black shirt into his chest. It looked as though when the darts had hit him, he lost control of his fireball.

On the other side of the street, I spotted an overhanging terrace. I jumped up, grabbing the railing. Pain in my arm and side felt like I had fallen onto a mound of broken glass. My left hand lost its grip, but I managed to hang on with the other. I hung there for what seemed an eternity. Eventually, I dragged myself up and over. As I did, I heard voices in the street. With Kasi's help, I made my way across several roofs to the next street and dropped down. On impact, I almost passed out. My head spun and every part of my body felt on fire. I wound my way through the streets to the outskirts of town, each step painful. While everyone was distracted by Ilka's return, I slipped into my wagon, stripped naked, hid my clothes, and collapsed onto my cot. I vaguely heard a knock on the door.

"Ryana, are you in there?" Marku whispered.

"Come in," I rasped. Even that hurt. I was alive but definitely not well. Marku slipped in, stopped, and spun to face away.

"You're naked!"

"Call Stela. I need salve for burns."

"Everyone will know you're…"

"Don't say anything except I'm hurt. I'll have a bedtime story." I laughed and immediately regretted it. Searing pain. I heaved but only a string of yellow bile came up. "Go."

He flew out the door. It seemed forever before Stela opened the door and came in. She knelt and examined my arm. "Those are bad. I've some salve that will help, but it's going to hurt."

It did. I could have suffered the pain in silence. But Stela would expect me to react, so I moaned, jerked away, and sobbed. I got so engrossed in the act that I almost forgot about the pain—almost. When she finished, she wrapped my side and arm with a cotton cloth.

"What happened? It had something to do with Ilka, didn't it?" She looked at me suspiciously. I could see by her wide-eyed expression that she had jumped to the correct conclusion.

Practice makes perfect, my Shadow-self mused.

"Yes. When that damn Wizard dragged Ilka off, I grabbed a good-sized rock and chased after them. I had some crazy idea that it had worked last time, so maybe it would work again. Sneak up and whack him in the head, but I lost sight of them. Then I heard a commotion one street over and ran there. When I turned the corner, the Wizard and Ilka were at the end of the alley. Two Shadows had him trapped. The one I was facing drew a knife at the Wizard as he threw a fireball at her. She got out of the way, but I didn't." I paused.

Good story, Ryana.

"At that moment, I understood why the Shadows made me leave and why I would never be good enough to be one. I'm far too impulsive. I act then think, and I'm far too slow. I thought for sure the Wizard's fireball would hit the Shadow. It didn't. She moved like a wraith. I knew she could save Ilka better without me, so I headed back." I closed my eyes. I wasn't faking the pain or dizziness.

"That was very brave, if not too smart. Rest now. I'll check on you later." She covered me with my blanket and kissed me on the forehead before she left. When I woke, it was morning judging by the dim light and the noise outside. Marku sat by the side of my bed, looking like he hadn't slept.

"Thank you, Ryana."

I motioned for some water. My throat was so dry I couldn't speak. He spoke while he held the cup to my lips. "Your story has been told a dozen times. You're a hero. You tried to get the Wizard to take you and tried to help. We stood around doing nothing but arguing what to do. If Ilka hadn't returned… Well, I'm afraid we would have gotten the clan killed. We owe you even if they don't know. We've everything packed and will be ready to leave shortly."

"Don't. Stay and do the performance tonight."

"Are you crazy?"

"My advice: never do what they expect. Do the opposite. If you run, they will think you're hiding something. If you stay, they will think you've nothing to hide; otherwise, you would have run."

"What about Ilka?"

"She should say that the Wizard wanted to know about the roadblock. On the way, two men in robes attacked him. She ran. She saw fire and heard noises but kept running. Play stupid."

Marku's eyes lost focus. After a few minutes, he shook his head, rose, and left the wagon. I could hear him shouting to unpack and everyone yelling at once. Bedlam reigned for a long time. I hoped the enemy reacted logically.

CHAPTER NINE

Adak—Saxis Province

I stayed in my wagon for two days sleeping, eating, and thinking. Had I done the right thing chasing after Ilka and confronting a Fire Wizard? I had risked my life, my identity, and my assignment. I could've stayed with the clan and listened to them argue. After all, no one expected me to do anything. I wondered if Ilka's life was worth the future of the Shadow Sisters. She wasn't, so why did I risk it? My mind exploded in chaos as I fought fear, regret, shame, recrimination, indecision, guilt, and another hundred emotions. Knowing the Fire Wizards were in league against the Shadows didn't justify my actions. I had no reason to kill one. Morag had told me to find who was killing our Sisters and get the information back to her. I could find no answer to my dilemma, so I tried to hide in my wagon. It didn't help. I was treated like a hero. Everyone in the clan visited at least twice. Food was brought to me. Stela stopped in several times a day to inspect my burns. And Ilka was a regular visitor. Sitting by the bed, she held my hand between hers.

"You were so brave trying to save me. Everyone wants to make you a member of the clan…only if you want. This the second time you've helped us."

The next day, Stela sat looking at me after she had finished her nursing routine.

"Marku told me that you convinced him to stay rather than leave Adak. That was very clever for a young…woman." I could sense where she was going: *You're a Shadow aren't you?*

"The one thing I learned at Ahasha was never to do what people expect. It confuses them when you don't and gives you an advantage."

Stela laughed. "We gypsies do that all the time with our games of chance, our acts of magic, and many other things. But we didn't when we needed it most. Marku almost had to fight the clan when he told us to unpack. Later one of the Wizards came by to talk to Ilka. He was eager to believe it was one of the other Wizards who attacked his friend and left after only a few questions. The clan owes you."

She seemed satisfied and left. I sat thinking. The clan was providing me cover and helping me investigate every city in Hesland—my assignment. Helping them allowed me to fulfill my mission. Morag was right. I should follow my intuition. With my turmoil resolved, I felt better and left the wagon. Although I wasn't well enough to take part in the tumbling or the skit with Yoan, I did help with the games. To everyone's relief, we saw no more Wizards and left on schedule for Lanpo.

* * *

Lanpo—Tuska Province

Lanpo was in Tuska Province, a two-day detour from the main road to Naze. The land soon became rolling prairie ideal for grazing cattle, which provided the town's main source of income. They supplied much of the meat for Adak, Naze, and Kaslos, the capital of Tuska.

Lanpo was a cattle town and the people boisterous and full of energy. As we rolled into town, men and women rode alongside, shouting greetings and making good-natured jokes directed at the clan's clothes, wagons, and individuals. As I had been taught,

I scanned the streets to get a feel for the town and its people. The men on horses and the people waving from the streets seemed normal.

The campground was flat and dry with a few small trees. The surrounding area consisted of grass and shrubs, which would make it difficult to leave without drawing unneeded attention. The clan unpacked quickly in preparation for the evening performance. Still not able to take part in the acts, I spent much of the time watching the crowd. I noticed what appeared to be thieves and assassins moving among the spectators. The thieves were easy to spot. Like the young woman who stumbled into a mark as her partner lifted his purse. The Sisters practiced similar techniques at Ahasha. It was one of many methods they used to acquire information.

A gangly young man in work clothes wove in and out of the crowd, examining each woman. Another, a couple of years older, passed him, intentionally ignoring him. I couldn't be sure whose side those two were on, if any. Many groups were involved, which indicated to me the Sisters were only an impediment to a larger conspiracy. I was faced with a dilemma. Had I accomplished what Morag asked me to do—find who was killing Sisters? Knowing what I knew, she might decide to recall everyone and let the game play itself out. Or should I continue and try to find the root of the cabal? I couldn't resolve it. Morag had suggested I rely on my intuition. After the Fire Wizard incident, reason dictated I run back to Ahasha as fast as my legs could carry me. But my intuition told me to continue. I decided I could put off the decision until I reached Naze. If I could find the Spy and her apprentice, I could send them home with the information. But could I trust them? The conflicting options gave me a splitting headache. Thankfully, Marku jerked me back to reality.

"Ryana, are you well enough to take the fortuneteller duty tonight?"

"I'd be happy to. It's kind of fun making up stories people want to hear." I chuckled.

"Your stories put us gypsies to shame." He made a small bow and wandered off.

I had been telling people's fortunes for over an hour when a gangly youth lifted the flap of the tent and came in. He put down his three coppers. I recognized him as one of the men who had been roaming the crowd and thought he might be in the assassins' guild.

"Well, sweet thing, what good things are going to happen to me?" He smiled as he sat down in the wooden chair across the table from me. Most customers tended to be apprehensive, not charming. He was either very clever or very inexperienced. Until I found out which, I had to avoid the kind of slip I had warned Zeta and Salma about.

"I see you've had a tough time in the past, and it's been difficult to get to where you are now. Luckily, I see success in your future," I said staring into my glass ball. Smoke swirled in it like clouds in a storm, a simple trick. Air was forced into the globe through a hole in the bottom. What I told him was easy to deduce. If he was an assassin, he had grown up on the streets—an extremely hard life.

"How quick?" he asked, a huge grin splitting his young but haggard face.

"Not soon. It'll be a bumpy road and will take time, but you'll have pretty women to smooth the bumps." The bumps and time would make the dream seem real. Just what a fortuneteller did—make the future look better than it would probably be. I thought he would be dead in a cycle or less. Belonging to the assassins' guild didn't change that he was a cocky amateur.

"Are you sure you don't –"

"Luix, you're supposed to be working. Get your ass out here." An older man stood holding the tent's flap open. His scarred face and whipcord-hard body suggested a dangerous man. Luix jumped up, knocking the chair over, and hustled after the man. I pitied Luix, a small sparrow trying to fly with hawks.

The rest of the evening proved boring. Most of the clients were women who wanted to know the future. I couldn't say I blamed them. They had hard lives and wanted someone to lie to them about tomorrow.

After we had closed the tents for the night, I wandered away from the camp to a small hill topped by a large-leafed tree and sat. I would never have felt Kasi and then Anil's feather-light landing if I hadn't seen them. For the thousandth time, I admired their large pointed ears, their small black eyes, and the silver-gray fur on their body, which gave the small creatures a wraithlike appearance. Anil's fur tickled as it crept toward my wrist, its sensitive nose searching for a vein close to the skin. Using razor-sharp teeth to make a tiny cut, it lapped up the warm flowing blood. I smiled. Anil had not found food. I didn't mind sharing.

I sat wondering what I should do now. The assassins were in the pay of or sided with whoever was planning to do something. I laughed. If I returned to Ahasha, what would I tell Morag? I didn't know who, what, where, when, or why. It was my move not theirs, as they hadn't found me. Suddenly, Kasi and Anil took off. I could see through their echoes that someone was coming. It turned out to be Marku.

"How are you feeling, Ryana?" he asked when he got closer. He looked tired. No one was near, but I was still wary of saying too much.

"I know it's been hard having me along. I'm ready to leave anytime you want." It was bad enough that the gypsies were distrusted and disliked by so many without having a Shadow along who everyone was searching for. It would be certain death if I were found traveling with them. He shook his head like a dog shaking water off. He reached out and took my hand.

"Yes, I'm tired, and I do fear for the clan. These are troubled times and not because of you or the Shadows. A storm's brewing that will affect all Hesland. I can feel it in my bones and so can everyone in the clan. You've been more a help than a burden. These people would be searching our wagons whether you were with us or not. You've thwarted the theft of our horses, which would have been a disaster, and you've risked your life to save Ilka. For that, the clan owes you a debt. Saving her had nothing to do with your assignment. You're welcome to stay for as long as you wish."

"I'll leave the second I think I might put you in danger. I won't have your lives on my conscience."

"The men in the crowd? Thieves or men searching for you?"

"Both. I don't believe they know I'm in Lanpo. They think I'm in Naze." I gave a small smirk. "They're just covering their bases. In Adak, it was Fire Wizards. In Lanpo, it's assassins. The funny part is that I always thought of assassins as experienced, clever, ghost-like people. They're a disappointment."

Marku laughed. "I've a woman still in her teens telling me that she's disappointed in the quality of the people in the assassins' guild."

I nodded. "Most have had hard lives growing up in the slums. They have had to fight to survive. That's made them hard men willing to do anything. It makes them killers, not assassins." I paused to consider what I had just said and how it might sound. As if somehow assassins weren't killers. "Marku, a person trains to be a soldier or a knight. I trained many cycles to be a Shadow. A person doesn't train to be an assassin or a thief. They are a collection of survivors."

Marku sat quietly for a while. "I see your point. You're saying an assassin could kill someone in a fight or sneak up on someone and kill him. They couldn't kill a Fire Wizard or wouldn't risk their survival to save a friend. And Shadows make terrible enemies."

The next day Yoan asked me if I wanted to start practicing again. I did, and the next night, we performed our skit to cheers and laughter from the crowd.

* * *

We left Lanpo at midmorning. On day two, Marku decided to stop early and make camp short of the crossroads to and from Adak to Naze in anticipation of a roadblock there. When he called a halt for the night, I sent Anil to check on the road ahead. As Marku had anticipated, the same bunch of mercenaries was searching everyone. Telling them where I planned to go didn't matter, since they had to know I would eventually go to Naze. My ploy had been primarily to divert suspicion away from the gypsies.

The early stop gave an excuse for a small party, a slow meal, and lots of talking and dancing. I spent time afterward in the forest with my darlings. By now everyone knew I stayed up late and wandered off by myself, which they attributed to my training at Ahasha. In part that was true. I could remain functional on four hours' sleep a night for a sixday.

The next day, we had been on the road to Naze for an hour when we came to the roadblock. Because the mercenaries were only searching those traveling toward Naze, the road north to Adak was moving freely. Ahead of us waiting to pass were horse-drawn wagons, several mule trains, and over twenty people on foot. There were more mercenaries this time. Judging by the loud grumbling and yells, there would have been a riot without the additional men. They were abusing every woman they encountered.

It took us three hours to make it to the front of the line. To my surprise, they looked each of us over, but no one was touched. I think they remembered us and were verifying we hadn't added anyone. Interestingly, they ignored the men. I would have to keep that in mind for the future. Maybe I could pass for a young man or older boy. With my figure and size, I barely passed for a woman. For this assignment that had proved fortunate.

CHAPTER TEN

Naze—Tuska Province

We reached Naze three days later. Even before we caught sight of the town, the stink of fish filled the air. As we drove nearer, I could see the harbor, which had a dozen ships coming and going with their sails billowing in the wind. They varied in size from small five- to eight-man fishing boats to larger oceangoing merchant ships. We stopped a league short of the town in an area designated for the gypsy caravans. It was surrounded by woods and near a moderate-sized stream, which provided good sanitation for the large audiences the performances attracted. We didn't try to put on a show that night. It was late in the afternoon and we were tired. Besides, our presence had to be announced. The next day several of us went into town handing out notices. I volunteered because I wanted to learn the layout of the town and the location of our Intermediate's house. It may help me find the Spy and her apprentice working in Naze. I hoped to contact them before I left.

The performance went well that night, and the clan made a nice profit. Afterward, I sent Kasi and Anil out to watch the Intermediate's house, a narrow two-story building in a row of similar houses. Most of our Intermediates had other businesses to supplement the money they made from arranging contracts with the Shadows. Tonight, men came and went while others loitered near by. Just after midnight, a Shadow entered. She moved quietly and stayed in the shadows but was easily seen through Anil and Kasi's echo-sounding sight. She slipped in, and shortly afterward three men followed. It felt like a trap and it was. The same three men exited dragging the woman by her arms and into a doorway three houses away.

I dressed in my blacks and collected my weapons. The peasant clothing went over them, and I faded into the night. The building was located well across town. Although it was late and the streets deserted, it took close to an hour to reach the building. When I did, it was the only house on the street with lights showing. I worked my way around to the back of the Intermediate's building and found a man leaning against a nearby tree watching the back door. Every now and then, he took a drink from a bottle he was clutching. I stood debating between a rocktail and rockberry dart, wondering if he had been one of the three who had captured the Shadow. It didn't matter. Morag said my assignment wasn't to avenge our Sisters, only to find out who and why. I loaded my blowtube with a dart laced with rockberry. The dart hit him in the neck. When I reached him, I picked up a good-sized rock and smashed him in the head. The darts had to remain a secret. With the lookout down, I slipped into the house through the back door. The Intermediate sat at a table with a mug in one hand a gold tora in the other. She smiled as she turned it in her hand.

"I guess this means you no longer work for us."

She jumped up, sending the chair crashing to the floor. Her face turned pale and she began to tremble.

"I…I was forced to do it," she said in a high-pitched squeal and took a step backward into the table.

"By whom?"

"A Wind Wizard… I had no choice…Shadow."

"As I have no choice." I said as I approached her. Whether she did it for pay or out of fear, she would sell me out at the first opportunity. As she held out her hand to keep me away, I grabbed it and twisted. When she bent from the pain, I drove my palm into her temple. Although she was unconscious, I gagged her and tied her arms and legs. To make sure she wouldn't be able to talk for hours, I stuck her with a rockberry needle. I slipped back out and dragged the outside guard into the house. Before I left, I blew out the candles, leaving the house dark.

Moving like a stalking cat, I slipped back to the building the men had dragged the Shadow into. The ground-floor lights were on, but it was dark on the second. Using ledges, terraces, and other protruding features, I climbed to the second story and peered through a window. The room was dark and neither Kasi nor Anil's echoes could penetrate glass. Inch by inch I opened it and climbed in. The room was empty, as was the one across the hall. As I exited the room, I heard screams and laughter from downstairs. I crept down the stairs, one foot at a time. Halfway, I froze at the sight. Two naked women hung like butchered cattle. The older, heavier one hung there covered with bruises and blood oozing from the many cuts to her body and legs. The young one's cuts and bruises were new and fewer. A young skinny man with a stick stood smiling as his eyes roamed over her body.

"Well, sweet thing, what other Shadows are in Naze? I'm in no hurry. I've all night." He laughed and struck her on the thigh. She jerked in pain but didn't scream. With her feet and wrists tied and suspended two hands off the floor, she could do nothing. A third man, sitting at a small table, laughed and lifted a bottle to his mouth.

A muscular man stood behind the older woman with his pants around his knees. His burly arms squeezed her to him, and his hands pulled at her breasts. I wanted to scream my outrage to the gods. I wanted to vomit when he squeezed her to him. Tears would come later. Ice flowed into my veins as I blew a rocktail dart into his neck. He froze for a second then fell against her, pushing her forward. She swung like a pendulum as he fell. The skinny one gapped at the man as he hit the floor. The man at the table looked up and pointed at me.

"There, on the stairs!"

The skinny one's head jerked toward me just as my throwing knife buried itself in his throat. I loaded my blowtube. The one at the table jumped up, knocking over his bottle, and drew his sword. He managed only a step before a dart hit him in the chest. He stumbled two steps more toward me before collapsing.

The ice in my veins melted and I stood trembling. I had killed three people in less than a minute. On the way to Miffin with Morag, I had wondered if I could kill anyone, even in self-defense or to save a Sister. Now I knew. I had become an Assassin who could kill without mercy, without doubt, and…without guilt. If our enemies wanted a war, so be it.

I dragged a chair over to where the older woman hung and reached up to cut the rope that held her. I tried to hold her as I cut the rope, but she was too heavy. We landed on the floor. Luckily, I managed to absorb some of the impact. I lay with my arms around her.

"You're safe. They will never hurt you again. I wish I could stay here with you and nurse you back to health. I can't." I could feel her trembling. Tears rolled down my face. "I can't. Worse, I must ask you to summon the strength you learned at Ahasha. To feel the strength and love of your Sisters, those still alive and those whose shadow we walk. I'm sorry. You must leave within the next two hours, and I can't go with you. Rest for a bit, while I attend to your apprentice and make arrangements."

I went over and cut the ropes that held her apprentice. She sat there trembling and quietly sobbing. I left her trying to gain control. There were things to be done. After recovering my knife from the man's throat, I cut it open. The gypsies had an act with throwing knives, and I didn't want even the hint of a connection. I picked up the chair and smashed the man on the floor in the head and broke the other one's neck—in case people wondered how they had died. Then I collected my darts and returned to the Intermediate's house. There I collected clothes and all the food I could find, which I stuffed in an old traveling bag. When I returned, Renee had Eshe in her arms and was still crying. Eshe looked awake. She looked up at me and tried to smile.

"I've clothes and provisions for you. We must get you dressed and gone within the hour." I felt inhuman asking and worse knowing I would force them if necessary.

"We can't leave. Look Eshe can't walk. Who are you to tell your Sister what she should or shouldn't do? You're a vicious killer. I saw what you did to those men after they were dead! Did you enjoy that?" She coughed and cried at the same time.

I guess she forgot I saved them.

I didn't mind. She and her Sister had been through hell. But it didn't change anything. I dumped the traveling bag on the floor and removed some clothing.

"Get dressed, Renee. You and Eshe are leaving. You can curse me after I'm gone." I knelt next to Eshe and began helping her put on the clothes. I died inside watching her pain as she tried to help. She grasped my hand. I could feel the two lines that proclaimed her a senior Spy as she could feel my Assassin/Spy sigil.

"Thank you, Sister. Renee, do as she says. It's her right."

"She's vicious. Did you see what she did to the men—after they were dead?"

"Your Sister knows what she's doing. You've no right to judge her. Anyway, if we don't, she has the right to kill us," Eshe said, choking as she tried to laugh. Renee dressed in silence and anger. I fed Eshe a little food and drink while I talked.

"I need you to carry a message to Sister Morag…" I went on to explain what I had found without mentioning the gypsies. "Tell her I'm ordering all Shadows home, except the rogue, who I'll kill. Tell her intuition rules her student. I hope it's what she wanted."

Eshe sat in silence, listening. "Our senior Sister has chosen wisely. What do you want us to do?"

"Here are twenty silvers our friends have donated for your inconvenience. It should help ease you on your way to Ahasha. They have also agreed to give you three horses for travel. Keep the third horse as long as you can. It's important. I want you to go north as many hours as you can. Find a place to camp for several days to regain your strength. There's a blockade at the Naze and Lanpo crossroads, though I believe it will be gone tomorrow. In any event, they are detaining those going to Naze, not to Adak."

"That's stupid. We'll go west toward Ahasha not north, and we don't need another horse." Renee scowled.

"If you don't go north, and don't take the third horse –" I walked over and grabbed her hand. I knew she felt the Assassin/Spy sigil. "Are you a Shadow Sister or a rogue? Do you obey your seniors or not?" I held her eyes until she dropped her gaze. North would be the one direction no one would look. Why would the escaping Shadows go north? They would be expected to head south to Kaslos or west toward Ahasha, since east lay the ocean and north went nowhere useful. It was illogical and, therefore, the right direction. The third horse would make their pursuer believe I had gone with them.

"Renee, she's thinking and we're not. Again, thank you, my Sister. May the shadow of our Sisters follow you wherever you go."

Was I thinking? I was drained of all emotions. I should feel something. I didn't. I felt detached. But for now, we had to leave before someone else arrived. Since Kasi and Anil detected no unusual activity, I sent them on their way. Covering my blacks with the peasant clothes, I returned to my wagon.

* * *

I let my visual-self relax into the clan's activities, refusing to think about my shadow-self's activities. Our skit continued to improve as I fine-tuned my accuracy. I could now, at twenty paces, put a knife in a one-inch circle every time. I think Yoan finally felt comfortable that I wouldn't miss. He had been brave to let me throw knives at him in the first place, especially since he didn't know anything about my previous training.

My tumbling improved as the group included me in routines that were more complex. It made me more flexible, and since I only took part as a member of a team, I didn't attract special attention. I also improved at fortunetelling. People seemed easier to read, and I enjoyed making up stories. As a result, I frequently found myself in the fortuneteller tent. Life felt good.

We left Naze at the end of a sixday stay. The clan had made five gold toras, which was a good profit. The two toras I had collected from the mercenaries, I gave to Marku. I had decided not to give them to my Sisters in case they were searched. That would have drawn too much attention. Marku gave me a strange look but said nothing. I knew he had heard a twisted version of the killings and was surprised he didn't ask me to leave. I had smashed the hornet's nest, and the killer bees swarmed Naze, looking for someone to kill.

We had no trouble on the road to Kaslos, which surprised Marku and me. We passed isolated pairs of mercenaries, who scanned the caravan as we passed but made no attempt to stop us. My ruse may have made our pursuers assume I had too much of a head start by the time they discovered the bodies and the missing horses. From the casual way the two-man patrols scanned our caravan, I would bet Kaslos seethed with angry people wanting me dead. Seemed fair; I wanted them dead, too.

* * *

Kaslos—Tuska Province

Along the road, we passed huge wagons being loaded with logs to be hauled into Kaslos, which was the main supplier of hardwoods used for making boats and furniture for the wealthy. When we arrived, the sun had begun to set, and the giant oak trees cast long shadows across the campgrounds assigned us. The site suited me because of the inconspicuous access. We spent the evening preparing for the performance tomorrow.

After most had gone to bed, I sat a few hundred paces away from the wagons contemplating my next move, while watching Kasi and Anil dart between trees catching bugs. I smiled at the thought. I had bugs of my own to find. An Assassin, Alina, and her apprentice, Carla, were operating somewhere in Kaslos, as well as a mob of angry people hunting me.

It wouldn't be easy finding two people in a large city when they were undercover. If they visited one of the performances, perhaps I could pick them out. In the meantime, I sent Kasi to watch the Intermediate's house. When nothing interesting happened after watching for a few hours, I walked back to the wagons. Ilka and Alida called out to me as I passed.

"Ryana, how do you stay up half the night and function the next day?" Alida asked. She and Ilka were sitting on the steps of the wagon they shared.

"Habit. It's a good time for thinking and dreaming," I lied and sat down next to her. "Thinking about going home and life after the Shadows."

"Yes, dreaming is good. I hear the Tobar clan will be here tomorrow. Pali is with them. He's very cute." She had a dreamy expression as she gazed off into the sky.

"What happens if Pali and you decide to marry?" I asked, curious about the clan's interactions. I had found peace among them. I couldn't stay, but for now, they were family. Alida's cheeks turned red. She lowered her head and giggled.

"When a man and woman decide to join, there's a gathering of the clans. Afterward, the woman's adopted into the man's clan." When Alida looked up, she was smiling. "Yes, Ryana. I'm in love with Pali and hope he feels the same. We've been apart for over two seasons."

"He would be a fool if he weren't."

Alida was a good-natured woman, with a kind and happy disposition. She would make a good wife and mother. I stood and yawned for effect. "We both need some sleep if we're going to be our best tomorrow."

"Good night, Ryana. You're a good friend. I'll miss you."

She knew her destiny. The clan's members had few choices except to marry within the clans, and their numbers were limited. I had heard there were five clans with maybe twenty-five to thirty eligible males and females whose genealogy were several generations apart.

* * *

I woke to a lot of shouting and jumped out of bed with a knife in hand. When I left the wagon, people were hugging and exuberantly exchanging greetings. I envied their simple life and the way they treasured family and friends.

"You must be Ryana," a tall man said from a few feet away. He had a thin face, high cheekbones, a hawk nose, and a pleasant smile.

"Yes." For a moment, I found myself speechless. He made me feel like I was part of the Dorian family with that simple greeting. "And you are?"

"I'm Luka from the Tobar clan. We've just arrived. Why not join us? We can learn about each other." He reached out his hand. I took it, and we walked toward the chaos. Food and drink had magically appeared, and the two clans formed a large circle.

"Luka, I see you've already found a new woman to flirt with. Don't trust anything he says, even if he swears it on his honor. He has none," Ilka said, invoking laughter from everyone.

"You've driven a stake through my heart, Ilka."

"You've no heart, Luka. It's a fable told to young innocent women," Alida said. The morning went quickly as the clans caught up on the other's experiences since they last met. Pali and Alida sat close, holding hands and whispering. I hoped Pali proposed or whatever clan men did to get married. I felt protective of Alida, like a much younger sister. That was funny because she was several cycles older.

"I hear many things about you, Ryana. I hear the Dorian clan has adopted you and that you take part in the acts. Do you plan to join a clan?" Luka asked, leaning near to me. That was an interesting question. Twice interesting. He just arrived, yet he knew my status in the clan and wanted to know if I planned to join a clan—not the Dorian clan.

As I thought over an answer, he went on: "I want to see your act tonight. The Dorian clan will perform first, then Tobar. Afterward I'll come and have you tell my fortune." He smiled as he rose and followed the others. Everyone needed to begin preparing for tonight's performance.

* * *

When we had finished our acts, I strolled over to the Tobar area to watch their show. They were the same as the Dorian clan but different. They had tumbling, knife throwing, tightrope walking, and other acts like us, yet each was unique. Even their games varied. After watching them, I realized we could duplicate the same routines with a little practice, but the differences allowed each clan to draw an audience. If they were the same, people might skip some clan's performances because they knew it would be the same as the last. It was the same reason we changed or added variations to our routines over the seasons. Luka walked the tightrope and performed a solo tumbling act with fire rings. It proved a clever variation on our tumbling.

I felt someone approach from behind me and spun around as he leaned toward me. I caught myself in time and slowed reaching for my knife. He caught my arm before my knife cleared my skirt. He smiled. "Was my act so bad you want to kill me?"

"Sorry, there are a lot of bad people around," I said, returning his smile. "I enjoyed it. You're exceptionally talented."

"Thank you. I enjoyed your skit with Yoan. I wouldn't like to get you mad. You're obviously very accurate…or Yoan's in love with you and willing to die for your attention." He looked at me intently.

"No, Ilka has designs on him. He has more to fear from her than me. I may miss; she wouldn't."

He threw his head back and laughed. "Come, let's sit by the fire and talk. I want to know more about you if you don't mind."

I'll tell you all you want to hear about my visual self.

We talked for hours. I told him some of my life at Ahasha and my subsequent life with the Dorian clan. He was attentive and asked many questions. In turn, I learned about his life growing up in the Tobar clan. I was disappointed when everyone returning from the evening acts interrupted us. I had enjoyed talking with Luka. After he left and everyone began to retire for the night, I wandered into the forest to relax. Kasi had returned to me as nothing of interest had happened at the Intermediate's house. I heard Luka long before he appeared.

"I had been told this is where you hide," Luka said as he walked up. "Notice, I didn't sneak up behind you this time."

"Probably a good thing." I was happy to see him but didn't want him doing this on a regular basis. This was my cover, providing me a convenient ruse to leave camp without any questions. "Do you have a heart, Luka?"

"Yes, but I protect it well. There are a lot of wily women out there." To my surprise, he didn't smile. It was a great line, or he was actually serious. We talked for another hour before he gave in.

"You don't seem to need sleep, but I do." He stood, lifted me to my feet, and kissed me—long and tender. I tingled from my head to my toes. I had never thought of myself as a woman. In the mountains, I was a girl-child. At Ahasha, I was a student and neuter. Here, an Assassin. Sex was something other people did, not Shadows. I melted in his embrace. He released me and took my hand as we walked back to my wagon. "Good night, Ryana. I'll see you tomorrow if you wish."

I nodded and climbed into my wagon to sort out my feelings. The Sisters had explained sex, its ram-ifications, and the drugs that kept you from having a child. I didn't know what would happen or what I wanted to happen. Mixing the drug, I decided better safe than sorry. A child didn't appear part of my as-signment.

CHAPTER ELEVEN

Kaslos—Tuska Province

For the next several nights, nothing happened at the Intermediate's house, but Luka seemed to be everywhere I was. We talked and laughed over the smallest things. He gave me lessons in tightrope walking, and in return, I showed him some of the finer points of knife throwing. We kissed, and his hands roamed my body, sending glorious tingles though me. I was relieved when he didn't press me to go further. Before he did, I needed to know more than I did, which bordered on nothing. Between acts, I cornered Alida and Ilka.

"I need advice about Luka and sex," I said, pulling them aside where no one could hear.

"Sex gets you kids. Kids before you're married means it's unlikely anyone in the clans will marry you. But every man will try to have sex with you because they think you're easy. Even if you don't get pregnant, word will get around, and it will be much harder to find a mate. Kissing and roaming hands is considered normal while you're trying to find a husband. The best advice is don't," Alida said. She seemed serious. Ilka nodded agreement. "We're a small community and everyone knows everyone else's business."

"Luka's the biggest liar in all the clans. More than one girl has succumbed to his charm. To his credit, he doesn't brag about it afterward. He isn't interested in marriage because he's having too much fun," Ilka added.

I left with much to think about. According to Ilka and Alida, the clan had a taboo on sex before marriage. I wasn't clan, but my visual self had to act in a manner consistent with their values. If I hadn't been adopted into the clan, I wasn't sure what I would be willing to do. I felt so confused.

I continued to see Luka. We talked a lot and had sessions of glorious kissing. He didn't try or suggest more. I was glad because it avoided a confrontation. I had decided I wouldn't have sex with him regardless of my own desires.

* * *

Four nights later, as I climbed into bed, Kasi spotted two figures ghosting along the street close to the Intermediate's house. A Wizard, his robe black with a silver swirl pattern on the hem and on the sleeves, stood at the corner. Dreading the inevitable confrontation, I threw my clothes on and hurried in a different direction than normal to avoid Luka. Using Kasi's eyes, I wove through the vacant streets.

When I reached the corner behind them, the Wizard had found the Shadows and stood smiling in their direction. The Sisters half crouched and pressed back against the wall in the deep shadows. I slipped up behind them.

"Go," I said. The nearest spun, her knife ready.

"You'll lose this fight. Run. I'll hold him as long as I can. Meet me two days from now, two hundred paces behind the Intermediate's house." I grabbed the back of her hand and could feel her Assassin's sigil. I knew she could also feel mine. "Go, Sisters, that's an order. You're interfering with my fun." I stepped past them as a gust of wind forced us back a step. "He and I have an argument to settle."

I meant it to be lighthearted—an Assassin/Spy's bravo. It was not. The Wizard wanted to kill Shadows, maybe already had. I wanted to stop the killing, the hunting of my Sisters. Yes, we had an argument settle. One of us would die here tonight.

"Come, Sister, you can't win," one said as they backed around the corner.

Another blast slammed me into a wall. I gasped for breath and dove, rolling as a blast of air blew past me. The force hit where I had been a moment before. I dove for a doorway. A gust of wind swept by, tearing shutters from two nearby windows. They scraped along the wall shattering windows and finally clattered to the ground. I stepped out and threw a dagger. The Wizard brushed it aside with a gust of wind.

I dashed across the street headed toward another doorway as I realized that, unlike the Fire Wizard, he didn't need to drop his shield to attack me. My hope of killing him like I had the Fire Wizard was gone. A blast of wind tore at the doorway where I had fled and threw me into the door. Pain shot through my ribs and arm. I jumped for a terrace jutting above but couldn't hold on as another gust tore my grip loose. The street cobbles knocked the wind from my lungs as I hit. I lay panting when another blast pushed me, scraping against rocks and rubble. My blacks ripped and skin shredded as I slid.

Voices reverberated in my head. My father shouting, "Worthless girl…" A softer voice, "These games will teach you the secrets of the Shadows…"

Kasi and Anil waited for my word to attack. I wouldn't give it. They couldn't survive the wind circling the Wizard. I rolled toward the wall, stifling a scream from the pain. Images flashed through my mind…at the table before bedtime, stirring a mug of hot milk…faster… The faster the outside turned, the deeper the center went—the vortex of the current. The Wizard laughed as I pushed myself to my knees. Another gust rolled me along the wall. On my knees, I sent a knife arching into the air. The wind spun it around. Another. It spun after the first. Another. A blast of wind slammed me into the wall and onto the ground. I lay there awaiting the end. The final blast that would end the contest. When it failed to come, I realized the wind had died. Looking up, I saw a knife stuck in the Wizard's head. Blood streamed down his forehead and over his eyes. He was only wounded and would have the wind back up soon. I groaned as I rolled onto my back.

"Attack," I mentally screamed. Kasi and Anil dove into the silence. They landed on his shoulders and sank fangs into his neck. The Wizard dropped to his knees. I struggled to my knees and blew a rocktail dart into his chest, and my lungs felt like they had imploded. I crawled on my hand and knees to him and pulled out the dart and my knife. Grabbing his hair, I pulled back his head. With no regret, I cut his throat.

Look inside yourself. Calm. Only the present exists. With the pain pushed back, I rose to my feet. No one saw me as I slipped silently through the streets. But my mind was on the arrogance of the Wizards, thinking themselves gods and the Shadows mere beasts.

Tonight, the gods would bleed.

At the tavern, I slipped behind the building and picked the lock. A few minutes' search and I had four bottles of brandy, some old rags, and a flint. I left a tora on the bar, relocked the door, and disappeared into the night.

Kasi's echoes guided me through the still streets and through a narrow stand of woods to the Wind Wizards' guild house, a two-story black and silver building with a wide grassy lawn and a scattering of trees. A dozen black flags fluttered along the rim of the roof. In the middle rose a circle of arches, each with a large silver bell clanging in the breeze. Since there was no wind now, the Wizards' power created the effect.

When a drifting cloud covered the moon, I managed a slow run across the lawn. At the house, I used a windowsill to jump and grab a rail on an iron terrace. I heaved myself over. After a few minutes to steady myself, I climbed onto the upper rail, caught a flagpole, and swung onto the roof. I lay there panting, knowing my body should be screaming with pain and soon would be. I rose and crept toward the front, emptying the first bottle as I went. The liquid ran down the roof and dribbled onto the wall. I pulled out the rags I had brought and stuffed one in each bottle after soaking them with brandy. I struck a flame to each one and they caught with a whoosh. I dropped one down one of the three chimneys. It crashed and exploded. Someone screamed. I threw another one to where I had previously poured the first bottle. Fire flowed over the edge of the roof and down the sides. At the same time, the flames on the roof lashed higher. As I dropped onto the terrace, a Wind Wizard came running around the corner. Looking up, he saw me, and wind began pushing me back against the wall. I flipped my remaining bottle arcing through the air, imagining him one of the narrow-necked bottles. It disappeared into the Wizard's growing vortex, and he flared like a giant candle. I dropped to the ground and staggered into the woods, hoping to hold out a little longer. A short time later, a thousand flaming arrows tore through me, and I collapsed.

* * *

When I woke, thin fingers of dawn lit the eastern sky. I was desperate to make it back to my wagon before everyone began the morning tasks. It seemed impossible as every step sent searing pain from my foot to my brain. Focused on one step at a time, I eventually reached the wagons. One of the lads was watering the horses, but I stumbled past without being seen. In the wagon, I stripped and passed out.

A loud knock on the door brought me back to consciousness. "Ryana, are you there?" Marku called. He sounded concerned.

I squeak out something close to "Yes," which I regretted instantly. Pains slammed into my chest and ribs.

"Can I come in?"

"Yes."

He peered in. "You're naked. I'll be right back. Don't move."

I couldn't stop a choked laugh or the resulting jolt of pain through my ribs. I didn't want to breathe much less move. I lay as still as I could, thinking. Had I done the right thing challenging the Wizard? I still hadn't located Sir Haris and Lord G. Now I had lost the chance. The Wind Wizards were supporters, not instigators. My assignment was to find the force behind the killing, not their supporters. Right and wrong were illusive, and I felt too young to differentiate between the two. A few minutes later, someone opened the door and closed it immediately. Judging by the voice, it was Stela.

"Marku, get me the satchel with my salves and herbs." She knelt by my cot and gently inspected me. "What happened, child?"

I hated to lie to her, but it couldn't be avoided. "I was walking in the forest behind the wagons when some large animal began chasing me. I ran. When I tried to look back to see how close it was, I tripped. It sent me tumbling over a rocky embankment. When I woke up, I found myself lying between two boulders." Each word took all my strength. My lie wasn't bad considering how hard it was to concentrate with my head spinning.

"That lie is almost plausible –" She stopped and got up when Marku knocked again. He handed her the bag.

"How's she?"

"Good considering she tripped while running and fell down a slope of rocks. Go, I'll call you when she's decent." She closed the door and returned to me. I hadn't realized I was naked. I hadn't had the energy to dress after I had managed to put my blacks away. "Not quite as good as the one about the Fire Wizard." She didn't say anything else while she applied a variety of salves and herbs, some cold, some burnt, and others that stank like a skunk. She was gentle, but I had to bite my lip till it bled to keep from screaming.

"Time for the truth, Ryana. You weren't asked to leave Ahasha, and we aren't taking you to Scio. You're a Shadow. Marku knew, didn't he? The truth."

"Yes." I didn't want Marku to get into trouble for protecting me, and I didn't want to put the clan in danger. "I'll leave tonight, Stela."

She laughed then sobered. "I believe you would try. I'm not mad at Marku. The gods know we owe Mistress Morag…and you for the horses and Ilka. I can't believe Morag sent a child to do whatever she wants. How did she expect you to survive?"

"She sent me because I was the best choice. I'm too young to be the one the Shadow Sisters would send on this assignment. And she doesn't expect me to survive." I looked into her eyes. Kind eyes. "Stela, would you give your life to save the clan?"

"Yes, without regret… I see. You do it for your clan. Are you an Assassin? Forget I asked, it's none of my business."

I had to decide what to say. She deserved honesty. "It's complicated. The Shadows have three ranks…" I spent a few minutes describing our system and its hierarchy. "I'm an Assassin/Spy working to find who wants us dead and why."

"You killed the Fire Wizard to protect Ilka, and the Wind Wizards to protect the Shadows?" she asked. She rubbed her temples, frowning, as she tried to come to grips with the situation and weigh the danger. I nodded.

"Morag doesn't know who's attacking the Shadows, then. Do you?"

"She sent me to find out. It's major. Rulers, Wizards, and guilds are involved. I don't know why or who's at the center of it. I told Marku, I would leave rather than put the clan in danger. You've done more than Morag could expect of your clan. I, in her name, release you from any debt to her."

Tears gleamed in her eyes.

"Mistress chose well. I don't envy you, child. No one your age should have to bear that much responsibility. You can't release us from our debt to the Shadows any more than you can forsake your clan. You may stay as long as you want. Now sleep. I'll repeat your story. It isn't as good as the Fire Wizard one, but it isn't bad." She shook her head and left mumbling to herself.

* * *

After sleeping the rest of the day and the next night, I awoke with the feeling it must be midmorning. To make it look like my injuries weren't very bad, I'd have to get up and out. It took forever to get dressed, with stops in between to rest. I climbed carefully out of the wagon, each step a reminder of the beating I'd taken.

"Ryana is up, everyone," Ilka shouted and instantly I had a crowd walking with me to the seats surrounding the fire pit. "How are you feeling?"

"Like you rode all of the wagons over me." I gave my best smile. I did feel a bit better than last night. Luckily, I was young and would heal fast. At least I could walk upright. "I twisted around to look back at something chasing me when my foot snagged on something, and I tripped over the edge of a cliff. I'm glad this is the last night in Naze; it will give me a few days to recover." It sounded like a reasonable story to me. Hopefully, no one would go looking for a slope with rocks.

"Sorry, Lord zo'Stanko is having a party five days from now and wants us to give the entertainment. He particularly asked to see Yoan and your skit," Alida said. That was fortunate as it would give me a chance to find Lord G and Sir Haris, if I could recover by then. Just then Luka came walking around one of the wagons. "Ryana, I just heard about your accident. I was worried when I didn't see you last night." He stared at me before giving me a kiss on the forehead. He looked around the circle of people. "Has everyone heard about the fight the Wizards are having? They say two Wind Wizards were killed last night. The Fire Wizards set the Wind Wizards' guild house on fire."

Marku nodded. "The Earth Wizards have joined the Fire Wizards. Between the three, they are destroying half the city. The Wizards are a law unto themselves. Even Lord zo'Stanko can't stop them. I don't want us mixed up in any of it, so stick close to camp."

"Ha!" Ilka snorted. "Let them tear each other apart. Serves them right." Talk buzzed. I sat trying to blank it all out. I had to think about Sir Haris and Lord G. The gods and Lord zo'Stanko had favored me with a second chance. Luka wasn't helping the thinking as he leaned over me.

"Am I going to see you tonight?" he whispered.

"Yes, I'll meet you at the edge of the forest, as usual." I gave him a weak smile. He kissed my forehead again and left.

* * *

I sat on a fallen tree trunk waiting for Luka, thinking about my life, the Shadow Sisters, the Dorian clan, and Luka. I loved all three. But in the end, it didn't matter. I'd eventually die for one or the other. I didn't mind. It would be worth it. Life was to be lived one day at a time—not yesterday or tomorrow. Marku was heading toward me through the trees. I could hear the difference between him and Luka, like Kasi and Anil heard the bugs they chased.

"How are you?" he asked as he sat down next to me.

"Sore and confused," I said. I needed someone to talk to. I wished it had been Sister Morag, but she wasn't here and Marku was.

"What about, afraid?"

"No, I'm resigned to my future. I can no more change that than you can change being a gypsy, and neither of us would want to."

"I wish you could. Everyone in the clan loves you. I think you've even captured Luka's heart." He sat silently for a while. "I know you put on an act and make up wonderful stories to hide behind, but you can't hide that you care for the Shadows, the clan, and Luka. That's real. I don't think Mistress Morag knew how well she chose."

"Yes, I do care. I don't know whether that's good or bad. I'm too young and inexperienced to know. She told me to rely on my instincts. I am and it feels right."

116

"Stela and I'll help as much as we can. I had better leave now, Luka will be here shortly." Marku kissed me on the forehead and walked toward the wagons. He hadn't been gone long when Luka waved to me as he strode between the trees.

"I missed your act tonight. I don't think you know how much a part of the show you've become." He sat and put an arm around me. My face didn't react, but I flinched in pain. He let go.

"What's wrong, Ryana?" he asked, leaning back to search me with his eyes. I opened my blouse to show my ribs and chest. Stela still had it wrapped, but purple bruises and scrapes went all the way up to my shoulders.

"I love your touch, but I'm very sore." I rebuttoned my blouse.

His face froze, his eyes wide, and mouth open. "What are you doing up? You should be lying down." He took my hand. "Come, I'll walk you back to the wagon."

"No, let's sit and talk. You'll be leaving tomorrow."

We sat and talked for a long time with me leaning back against his warm chest. I felt protected from the world.

"Ryana, you're like no other woman I've ever met. Alida's right…" He smiled a little smugly. "I flirt and lie to all the women. But with you, it's real. I'm sick about leaving tomorrow without you, knowing I may never see you again." He paused for a moment. "My love, join our clan. Marry me." He turned my face enough to look into my eyes. My traitorous eyes misted. My training had deserted me.

I blinked them back. "I'm confused, Luka. You know I grew up among women. This is so new. I love being with you. I wouldn't let anyone touch me like you have and love the clans, but… How can I be sure it's the life for me? I love you, but… I'm not sure that's enough." I kissed him on the lips lightly. "I need to go home and sort out my feelings."

"I'll never see you again if you do." His voice was a whisper.

"Yes, you will. You'll stop in Scio in less then a half-cycle. I'll be there. By then we'll both know." I wondered if that were another lie or somehow the truth. He nodded, stood, and pulled me up to my feet. Then he held me against his chest. It hurt but was welcome. He surprised me when he let me go and ran toward the wagons.

I waited until near midnight and then slid into the forest. With Kasi and Anil's help, I ghosted toward the Intermediate's house. Kasi showed me the two Shadows were hidden two hundred paces behind the house. I snuck up behind them. Each had a small cat on her shoulder.

"Evening, Sisters," I whispered. The Assassin's apprentice Carla jumped and spun around; knife drawn. Assassin Alina turned and smiled.

"It's good to see you alive, my senior Sister. Thank you for saving our lives," Alina said. She put her hand on Carla's arm, lowering it. "I hear a Fire Wizard killed two Wind Wizards and burnt down their guild house—a story that will be told for generations. A dream for every aspiring Assassin."

"Return to Ahasha," I said. "Tell our senior Sister I believe we are being killed not because of what we've discovered but what we may discover. There's a plot of some kind. Province rulers and the guilds are taking sides."

"I acknowledge your right. We'll leave tonight. May we help you in anyway?"

"Yes, I would like your apprentice's blacks. Mine are getting shabby." I grinned at Carla's expression. She shook her head, no. "She's closest to my size."

"Our Sister needs a change. She's staying. We're going home."

Carla reluctantly stripped and handed me her blacks.

"I'm sorry. Please turn your backs," I said and waited as they did. I stripped and put on Carla's clothes. "Thank you." I handed her my bundled clothes.

"Why?" Carla asked.

"Carla, she's our senior Sister's avatar. She would…did…risk her life for us, but she can't risk her secrets with us." She gave me a small bow. "May you walk safely in the shadow of our Sisters."

CHAPTER TWELVE

Kaslos—Tuska Province

The next few days flew by. Although I was still sore and every move either painful or uncomfortable, I began practicing on the third day. The Sisters had taught me to tolerate pain as little more than an inconvenience.

Yoan and I practiced the skit, and I joined the tumbling act. For my assignment, I needed to join the clan for their performance at Lord zo'Stanko's dinner party.

We arrived well before the dinner to set up for the acts. We had more than enough space. The hall could accommodate several hundred. But the dinner had been restricted to royalty and influential people— less than a hundred. We waited in an adjoining room while they ate. After they had finished dinner, a uniformed chamberlain motioned for us to come in. Alida and Ilka spun through the door with cartwheels. The rest of us paraded in behind them. Baldi went first with feats of balance on the tightrope. Next, Stela made balls, scarves, and birds appear and disappear. Yoan followed with his precision knife throwing, finishing with several throws blindfolded. Finally, it was Yoan and my turn.

Yoan led the way onto the stage. "Are you ready for the show, Kati?"

"Of course, Adami. Just make sure you stand still," I said. "No scratching and no making faces to throw me off."

Yoan went to the wall and assumed a position inside the outline drawn there—legs spread, and arms extended straight out from his sides. "Ready."

I stood twenty paces back, knife in hand, staring at him. My hand whipped back and then forward. The knife slipped out on the way back, dropping to the floor.

"Damn, Kati. You said you practiced."

"I did. Well, sort of. It's so boring. Anyway, the knife slipped out. My fingers are greasy from the chicken. I'll be fine," I said while wiping my hands on my shirt. Now the audience was leaning forward and snickering. My second knife hit the board a foot away from him. I looked at him and waved.

"More grease." I said again wiping my hand and the knife on my shirt. "I'm not worried."

"No, you have the knives. It's me that should worry."

"Quit fussing!" The knife flew and hit with a thud, hilt first, and dropped to the floor. "Don't give me that look. I didn't hit you, did I?"

The audience was roaring.

"I think that's enough –" Yoan said stepping away from the board. I held my knife pointing toward him.

"Get back, you worm, or I'll skin you like a chicken."

Yoan stepped back. The second he was against the board, a knife thudded two inches above his head. I put my hands on my hips.

"That was good, Kati," he said, beaming a smile.

"Well, sort of. I aimed for the outside of your hand."

By now, everyone was shouting for Kati to throw another knife. The next knife went between his legs. That got gasps and more chanting to throw. Now the audience was well into the skit, feeling like it was real. The next knife went wild, hitting the floor first.

"That one doesn't count, Adami. I was looking at the handsome man over there." I winked at a young man at a far table.

"Pay attention to me, not him!"

The next knife stuck six inches below Yoan's crotch.

"But he's cute." I smiled in the table's direction, turned and threw again. This time two inches above his wrist. "I got it, Adami!" I jumped up and down clapping.

"What?" Yoan said.

"If I aim for your arm, I miss. Watch." The audience gasped as I threw. A knife thudded above one wrist and then the other. Then one after another struck next to each shoulder and then an inch from each ear.

The room was silent, and then clapping exploded.

We took our bows to shouts of "Bravo!" Lord zo'Stanko motioned Yoan and me over.

"You are a very brave man, gypsy." He handed us each five toras and waved to his chamberlain, who led us toward the door. We paraded out, waving, to applause.

Two serving girls carried in a tray of roasted chickens redolent with the scent of onions and another piled with loaves of white bread and apples. We stuffed ourselves while waiting for the party to break up, so that we could remove our makeshift stage and props. I caught one of the servers as she was leaving.

"Do you know Sir Haris and Lord G... I forget his name." I hoped they were regular visitors or important enough to be well known. She nodded.

122

"Yes, Lord zo'Goran. He's zo'Stanko's son. He lives out of town. Sir Haris is chief of his guard."

"Thank you. I had heard Lord zo'Goran is an important man. He may be interested in our performance." I slipped her a silver. "Thank you for your help."

She gave a small curtsy and left smiling. Now that I knew them, what did I do with the information? I decided to do nothing and let him think they were anonymous. That might lead me to others involved in the plot.

We packed and left Kaslos as dawn broke the next morning. Our next stop was Bywick, a small town on the Tuska border with Calion.

* * *

Bywick—Tuska Province

On the way to Bywick, we rode past pairs of mercenaries, who stopped to watch us pass but made no attempt to search us. We passed a merchant's train of two wagons being searched by two mercenaries. One had a woman backed against one of the wagons, blouse torn open. The two merchants didn't look like fighters and were making no attempt to interfere although clearly furious. There was nothing they could do as the other mercenary stood guard with his sword drawn.

When we stopped each night, we built a fire in the middle of the camp and everyone sat around eating and talking. A lot of the talk the first night was about the Tobar clan, sharing what each had learned. Talk centered on their acts, possible changes in ours, and potential new acts.

"Everyone," Alida stood, shifting from foot to foot. "Pali –"

"Proposed!" Ilka shouted and everyone started laughing, crowding around, and hugging her. Soon a party began, and drinks and snacks appeared. Confused, I leaned over to Ilka.

"Why is Alida staying with us if she is going to marry Pali? Shouldn't she be leaving with the Tobar clan?"

Alida laughed. "And live with who? Pali is living with his brother in their family's wagon. Pali will have to buy his own wagon before they can get married. His family and friends will help, but it will take time. Alida hopes that he will have everything settled by the time we meet up with the Tobar clan next. Then there will be a wedding and a big party. And no acts for a few days."

I wasn't only learning about gypsy life but life in general. At Ahasha, there was no social life and no men. I owed the Dorian clan much. Without them, I wouldn't have survived more than a few weeks. I would have been on my own and noticeable. I didn't know the price of anything and wouldn't have known how to interact with people. Even now, I would have trouble on my own.

They were helping me to understand how complex life was outside Ahasha. Right now, the main complication was named Luka. I had an assignment that could impact the Sisterhood and didn't know how they dealt with...love. I had lots of questions and no answers. I guess it didn't matter, since my assignment took precedence. Yesterday was gone and tomorrow might never happen. Today and my assignment were all that mattered.

We entered Bywick toward evening and made camp a half league out of town. The town's income came from lumber and wood products. Ironically, the town made the wagons that Alida and Pali needed to get married.

Bywick tended to be a convenient stop between Kaslos and Slicci, which meant visitors often outnumbered the town's permanent population. It also meant that the town had more nobles than justified by its size.

Marku planned to stay five days but only put on two acts. The stop would give the clan time to work on new acts before we reached Slicci, in Calion Province.

I sent Kasi to monitor our Intermediate's very modest house. Because of the limited demand for Shadows, she had a small business providing herbs and drugs. The second day, two men visited her. One was a noble, dressed in silks and leather boots and carrying a gilt sword. It seemed strange, a noble visiting a modest herbalist. I shook my head. The other wore leather, had a well-worn scabbard, and walked with a fighter's swagger. Kasi couldn't tell what they said while inside the house but did catch parts of the talk as they walked away.

"She would have to pass through here on her way to Slicci."

"The money we offered should be plenty of incentive. We'll know if she comes."

The next evening, I waited by the fire until everyone had gone to their wagons for the night, then dressed and disappeared into the night. When I reached the house, I slipped through the bedroom window. The Intermediate sat at her small kitchen table putting some sweet-smelling herb into small bags.

"Clarra," I said quietly from behind her.

She jumped, dropping a handful of herbs on the floor. She rose and bowed.

"Shadow," she said. "I didn't know a Shadow was in the area."

"I'm not, Clarra. I leave for Ahasha tonight. I would like some guarana powder." The powder was used to stay alert and awake when having to work or travel for long hours. Clarra went over to a row of jars, selected one, and put a few spoonsful into a folded paper pouch. I gave her several silvers and turned to leave. "I wasn't here."

I left Anil to watch and returned to the camp. It was a risky gambit. If she worked with the killers, she would report my visit to the noble. Implying that I was only passing through, I hoped to avoid any connection to the gypsies. There was still the chance they might connect the presence of gypsies when and where I had been. Even with the risk, I felt it necessary to know whom we could trust and whom we could not.

The next morning, Yoan and I played around with our skit, which had been such a success with zo'Stanko and his guests. Currently, it was different from anything the other clans were doing, although I suspected similar acts would soon appear.

That night I returned to watch the Intermediate's house. No sooner had I arrived than the same two men appeared. As they pushed open the front door, I slipped in the back.

"Have you heard from a Shadow?" he asked more as a demand than a question. "Lord zo'Stanko will be very upset if he finds a Shadow was in the area, and you hadn't let us know."

"No, Sir Haris. I know of no Shadow in the area. Two sixdays ago one passed through headed for Ahasha. Mistress hasn't told me of any Shadows coming to Bywick or going to Calion."

"Remember, Clarra, Lord zo'Stanko will pay five toras if you can locate one. The lord's in desperate need of a Shadow." After glaring at her, he and his fighter companion left. I waited while Kasi followed them for a league.

I stepped into the kitchen. "The Shadows appreciate your loyalty."

Clarra knocked over her chair as she tried to rise and turn around at the same time.

"There isn't much business in Bywick for an Intermediate, and you could certainly use the five toras."

"Yes, but it would be blood money. They're looking for Shadows to kill. Several have already died at their hands. I hear that there's a Shadow loose that has them extremely nervous." Clarra sat back down. "I'm not as stupid as Sir Haris thinks."

I walked over to the table and laid five toras on it. "The Shadows have been negligent in Bywick. Mistress wishes you to have this as a token of her appreciation. Loyalty's a precious value." Five toras was more than Clarra could earn in a cycle selling Shadows' services in a large city. "I wish you to send a message thanking Mistress for her modest gift. If Sir Haris is watching your house, he'll know you sent a Kite to Ahasha. If he asks, tell him that it was to let Mistress know you are looking for a Shadow and to let you know if one is in the area. If he questions you, say selling a Shadow's services is your job, and you want to earn the five toras."

She nodded.

I left the way I had come and worked my way back to the campground. There, I saw Stela sitting on a fallen tree trunk far away from the wagons. I changed out of my blacks and decided to join her.

"Good evening, Ryana. Were you out for your late-night stroll?"

"Yes, it takes a long time to get over the Shadows' ridiculous training. I can't be walking the streets of Scio all hours of the night, can I?" I shrugged. She smiled.

"You know Luka's in love with you."

"No… I don't know. I can't say I understand men." I hadn't known what to think when he ran off. "I've no one to give me advice. There are no men at Ahasha. I need Mistress's advice, but she isn't here."

"You've stolen the heart of the one man every woman in every clan has been trying to catch. But that's a problem, isn't it?"

"Yes, mother…Stela. I'm sorry." Stela felt like a mother, just like the clan felt like kin. My visual and shadow selves had become confused—a bad thing.

"Don't apologize. You're beginning to feel like a daughter, if a bit wild." She folded her hands together. "Everyone considers you clan. I can give you advice about men and people, but not about…your duty. That you understand well."

"Yes. I can't change the past. I'm a Shadow. And I can't know the future. All I can count on is the present. I'm sitting here talking to you. If tomorrow comes and I'm still here, who will I be? I won't be the Ryana who left Ahasha. It terrifies me."

"All of us change. Usually, it happens slowly. We become different yet remain basically the same. But sometimes life-changing things happen. Think about Ilka. Without you, she would have been raped. If she had lived, that would have turned her life upside down. She would have gone on with her life, but she would never be the same person.

"In a sense, that's how things are for you. Unlike Ilka's, your experiences are occurring every day. It's more than an older Shadow could handle. If you need someone to talk to, daughter, you can talk to me –"

"Fire! Fire!" I shouted and took off running toward the wagon. Anil had seen the fire on the side of one of the wagons. A flaming arrow was stuck in the side. Kasi found three men hiding in the woods.

"Stop!" I shouted. "It's a trap!"

As Baldi ran around the corner of the wagon with a slashing bucket of water, an arrow hit his shoulder. Others thudded at his feet. The bucket clattered to the ground as he staggered behind the wagon. Since the clan didn't use bows, they had few means of chasing the men off before the wagon was destroyed.

I changed direction, angling left into the trees to circle around them. Dawn was breaking, and with the gypsy clothing I was wearing, one noticed me before I was within knife-throwing distance. He turned and loosed an arrow at me. Fortunately, all three were poor archers. I darted from tree to tree with random moves. His accuracy improved as I moved within knife-throwing distance, but he was slow to respond to my moves. The other two men were concentrating on the camp, keeping the clan pinned down so they couldn't put out the fire. The fire had climbed up the side, and every time someone attempted to throw water on it, an arrow flew in their direction.

I closed my eyes and let Anil give me sight. I slid partway from behind the tree and waited. When the shooter stepped out from behind a tree and loosed the arrow, I threw. My knife missed by a finger's width as he jumped back behind a tree.

I threw myself into a roll as he shot at me again. At the same time, a second man spun toward me. I rolled to a standing position. While the first one reached for another arrow, the second man took aim. He loosed his arrow as I threw a knife and rolled again. The shooter missed. I didn't.

He shrieked and dropped his bow. "Let's get out of here. The bitch hit me."

He ran with a hand pressed to his shoulder. I had a clear shot at one of the men's backs but held my throw. If I killed one, it would call attention to the gypsies, and that would hurt future relations for all the clans—the realities of being gypsies. Besides, they had come to damage the wagon and had killed no one.

"It's all clear. You can put out the fire." I shouted. While I stood with my eyes closed reaching for peace, Stela ran up behind me.

"Once again, you're our guardian angel. Are you hurt?" she asked, holding me at arms' length before hugging me hard. "How did you know they were there? Oh, each of you has a familiar. Where? Never mind, Ryana. Thank your friend for me."

* * *

Our performance that night was well received. Afterward, Marku posted extra guards, but nothing happened that night or the next. We left the following morning for Slicci, a three-day journey. During the morning, Yoan rode with me, going over our skit and possible changes.

"How did you know three men were attacking?"

"I didn't. I was sitting with Stela when I saw the fire. When Baldi came running around the wagon, I saw the arrows and knew the men were still in the trees."

I had always been good at making up stories. The real trick was making them so close to the truth they were easy to remember but the lie difficult to detect. I had seen the fire through Anil's eyes, and I had seen the men before they shot at Baldi. If someone had been paying attention, they would have realized I shouted before anyone had shot at him. A small detail that gets lost in the excitement. People heard what they wanted to hear.

"You seem to be our lucky totem. You are clan whether you want to be or not," Yoan said, as he jumped off the wagon.

Two, sometimes three men followed the caravan far enough back as not to be noticed.

The land was heavily treed until the last day, when the soil became sandy and the trees smaller and fewer. Slicci was located on the coast and a major trade route, one of only three ports along the Calion and Tuska coastline.

The first night we sat around a fire in that family way I had come to accept as normal. Everyone joined in the cooking, except me. I helped fetch, peel, and stir, but I watched closely. I didn't know when or if I might need the skill. Shadows survived and became successful because they could blend in. No skill could be ignored.

"I hear you turned down Luka. Is that true?" Alida asked as we chopped up carrots for the stew. "It took me three cycles to find a husband. It will take another cycle to be married. You snagged Luka in a few days."

I chopped, smiling. "I may have snagged more than I can handle."

"I can understand him wanting you. Everyone in the clan loves you. I'm not sure if the women in the other clans will be jealous or relieved. Some won't mind if Luka finally knows what it feels like to be rejected."

"I don't know if I turned him down exactly..." I was no longer sure about anything. Scio, in a cycle? The past existed but tomorrow did not. I hoped Luka found someone rather than wait for a tomorrow that would never come. Or did I? The thought of him kissing another woman made my chest ache.

"You didn't exactly?" She laughed and shook her head as if I said something funny. "You're going to keep him guessing until you meet him again, in a half-cycle? That's justice and cruel. What about your boyfriend in Scio?"

"I've no boyfriend in Scio. Please don't tell Yoan. I didn't do it to hurt his feelings."

Alida laughed for a long time. I didn't think I had done anything funny to Yoan or Luka. I had lied. Telling the truth would have been cruel.

"You put us gypsies to shame. I not only thought you had a boyfriend, but I felt sorry for him." We lapsed into silence.

CHAPTER THIRTEEN

Slicci—Calion Province

The clan had planned to stay six nights in Slicci, putting on a performance every other night. I watched the audience each night, trying to determine Calion's allegiance. I spotted cutpurses at work in teams, although most of the people in the audience didn't seem worth stealing from. But then, thieves pitied no one. Most had begun stealing out of desperation to stay alive. I also thought I recognized assassins in the crowd. They weren't very subtle, walking through the people scanning every woman, young or old. Based on their interest, I surmised that the assassins' guilds in Calion and Tuska were part of the conspiracy. Perhaps they were just paid for their services, or more likely they were promised something to make it worth their cooperation. Two Wizards, a Fire and a Wind, were present. They didn't look friendly, but then Wizards thought themselves above the masses and nobles and therefore tended to be aloof. Ironically, the Wizard's allegiances didn't seem to carry across province boarders. The Fire Wizards appeared to be with the cabal in Saxis but not in Tuska, whereas the Wind Wizards appeared part of the plot in Tuska but not in Saxis. The Earth Wizards appeared neutral in both provinces. But then, appearances could be deceiving.

I had Anil watching the Intermediate's house, but no one had gone in or out except the Intermediate to do her shopping. Rather than relieved, I was frustrated. I should be doing something.

That evening, I took over the fortuneteller booth. I brought in the most money, so I frequently drew the duty. A line of women desperately hoping something good would happen in the future lined up at the front. Their current lives were hard and sometimes abusive. I tried telling what I perceived to be true, leaving a tread of hope that I wished for them.

The next customer was one of the older men who I had identified as an assassin.

It would be nice just to kill him and get to the next customer.

Of course, it just meant I'd have to be extra careful.

"Well, fortuneteller, what's my future?" he said as he sat. No small talk to help me determine a little about him—not that I needed it.

"You're an aggressive man, used to getting your way –"

"I already know that. You fake."

"Why waste your time if I'm a fake?" I looked him in the eye. "Aggression and experience protect you while you are vigilant. But another waits –" He rose quickly, lifting the table. My first reaction was to roll back with chair, flip to a standing position, ready to put a knife in his throat if necessary. Instead, I fell backward and lay there with a knife in my hand, as any female clan member would do, and shouted.

"Clan, to me." A clan call would bring everyone within hearing. I palmed a rocktail needle in my other hand.

He stood there looking at me as Yoan ran in, knife in his hand. Baldi stood behind him in the open flap, knife in hand. When he spun toward them, I switched my knife to a throwing position.

"Trouble, Ryana?" Yoan asked, crouched and never taking his eyes off the man.

"I don't think he liked his fortune. Sir, I can only tell you what I see," I said innocently. He reached in his pocket and threw a silver at my feet.

"Do you see into my mind or the future?" He turned and walked past Yoan and Baldi.

"Are you all right?"

"Yes, sorry." I gave a rueful smile. "It would ruin business if I killed a customer."

* * *

The next night, as I stood watching, the assassin with whom I had the incident returned. There were more assassins than last night. I hoped he hadn't returned to cause trouble, or worse, because he suspected I might be a Shadow. Four were obvious. A mid-aged man, experienced and confident, roamed the crowd along with three younger men. I almost missed a young woman standing quietly off to the side. She appeared to be watching the acts, smiling and clapping at the appropriate times. She was scanning the audience and stopping to evaluate each person on and off the stage. Perhaps I should warn Marku but pitting the clan against assassins wouldn't be fair and could cause more problems than the assassins would.

After our nightly performance, I again drew the fortuneteller tent. The first customer was the assassin from the night before. I palmed a rocktail needle. He sat quietly.

"I'm sorry about yesterday. You were too close… I won't cause you any trouble whether you're a fake or really can see more. I'm not here to cause you trouble." He dropped five silvers on the table. "If you can tell the future, I want the truth, not stories to make me feel good."

I studied him while my mind raced. He seemed sincere, but even if he were, that didn't make him less dangerous. Should I just admit I was a fake? That would make him happy. On some abstract level, I felt sorry for him. He had grown up in the slums and survived by becoming an assassin. He stood alone, surrounded by danger, with no one he could trust or turn to for help.

"I can't tell the future," I said and held up my hand before he could say anything. "There are too many possibilities. I can give you the advantage of my insight."

He nodded. I cut the smoke in the globe.

"Put your hands on the table." When he did, I placed mine over his. That assured me his hands were empty and that I would know if he tried to move. I closed my eyes.

"You lead a dangerous life and feel there's no one you can trust. You're wrong. You can trust the one you've known longest. He does not want what's yours. You've met a woman. She's dangerous. She wants something from you but not what's yours. The others are young with little experience. They are more dangerous to themselves than to you." Before I could continue, he gave a snort. "One thinks he's smarter than you. He's stupid but wants what's yours. That's all I can see. The future is yours to make."

I opened my eyes. He sat for several seconds, then nodded.

"Yes, I brought them all. If you were a fake, you would tell me a story based on my looks and clothes. If you were real, I hoped you could see them for what they are. You have. I should slit your throat, but of course, you already know I won't." He laughed this time and dropped a tora on the table as he left, brushing past Yoan and Vali as he strode out.

After we closed for the night, I sat thinking about the assassin. He hadn't been in my tent looking for a Shadow. He was desperate, looking for help from

136

someone, anyone. He would now rely more on his old friend and kill the cocky young man. It would serve as a good example for the other youths. The woman was the dangerous one. She carried herself like an Assassin. If she was, she was assisting the assassins and had indirectly confirmed she was helping those responsible for the killings. The thought that a Sister could betray the Sisterhood brought tears to my eyes. I buried my face in my hands. How could a Sister betray us?

Later that night, while I was sitting around the fire pit eating a chicken stew, Yoan sat down beside me.

"What did he want this time?"

"He was a sweetie and gave me a tora." I picked it out of my purse and flipped it to Stela, who kept the clan's money. I spent the next hour talking about my encounter. As usual, I sprinkled a little truth along with a few lies and wove it into an interesting story.

* * *

I didn't know what to do about the Assassin, who I refused to think of as a Sister. Kasi continued to watch the Intermediate's house for me while I tried to decide.

The evening performance had a good-sized crowd. In the middle of the tumbling act, someone screamed, "Fire!"

Everyone scrambled off the stage. Flames shot above the trees in the direction the horses were tethered. Marku formed us into a line to get water to the blazing hay. Choking smoke spread, but we couldn't stop without it spreading to the wagons. The next two hours were chaos. Every bucket with water or any other liquid was thrown on the burning hay.

Yoan and Vali threw blankets over the heads of the screaming, plunging horses. One jerked loose and galloped by wild with terror and covered with lather.

Just as things settled down, Ilka jumped from her wagon shouting, "My earrings are gone!"

That wasn't the only thing missing. We found items had been stolen from the tents and stage. It was late when the clan finally gathered around the fire to have their evening meal.

"Did anyone see who started the fire?" Marku asked. Everyone was shaking his or her head.

Ten-year-old Kata held up a burnt arrow. "Look! I found this next to the hay!"

Little Tania jumped up and down, waving her hands, and pointing. "Three men ran that way when the fire started."

I wondered if the three men had followed us from Bywick. Would they continue to follow us? And what would they do next?

A schedule was prepared to ensure the camp was guarded each night during the performances and during the night. Everyone was exhausted, but the wagons had to be packed to leave at dawn the next morning. When we finished, I fell into bed still not sure what to do about the Assassin.

* * *

Kadal—Calion Province

I drove my wagon lost in thought. The three men who had attacked the wagon were intent on destroying property. They weren't trying to kill anyone, just to keep us from putting the fire out. The second attack was meant to stampede the horses, injuring or killing them. The attacks were escalating. The next attack would be against one or more clan members. If the predators were to be stopped, it would have to be away from any town. The people of Hesland tolerated the gypsies for the entertainment they gave, but they would be quick to blame the gypsies for any troubles.

Capturing whoever was attacking the clan would be useless. The town would at best give them a small fine and release them to continue the attacks. I concluded they wouldn't stop until they were killed. To avoid implicating the clan, it would have to be away from any town and made to look like… I wasn't sure. Vali interrupted my musing.

"Mind if I join you?" he said jumping from his horse to the wagon. Stela was right, everyone did consider me clan. To an outsider, Vali would have waited until invited. For clan, the question was rhetorical. Family wouldn't object.

"Why didn't you call for help when that man came back? Yoan and I would have thrown him out."

If I told the truth, it would tell too much about me, so I played with the truth—lied. I found myself doing a lot of that lately. At the time, I had wondered why Sister Rong had spent so much time teaching us how to come up with plausible stories.

"He was quiet when he came in and dropped a silver on the table. No one willing to pay a silver can be all bad. Besides, if I killed him, I wouldn't know his future."

Vali laughed.

"He looked to be a hard man. Someone nobody would want to mess with, so I decided to wait to see what he wanted. He thought I told the future. I think that's what upset him the previous day. He expected a fake."

"But you're a fake…even though you do tell good stories."

"I'm hurt, Vali. To think you don't believe I can see into the future." I closed my eyes. "I can see that in the near future, you and a woman from the Sorin clan will be married."

He jerked around to stare at me, his mouth open. "How did you know?"

As though everyone hadn't noticed. He only thought they were being coy. Clan knew everything about each other.

"I can see the future." I laughed. It had taken the focus of the discussion off the assassin. We talked about the woman, Rodica, for a long time. Rather, he talked, and I listened.

* * *

I stayed up late that night, watching for the three men stalking us. They would attack soon. Success would give them a heightened sense of being invincible. What was their motive? It didn't seem to make sense. Nothing happened. The second day's ride also proved uneventful. The clan was taking its time: up early, ride until noon, rest and eat, and ride until dusk.

I went off into the woods as usual. By now, my nighttime wandering was ignored as normal. Sitting with my eyes closed, I listened to Kasi and Anil hunt. After a while, I nudged Kasi and Anil further out in opposite directions. Then Anil found them. They were sitting around a small fire about a league away.

I moved a half league closer and stripped down to my blacks. Like a wraith, I flowed through the trees using Kasi and Anil's eyes to home in on the men. Before too long, I lay a few paces away.

"What next, Borin?" a thin young youth asked as he took a bite of some meat on a stick. "I'm getting tired of this. The stuff we took isn't paying for our time."

140

"That bitch Lucija still needs a lesson. A silver's more than any gypsy's worth. The nerve of her putting a knife to my throat. Guys were laughing at me for days."

"Maybe we could kidnap her and share her between us," the third one, a muscular youth, said rubbing his crotch.

Borin shook his head. "Although that would be fun, they don't go far from the wagons. I suggest we show them what happens to trash like them when they start thinking they are better than us Heslanders. They'll probably post a guard now that we have them scared. We'll kill him tonight and another the first night in the next town. No one will do anything to us. We'll say they attacked us. The town people will run them off after destroying their wagons."

I agreed with Borin. In town, they would assume the gypsies had started any trouble and that these three were telling the truth. The gypsies would suffer the consequences. A rocktail dart took Borin in the neck. He grunted and slumped forward. The thin youth jumped up. He joined Borin on the ground, a dart sticking in his back. The muscular youth spun around, jerking out his knife. A dart took him in the eye.

I lay there, eyes closed, wanting to question my logic, but logic wasn't involved. My actions had become pure unequivocal intuition. I did what felt right not what might be right.

Forgive me, Sister Morag, but I had to protect the clan.

I put an arrow or two in each one, took any money they had, released the horses to run free, and left the fire to burn itself out. It looked as much like a robbery as I could make it. The arrows would turn suspicion away from the gypsies since they didn't use or own bows. I made my way back to my clothes, changed, and walked back to the camp. I slipped past Baldi, who was standing guard. Borin might just have succeeded in killing him. I stopped. Stela sat on a stump looking toward the camp. Or they may have killed Stela. I shuddered. Without realizing how quietly I walked, I stood only a few paces from her when she saw me—and then only because I wasn't in black.

"Good evening...mother. You're out late."

"Good evening, daughter. Even in that bright dress, Baldi missed you, and I would have if you hadn't stopped to greet me. Have you finished your business?" she said more like a statement than a question. I nodded. "Sit, Ryana."

"Lucija insulted and embarrassed one of the three men when she wouldn't bed him for a silver. They planned to kill tonight's guard and another of you in Kadal. I'll leave if you wish." To my astonishment, she hugged me. I felt her tears on my cheek.

"Daughter, you kill, but only to protect others and without concern for your own safety. Leave? I wish you could stay with us forever. Unfortunately, there's a storm coming, and I'm afraid you're caught in it. Come, it's late. We both need our sleep."

CHAPTER FOURTEEN

Kadal—Calion Province

We drove past wide fields with ripening wheat and rows of turnips, carrots, and onions, produce for Slicci and Zeles, the capital of Calion. The clan planned to stay in Kadal four days but conduct only two performances. The extra time would give everyone a rest from the many days on the road and offered a chance to work on new acts or improve existing ones.

The ubiquitous thieves and two assassins strolled among the audience. Unless they had a target, I surmised they hoped to get lucky and find the mysterious Shadow—me. The Shadow Sister who had been at Slicci stood off by herself scanning the crowd. If I were right, she was Leela, the apprentice Assassin/Spy to Indira, who was assigned to Zeles. She was good but still an apprentice. I laughed. What was I except an apprentice without a senior Sister for a mentor? I sobered. I was an apprentice but with experience: an apprentice Assassin who had killed many times, and an apprentice Spy who had learned to see the difference between acting the part and being a part of the act. I couldn't help but wonder if my experience was helping me learn to fly or sending me rushing toward the rocks—Sister or rogue?

For now, I had no worry of her identifying me. Besides her being too inexperienced, I wasn't acting like part of the clan—I was clan. Confirming my observation, she ruined her act when she shook her head "no" to a Fire Wizard standing some twenty paces away.

My head throbbed with questions. Was Leela working alone or with Indira? The fact that she appeared to be on her own suggested either Indira was dead or Leela was working under her direction. Until I knew for certain, I couldn't decide what to do about her. If one or both were in league with those killing Sisters, should I return to Ahasha and report what I'd found, or should I kill them? Would that be revenge or necessary to avoid more deaths? Could there be more rogues? With all my recent experience, I was still an apprentice who needed a mentor. The answers would have to wait until I found Indira, and Leela was my sole link to her.

The acts went well. Afterward, I went to the fortuneteller tent, a duty I had come to enjoy. To my surprise, the first customer was the Fire Wizard. I shut down my emotions.

"Yes, Master Wizard." I gave a small bow of my head. "You wish to have your future told?"

"You're incredibly young. Do you claim to tell the future?" His eyes studied my face as he waited for my answer.

"There are many possible futures. I can only tell the one I think most likely."

He laughed. "I've heard you're exceptionally talented. The question's whether it's in lying or in seeing that which most can't."

He was looking for something, but what? He would have to tell me.

"Someone killed a Fire Wizard in Adak and a Wind Wizard in Kaslos. Who?" His stare intensified. It was a dangerous question. What did he expect? I didn't have a clue. I was tempted to laugh. It felt like one of Sister Rong's games, which drew me like a bear to honey.

144

"Most come to me to look into the future. I can only give them a glimpse into the most likely one, although they interpret it as the only one. You're the first to ask me to look back into the past. The past is written in stone but shattered so that the pieces, over time, must be reassembled from the many fragments."

He smiled. "Yes, I had never thought of it that way. A story does tend to change from person to person. The inverse of the future."

I nodded. I liked him, although it didn't make him any less dangerous. "Well, can you reassemble the pieces?"

"Put your hands on the table," I said. *This will have to be the greatest lie of my life.* He hesitated before complying. When I placed mine over his, he flinched but didn't move them. I closed my eyes and became the Assassin/Spy—two killers dancing with death. "You Wizards are at odds with each other, and allegiances differ from place to place. Your guilds aren't aligned across Hesland. I see fire quenched by land and wind. A third, loyal to the tora, stands to the side. A shadow watches." The Wizard's hands tensed. I waited for him to relax. "I see the wind quieted by land and water. Again, a shadow is there. It's a complex past and only one interpretation." My hands slid off his as I sat back and opened my eyes. He sat with his eyes narrowed, frowning.

"That's an interesting past, and you're an interesting…fortuneteller. Did you leave out fire because I'm a Fire Wizard and would know we didn't take part?" He gave me a knowing smile. The dance was coming to an end. He was trying to resolve his indecision about me while I tried to decide which course best to pursue.

"It's one of many possibilities. It's the past I see. You're a Fire Wizard and would know better than

I. As you pointed out, I'm young." I waited. The dance was over. He said nothing as he rose and dropped two toras on the table.

* * *

We sat around the evening fire discussing the events of the day as I pondered my encounter with the Wizard and his relationship to…it pained me to think of them as Shadow Sisters. The question was whether I had overplayed my part.

"Hey, Ryana," Vali waved to get my attention, "tell us about your session with the Fire Wizard. I've never seen a Wizard go to a fortuneteller before. He didn't burn you and the tent down, so he must have been pleased."

All eyes turned to me.

"I told him he was handsome, intelligent, powerful, and would soon be the head of his guild. I saw it in my glass ball." I gave a big smile and bowed to the laughter and applause.

"That for two toras?" Yoan asked.

"He probably thought I would follow him home for that."

"Alida, yes. You, no," Vali said looking from me to Alida. That got lots of good-natured cheering and laughter. "Sorry, Ryana. I couldn't resist."

"That's all right, Vali. I'll remember that when someday you fill in for Yoan in our skit." Everyone began cheering and laughing. I was happy for the diversion, as it derailed the incident with the Fire Wizard.

I didn't see the apprentice Assassin at the next performance. Since she hadn't tried to kill me, I assumed she had moved on to Zeles. The fact that no killings could be attributed to me had them stymied. Where was she? Whom would she strike next? When? Did Ahasha send only one Shadow?

* * *

146

The road to Zeles was heavily patrolled. We were stopped three times by large groups of mercenaries. There were rude remarks and gestures toward the women—including me—but no one was touched. I suspect they knew they could win any confrontation, but a fight would be costly—many would die. They would have to fight not only the men but also the women, who knew how to fight.

* * *

Zeles—Calion Province

We arrived in Zeles a sixday after leaving Kadal. The capital of Calion, Zeles was a major city with its extremes of wealth and poverty. The campsite set aside for entertainers, like the gypsies, lay on the outskirts of the city next to the slums. Marku planned to rest for two days to give us time to advertise we were in Zeles.

A large, diverse crowd turned out for the first performance. Between acts, I scanned the audience. An Earth and a Fire Wizard stood at the back of the crowd with a good space around them. Gypsies weren't the only ones they made uncomfortable.

Although the city police in their blue and gold uniforms were stationed around the perimeter, I saw at least six thieves and two potential assassins roaming the crowd. The latter were harder to detect in a large crowd. The audience was mixed: a few minor nobles in silk pants and tunics, well-dressed merchants, and commoners in sturdy work clothes. As we put up the amusement tents, I spotted Leela. After looking at the woman standing next to her, she nodded her head toward me. Very sloppy, she needed more training; however, if she had made me as the Sister they were after, maybe she didn't. In either event, I had found Indira, and it was obvious they were working together.

Toward the end of the evening, Indira entered the tent. My visual and shadow selves fought for a second. My visual self won.

"Mistress, how may I help you?" I smiled and looked up with genuine interest.

I was clan. I told fortunes for money.

"I hear you're very good at telling the future and the past."

"Thank you, Mistress. What would you like to know?"

"What did you tell the Fire Wizard in Kadal?"

Did she know or did she want to know? And why?

"I can tell you yours but not someone else's. Besides, he's a Fire Wizard. It would be bad for all the clans to have his guild mad at us. I'm sorry, Mistress." I shook my head, thinking about one flaming the wagons and the men, women, and children burning. My eyes misted. "No, Mistress. Not as long as I live. Please leave."

She stared for several seconds trying to decide something. She stood and threw a silver on the table before walking out.

I was clan.

I smiled, picked up the silver, and dropped it in my blouse. Although I didn't look up, I know she saw. I sent Anil to follow her. So long as it was dark, the apprentice's hawk would be blind. Familiars were tuned to their soul mates, not to other familiars.

* * *

Late that night I made my way around the outskirts of Zeles and then slipped into the town. I had studied the young girls in the audience and dressed like one. They tended to wear drab colors. That suited me fine since it helped to make me less conspicuous. I made my way toward the Earth Wizards' guild house. It was a risk but sitting on my wagon wasn't going to help me discover the opposition's goal.

"Hey little girl, you looking for us?" two thin, scruffy men shouted. They were back several dozen steps, walking a bit unsteadily. When I kept walking, they began a slow weaving run. I turned at the next corner hoping to lose them, but there was nothing but row houses and nowhere to hide. My options were to run or fight. I decided fighting could alert those looking for me. It wouldn't be hard to lose them the way they were weaving, so I ran, maintaining the general direction I wanted to go. Not too long afterward, they turned around and staggered off. I assumed they had given up because I had entered a better neighborhood, which would be patrolled by the city police.

The houses were still attached, but they were brick and better maintained. Further along the houses were detached and had gates that enclosed the property; some even had horses and carriages. I ducked into a narrow separation between two properties and changed. Back on the street, I flowed through the shadows. The few persons and police I saw were easy to avoid by keeping to the shadows and using trees and fences to shield me. I doubted anyone would bother a Shadow, but I didn't want to be noticed. Eventually, I arrived at my destination, a single-story house in the center of a multiacre field filled with old trees. The house looked to occupy several acres. Although a single-story structure, it had a dome three stories high. The walls appeared to be a combination of stone, dirt, and thick vines. It made for a strange sight. I found a large tree next to what appeared to be a well-travelled path, scaled it, and sat waiting.

I began to think it had been a waste of time when a rotund man in a brown robe with vines for trim came walking in my direction. When he was still twenty steps away, I dropped out of the tree. He stopped and the ground began to tremble. Then it stopped.

"Well, a Shadow Sister. I thought the tree felt a little different. Your stillness and lack of emotions fooled me. I'll have to remember that in the future. Are you here to talk or fight, Shadow of Death?"

"Shadow of Death?" The title made me shiver. Is that what I had become?

"Your path seems to be filled with chaos and dead people, maybe even a Wizard." He smiled at something. I could still feel the earth shivering beneath me, waiting on the Wizard's command.

"Some group is killing Sisters, although we've never supported any employer against a province's sovereignty. It would appear we are an inconvenience rather than a part of what is happening. The Shadows are upset," I said. He nodded but remained silent. "The Wizards' guilds in the various provinces appear split in their allegiances; however, I believe the Earth Wizards aren't part of whatever is developing. Furthermore, I believe your guild is united. I seek answers and allies."

"And you're willing too…?"

"I'm willing to share my findings and commit the Shadows' support to the Earth Wizards."

"You can do that?"

I offered my hand. I sensed he would be able to feel Morag's sigil. He came closer and reached for my hand. The ground under me felt ready to explode.

"Your senior Shadow has placed much faith in one so young. We'll admit you tomorrow at this time. I can't promise you anything." I turned and like a

150

shadow worked my way back to the clan's campground. No one was waiting.

* * *

Anil had found little while following the Assassins. The two stayed at a tavern and rooming house called the Sickle. I couldn't determine what jobs they were working at, not that it mattered. They didn't attend the evening performances the next day. I hoped that meant they hadn't guessed I was a Sister. On the other hand, they wanted the information I had given the Fire Wizard or, more likely, what I might know. After the performances and evening meal, I slipped out and into the streets. I avoided the few people I encountered. When I reached the guild property, I made no attempt to hide. It would have been pointless. They could feel the ground and would know I was coming long before I reached the house. As I neared the door, it opened. The same Wizard stood inside. He waved me in.

"What happens if we decide we don't trust you, Shadow?"

"I die."

"That doesn't disturb you?"

"We'll all die. That's easy. It's living that's hard."

He laughed, a pleasant sound of genuine mirth. I followed him down a wide dirt hallway past closed doors into a round assembly hall. The floor was covered in a rich, dark soil, and the trees were sculptured into intricately twisted vines and branches to form seats, which surrounded a cleared center area. Each seat, a unique shape and color, held a brown-robed Wizard. My guide directed me into the middle, where a small gray boulder rested, and indicated for me to sit.

"My brothers and sister, a Shadow has asked to speak to us. She believes we can help her identify the person or people responsible for killing Shadows. She believes our guilds are united across the provinces and that we're not involved in the killings. She's willing to share her findings and commit the Shadows' support of the Earth Wizards." He turned and walked to an empty seat and sat. An older female Wizard in an ash-colored seat smiled at me.

"The earth tells me you're very young. Press your hand against the ground, please." Her voice was soft yet like stone. I leaned over, placing my hand on the ground, and remained still, waiting for her to speak. "Thank you. You aren't what you appear or what your enemies are looking for. They are looking for an older, experienced Assassin. Under those blacks, which make you look older and mature, lies a young, thin, senior Assassin/Spy who speaks for the Shadows. Of course, that's impossible…" She stared at me for a long time. "… yet true. The earth doesn't lie. If you're honest with us, we'll share what we know."

She received nods from the other seven Wizards in the room.

"I'll be honest except for anything that may expose my identity."

She nodded.

"It started in Adak…" Long after I finished, there was silence.

"I'm humbled. You've taught my brothers and me that…what were your words…dying is easy. It's logical to conclude other Wizards killed the Fire and Wind Wizards, because we assume only Wizards can kill us in a fight. Just as your enemy assumes the Shadows have sent an experienced Assassin.

"We accept the Shadows' support. It's our belief that there are groups in Tuska and Calion and others that intend a revolution to depose the king. It will be bloody, and many will die. That is a certainty. Why are they killing Shadows? We don't know, but the chance you may learn about the plot doesn't appear reason enough. As you guessed, the Earth Wizards stand united behind the king. I'll pass the word that you're a friend."

A younger man with a bushy beard and round face leaned forward in his chair.

"We believe one of the Shadows is working with the conspirators. Can you kill another Shadow, or will she be allowed to live?"

"Two. They will die before I leave Zeles. To answer your question, no, I could not kill another Shadow. The two you speak of have forfeited their right to be called Shadows by my authority."

* * *

I sat in my wagon shaking. I had given away information that could jeopardize my assignment. I could have been killed and two corrupt Sisters would have gone unpunished. I had risked much tonight. Fortunately, I had gained much in return. They had given me names and information about the other guilds and someone to turn to for support. But I continued to worry. Relying on my intuition might not replace thoughtful consideration. On the other hand, planning based on known facts might result in being too late to help. All night, I tossed and turned.

With the morning came the realization that the two Assassins would be coming after me. Not because they knew me to be a Sister but because I had information they wanted. I didn't have to find them. They would find me.

CHAPTER FIFTEEN

Zeles—Calion Province

I knew the rogue Shadow and her apprentice would be coming to see the fortuneteller soon, probably tonight. She appeared desperate to know what I knew and for the information I had given the Fire Wizard. I decided to wait in the woods to keep the encounter away from the clan. Otherwise, someone might get hurt trying to protect me. Besides, I needed to maintain my cover. I wandered into the woods earlier than usual and changed into my blacks. Resting my back against a tree, I sat and waited while Anil and Kasi roamed the woods. An hour later, Kasi found two figures in black working their way toward the wagons. As I watched thru Anil's eyes, they moved like ghosts. A gray-black wolf ran parallel to them some twenty paces to their right. When they reached within knife-throwing range, I stood, back pressed against the tree, invisible in the darkness. I felt I stood in the shadow of my Sisters, and peace settled over me. I existed for the moment. The second before was the past. The second to come the future. I existed somewhere in between, where no thoughts of life or death, hate or revenge, victory or defeat could exist.

"Hello, Shadow. I presume you're the one they call the Shadow of Death. How appropriate since you're going to die shortly," Indira said. I recognized her stance. It resembled Sister Hajna's posture—relaxed and deadly. "Strange, I don't recognize you. Morag should've sent Hajna. That would have been a reasonable match. Any last words before you die?"

The shadows whispered to me.

Speaking distracts. They are Shadows only in their minds.

They stood a few paces apart. Indira had a knife folded back against her forearm, out of sight but ready to throw. Leela had her knife in plain sight. Instinctively, I knew Indira had killed before, but Leela hadn't. When the fighting started, Indira wouldn't hesitate. Leela would be a second or two slower. Her targets to date had been dummies, which didn't move or shoot back.

As Indira's hand moved, I rotated to my right behind the tree. Her knife hit the tree a finger's width from me. I continued rotating around the tree, my blowtube to my lips. As I came out on the left side, Leela stood there, frozen. I blew the rocktail-laced dart and twisted back. One knife, probably Indira's, ripped through my shirt, opening a deep gash. A second later, another knife came wobbling by.

Leela's final act.

I loaded another dart. Kasi showed the wolf attacking from my left, mouth wide open with fangs exposed. I blew. A piercing scream reverberated through the forest as the wolf stumbled and fell. I took two steps and dove over the wolf, rolled, and came up standing next to another large tree. As I rolled, an arrow ripped through my calf. The death of her familiar had delayed Indira a second and the arrow meant for my side had hit my leg.

When Indira stepped out to shoot, I threw another knife. She jumped back. Too late. The death of her wolf had dulled her reactions and the knife sliced a gash in her arm. I had just slid behind the tree to load my blowtube when an arrow scraped the side of the tree where I had just been standing. Anil and Kasi showed her charging the tree. I stayed behind the tree, knowing I couldn't win a knife fight with her. I took a deep breath and called my darlings as I dove out from behind the tree, rolled, and landed on my back with my blowtube to my lips. With my neck arched, I could see her charging me. She looked like a demon with her face flushed red and mouth twisted in rage. As her hand went back to throw, Kasi and Anil struck. She stumbled and threw as I blew a rocktail-laced dart. Her knife cut deep into my thigh. If Kasi and Anil hadn't stuck when they did, both Indira and I would be dead. Her knife had missed my chest only because she stumbled as the poison took hold. Her eyes were wide with hate as she hit the ground.

I lay there in pain as I returned from the moment to the present. All three wounds were bleeding. Just then, Kasi and Anil landed softly on my chest.

"Drink, my darlings, the blood's only going to waste." Dizzy and weak, I tied off my wounds and limped to Indira and Leela. After stripping them of their blacks, I redressed them in clothes they had carried with them in a pack. I jammed an arrow into Indira's chest, a knife in Leela's, and dropped the bow and quiver next to her. Hopefully, it would look as though they had fought and killed each other. Afterward, I made my way back to the wagons. After removing my blacks and hiding them along with the extra blacks and weapons, I staggered to Marku's wagon, banged on the door, and shouted "help" several times. I wanted to wake the camp. A good story required an audience.

* * *

Stela cleaned, stitched, and bandaged the wounds. Then she half carried me to my wagon. On the way to the wagon, I claimed I happened upon two women fighting. One had knives and the other a bow and arrows. When they saw me, they stopped and turned their attention on me. One threw a knife and the other shot an arrow. When I staggered away, they

156

returned to their fight. A minute later another arrow grazed my arm. I didn't stop but assumed the one still alive wanted me dead so I couldn't identify her. I lay there certain I was about to die. When I looked back, both were lying on the ground, one with an arrow in her chest and the other with a knife in her chest. Of course, Stela wasn't buying it, but I was too tired to explain.

The next morning everyone wanted to hear what had happened. By now the clan was beginning to think bad luck followed me. I think the clan would have gone looking for the two women, except they were afraid if they got caught there when someone found the bodies, the gypsies would be blamed. I didn't take part in the performance that night, but I did take my usual place in the fortuneteller tent. Although the tent and wagon belonged to the clan, I was beginning to think of them as mine. Just as I had begun to believe I was clan. That had saved me more than once. I now understood the difference between playing at being something and being a part of it. Playing at a part would be easy to detect if you knew what to look for. That could be the difference between being successful or failing—between life and death.

Nothing happened for the next two days, thank the gods. I didn't feel in condition to fight a child. Kasi watched the Intermediate's house, but so far, nothing out of the ordinary had happened. He ran a small shop selling handmade jewelry. Judging from his customers' clothing, he sold to merchants and commoners. Two days after my encounter with Indira and Leela, a man dressed like a noble entered his shop. Since Kasi couldn't hear the conversations, there could be several possibilities. It could be part of his normal business, or a noble was seeking a contract with the Shadows, or he was in league with the killers.

That night I decided to visit his shop. I arrived after he had closed for business and, with some effort, used two windowsills to climb to the second level. I opened a window and slipped into a small bedroom. The polished chest and four-poster bed looked expensive. In the dimly lit room, I waited in the shadows next to the bed. A few minutes later, I heard footsteps coming up the stairs. Although he had a lantern in his hand, he failed to notice me standing in the shadows. When he closed the door, I spoke.

"I see you live well, Samal."

He stepped back into the door, almost dropping the lantern. His head jerked back and forth looking for me.

"Who are you?"

"One you work for."

"Shadow, you scared me." Then in a rush. "Are you looking for work? If so, I've a noble looking for an Assassin."

I handed him two pieces of thin paper.

"Send this message to Ashtol and this one to Ahasha."

He snagged the tora I flipped toward him.

I backed up to the window and sat. Rolling out backward, I caught the windowsill, dropped to the ground, winced with the pain, and faded into the trees.

He stood by the window watching until I entered the trees. When I was sure I was out of sight, I sent Kasi and Anil to keep watch while I waited. I had given him two messages. The messages to Ahasha read:

OUR APPRENTICE KILLED THE ROGUE SHADOW AS YOU DIRECTED. SADLY, SHE DIED TOO. I'VE TOLD YOUR SPECIAL SHADOW I'VE FOUND AN INSIDE CONTACT WHO'S WILLING TO GIVE HER NAMES AND PLANS. I'M FINISHED HERE AND LEAVING TONIGHT FOR HOME. H.

The message to Ashtol read:

SHADOW, RETURN TO ZELES. I HAVE A CON-
TACT FOR YOU WHO HAS THE NAMES YOU'VE BEEN
SEARCHING FOR.

HE WILL MEET YOU ONE LEAGUE IN BACK OF
THE INTERMEDIATE'S HOUSE TWO SIXDAYS FROM TO-
DAY. GOOD HUNTING. H.

When Samal left the house, my darling followed. He headed straight for the castle and was ad-
mitted. Shortly after he returned to the house, two
swift-wing hawks flew from his window. One headed
to Ahasha and the other to Ashtol. I smiled. I had been
right.

Several hours later, Kasi, who had stayed at the
castle, followed a noble and two riders when they left
the castle. A league out of town, they stopped at a large
camp of mercenaries, who looked to be the same group
who had blockaded the road to Zeles. Kasi settled in a
nearby tree.

"Lord Kerller, what do you have for us?" a
large man with wild black hair and a scarred face
asked. Kerller dismounted, tossing his reins to one of
the other riders.

"There's a traitor in our ranks. A Shadow will
leave Zeles tonight on her way to Ahasha, who knows
his name. Have half your men set up roadblocks on the
road to Kadal. First Lord se'Dubben is sending fifty
soldiers to help. Take her alive if you can."

"Fifty soldiers?"

"Yes. Take the other half of your men and set
up roadblocks on the road to Ashtol. Another hundred
soldiers will be sent to help there. In both cases, your
men will man the roadblock. The soldiers will fan out
on both sides of the road in case she tries to circle
around. The Shadow of Death will be travelling from
Ashtol to Zeles. She must be stopped. Se'Dubben is of-
fering a reward of fifty toras for the Shadow leaving

Zeles and two hundred for the Shadow heading to Zeles—dead or alive. He'll be extremely upset if you let the Assassin Shadow slip by you—again."

"Yes, sir." The mercenary banged his fist into his hand. "That bitch won't get by us this time. We didn't have enough men last time. She must have circled our roadblock. When my men have had their fun with her, I'll personally strip the skin off her, bit by bit. She'll tell everything she knows and beg me to kill her."

"If you don't stop her, you may be the one who begs to die." Kerller mounted and the three rode off.

Shuddering, I called Kasi back.

CHAPTER SIXTEEN

Road to Ashtol—Calion Province

We left Zeles for Ashtol two days later, a sixday trip. One day out of Zeles, we encountered a roadblock. The traffic to Zeles was jammed a half league back to Ashtol. Ten mercenaries were tearing apart every wagon and bag they found. Piles of clothes lay in the dirt. Crates were pried open with their contents pulled out. A woman shrieked as a mercenary pulled her from a wagon. Another clutched her breasts, her shirt ripped off. A huddle of men muttered and cursed, but they didn't dare challenge the heavily armed mercenaries. On the other side of the road, a few mercenaries watched the flow of people to Ashtol. One waved us through with little more than a casual look. Anil and Kasi showed me a long line of soldiers off to either side of the road.

After we passed the roadblock, Marku rode up, nodded to me, and stepped onto my wagon. "What's happening, Ryana?"

"They are looking for the Shadow…of Death. They believe she's returning to Zeles from Ashtol to talk to an informant. I guess they're misinformed, since I'm headed to Ashtol." I smiled.

"Death?"

"That's what they have begun calling me. Although I don't like it, I am leaving a trail of bodies. Are you certain you don't want me to leave? I'm dangerous to have around. Se'Dubben has offered two hundred toras for me—dead or alive. Besides, I'm not the innocent young woman you agreed to take to Scio. I'm someone else that I'm not sure I like." My eyes misted and I looked away from Marku.

"I don't know who you're killing or what's going on, but I do know you aren't killing innocent people. You're welcome to stay as long as you want. Besides, everyone would miss you." He vaulted onto his stallion.

We passed through two more roadblocks along the way. Each time they ignored the traffic going to Ashtol, whereas the people going to Zeles were brutally harassed. I felt guilty for having caused the problem. For the next few days, I remained quiet, my visual self afraid to examine my shadow-self and what she had become. Had Morag known what would happen, or what could happen, and prayed it would not? Would she approve? Did I approve? Was I saving lives or…? It had become too easy to kill.

"Why are you so quiet, Ryana?" Alida asked as she sat down next to me that evening.

"Just thinking of home and what life will be like when I get there." I almost laughed. This time it was the truth, although Alida would assume I meant Scio.

"I wonder about my life with Pali and the Tobar clan." Alida too lapsed into silence.

"You two look like you need cheering up," Ilka said as she sat down next to Alida.

"We're wondering about our futures. Me with Pali, and Ryana at home."

"Oh… I think about having a husband and children and…" With that Ilka went silent. The three of us sat quietly, each wondering what life had in store for us.

As we approached Ashtol, I managed to liven up. My visual self found joy being a part of the clan. My shadow-self focused on Ashtol and my assignment. Se'Dubben was clearly involved in the killing of Sisters. I needed to know if that meant the entire province supported him and which, if any, Wizard guilds.

Ashtol produced a variety of clothing from their herds of sheep and fields of cotton and were the primary source of cloth for Hesland. The people were a strange mixture of merchants, farmers, and herders. In a way, I felt the pain of my youth when I saw herders watching our performances. Most were in town to buy supplies or for entertainment of one kind or another. Because of the importance of the clothing industry, the town supported many guilds and nobles.

Marku planned to stay a sixday, putting on a performance every other day, leaving three days to rest. The first day, I wandered the streets posting notices of our arrival. I took the part of the town where our Intermediate lived and worked. She had a modest business spinning yarn. I wondered about her loyalty. So far, most of them supported our adversaries, probably for the money. Ironically, that had proved helpful in locating those responsible for the killings. Our Intermediate here lived in a working-class district. Through Anil, I saw no usual activity at her house as I wandered the streets putting up notices. I wore a traditional embroidered white blouse and a bright, multicolored, flared skirt favored by the gypsies. The reaction was mixed. Most were friendly, some indifferent, and a few unfriendly or hostile.

"Hey, girly. How about a silver for a roll in the hay? That's more than you're worth, but I feel generous today." He laughed as he approached. A big man, he wore dirty homespun with a leather vest, stank of whisky, and hadn't shaved in weeks. For the hundredth time, I pitied the gypsies. Of course, this kind of behavior wasn't exclusively directed at them, but it seemed more prevalent in their case. I would have enjoyed dumping this clown on his ass. Unfortunately, in that case, the gypsies and I would be blamed for harming a law-biding citizen of Ashtol.

"Five toras."

"You're not worth a silver." His lips and eyes narrowed. "How about nothing."

"Too bad, I'm good." I turned and began walking away, knowing he would grab me. He did. I let him drag me toward an alley filled with garbage. Three steps into the alley, he spun me around and pulled me to him. I jammed a rockberry stick into his stomach. Within seconds, he collapsed. If I had to, I could claim he was drunk and passed out. I left him lying in the alley with the garbage.

I couldn't help but feel like I should be doing something. I had to avoid killing anyone, since my adversaries believed me in Zeles or at least heading in that direction. I decided to find out if our Intermediate still worked for the Sisters. That night I wandered into the nearby trees and changed into my blacks. It was late and I encountered little traffic. With Kasi's help, I had little trouble reaching the house without detection. I entered through a side window near the rear of the building into a room containing a loom, baskets full of cotton and wool, and balls of finished yarn. I opened the door a crack and scanned the room. A woman sat examining several balls of yarn. I crept into the room and blew out one of her lamps. The remaining one left the room in shadows.

"Don't turn around, Evita," I whispered from only a few steps behind her. Her whole body tensed, but she didn't move.

"It's fortunate you're here. Se'Dubben is looking for an Assassin," her voice rose with excitement. I smiled.

"Neither I nor my apprentice are Assassins, but I understand one of my Sisters is in Zeles. She should be right for se'Dubben."

"How fortunate for you. A local noble is looking for a Spy. Would you be interested?"

It was becoming obvious that she had been commissioned to find Sisters. A cat-and-mouse game; however, she was confused about who was the cat and who was the mouse.

"Yes, if the price is right. I'll check back in a day or two for his requirements and terms." I slipped back through the door and out the window. I left Anil to monitor the house. Since they couldn't know when I would return, they would have to watch the house every night until I did.

* * *

The first performance went well, and our skit was again a success. The games netted a tora, a good profit for one night. I noticed the usual thieves, no assassins that I could identify, and three Wizards: Fire, Water, and Earth. From what I knew, it made for a strange combination.

The next day Marku was informed that a local noble, Lady Roshan, wanted us to perform for her and her guests, five nights hence. That would require us to stay an additional two days but gave the clan a day's rest between our last scheduled performance and Lady Roshan's party. Performances for nobles always proved lucrative.

That night Anil hung on the Intermediate's roof watching as six men arrived. Four stood in the shadows or behind the building while two went inside, confirming my initial impression. I intended to take no action but would like to determine who hired them. I pushed Kasi to follow them when they left. To my surprise, they were soldiers disguised as commoners and employed by Lord se'Dishad, a nephew of se'Dubben and the ranking noble in Ashtol.

The next night's performance went off well. Afterward, I again worked the fortuneteller tent and Alida the dart-throwing tent. When my next customer didn't enter, I opened the flap and peered out. Everyone stood staring toward Alida's tent. I moved closer. Marku and Yoan stood facing a Water Wizard who had hold of Alida's arm.

"I found her cheating. I'm taking her to Lord se'Dishad for judgment," the Wizard said. He looked middle aged and amused. He smiled at Alida while his eyes roamed her body. I headed for my wagon, sending Kasi to follow him. I had just finished putting on my drab clothes and had my blacks in my hand when Stela entered.

"No! Don't go. He will kill you… Alida needs help…he will rape and kill her if you can't save her and the clan will do something stupid…the clan will be destroyed…leave now, save yourself…by the gods I don't know what…"

I finished dressing as she dithered, then gave her a hug and a kiss on the cheek before climbing out of the wagon. Alida wasn't going quietly. The Wizard just laughed as he dragged her along while she struggled to get loose. I hurried to get ahead of them.

The street where I waited in the shadows was filled with well-maintained row houses. I didn't know what I would or could do to save Alida. I had been lucky with the Fire and Wind Wizards, but intuition ruled not logic. Alida was family.

When he was close, I threw a knife and then another. A wall of water swirled around him, and the knives lost their power and spin when they hit the water. It was obvious that knives would never make it past that swirling wall of water. I stood there out of

166

ideas when a wave of water hit me, driving me into the cement stairs leading to one of the houses. I lay there fighting for breath, knowing I had to move before more water slammed into me again. I leaped onto the stairs and over just as a huge wave hit where I had been. The stairs saved me from being smashed against the cement a second time.

He continued moving toward me. Knowing I would soon be exposed, I ran toward the other side of the street and at the last moment dove onto my stomach as the next wave came roaring down the street. The impact missed hitting me directly, as it would have if I had been standing, but the undercurrent sent me sliding down the street into a tree trunk. The skin on my stomach and chest was scraped raw from the street and my ribs throbbed with pain from hitting the tree. I was losing this confrontation. Unlike the Fire Wizard, this Wizard didn't need to drop his water shield to send each new wave. Although the swirling action around him created a weak vortex, he stood safely five hands under water. Even if something entered the vortex, it would lose power before it hit him. There had to be air inside the water surrounding the Wizard; otherwise Alida would drown.

Before the next wave hit, I managed to rotate behind the tree, although it would only provide a temporary refuge. After another wave, I ran toward a house with cement stairs and used them to jump up and grab the bottom of an iron terrace. As I did, another blast of water hit. The force of the wave lashed over my legs, nearly tearing my hands lose. Before the next wave, I pulled myself up onto the terrace, caught hold of a cement gargoyle projecting from the roof gutter, and dragged myself up onto the roof. His next wave was wasted on the house. By then there were uprooted trees, houses with broken windows, doors, and fences, and the sides of several buildings showed signs their foundations had cracks. The street was being torn apart.

I scrambled up the roof as the rain started. Slowly, it increased in intensity until the roof resembled a river with a strong current. I dug one of my knives into the roof and hung on as the racing water worked to rip my hold free. The Wizard stood in the middle of the street with water from the roof splashing around him. Soon I'd lose my hold on the knife and would be swept off the roof to the ground below. If the fall didn't kill me, the Wizard would.

I rolled on my back and let go, letting the water propel me down the roof with increasing speed. As I slid ever faster, I drew two knives. As I flew off the roof, I flipped over in the air and plunged headfirst into the center of the swirling water. My speed slowed as I slid into the water. Then I collided with him, my knives driving into his shoulder and neck.

The wall of swirling water crashed to the ground with Alida, who lay unconscious. The Wizard lay dead. I raised his head and twisted until his neck snapped. I grabbed a leg, twisted, and threw all my weight on it. It cracked. I gasped for breath as my battered ribs shot pain through my chest. Next, I jumped in the air and came down on his ribs.

I knew I would regret it and did. The impact nearly caused me to pass out as my body exploded in pain. Everything hurt. Although drenched, even my hair seemed on fire. I stood there waiting for the dizziness to stop. When my head cleared and the pain dulled, I dragged him over to a large tree and smashed his face into it several times before draping him around it. In the shadows of the tree, I quickly shed my blacks. When I got back to Alida, she was sitting up, holding her head. By now, lights were appearing, and people had gotten enough nerve to look out their windows and doors. Gasping for air, I put my hands under her arms and, with her help, lifted her to her feet.

"What happened, Ryana?"

"Come on. We need to get away from here. The Wizard is dead. I think another Wizard killed him."

Alida wasn't hurt, just dazed. When she saw me limping, she put her arm around me, and we limped as fast as we could back to the wagons. The audiences had left, and the clan had gathered around Marku as we staggered in. They rushed us with hundreds of questions. I quieted everyone by collapsing. Although faked, it had the desired effect—they stopped asking questions. Marku carried me to the wagon with Stela following. He laid me on the cot and left. As Stela began undressing me, my blacks dropped out.

"Just put them in my bag for now. I'll put them away later."

"You collapsed on purpose? How did you save her? How badly are you hurt? I'm sorry I made you go." She stopped to take a breath. "Thank you, Ryana. We can never repay what we owe you."

"Alida's in shock, not hurt. Like before, you must stay in Ashtol. Alida's story goes like this," I said with a weak smile. "She doesn't know what the Wizard wanted, but somewhere along the way, the Wizard raised a wall of water and chaos broke out. She fainted and only came to when it was all over, I was there, and we helped each other back to the wagons. Make sure she keeps to that story. I've made it look like a Wind Wizard did it."

I lay back to catch my breath. Pain seemed to come from everywhere. "Now for my story. I raced after Alida thinking to kill the Wizard. This time I had knives—not a rock. When I caught up with them, I threw three knives at him. A wall of water came up and washed away the knives. Then a wave of water smashed into me, knocking me out. When I woke, it was all over. I found Alida in the street, and she helped me home." It hurt to talk. Stela shook her head.

"Not a bad story. Better than last time. You have cuts and bruises from head to foot. I'll bring something to bandage the cuts and salve for the bruises. It'll speed up the healing." She paused for several minutes and had a faraway look. "Why did you do it, Ryana? You could've just left. You risked your life in a fight that should've been certain death." She stared hard at me as if my eyes held the answer. I didn't know. Certainly not logic. I should've lost a battle with any Wizard—intuition ruled my actions.

"Alida's my friend…and family."

She held my head between her hands. With tears rolling down her lightly tanned skin, she kissed my forehead. When she left, I drifted off to sleep.

CHAPTER SEVENTEEN

Ashtol—Calion Province

Once again, everyone in the clan visited me at least twice the next day. Alida came in the afternoon. She gave me a hug, and pain scored a direct hit to my brain and ricocheted around inside. I moaned to maintain the visual-self illusion. She let go and jerked back.

"Sorry, Ryana." After a minute, she took my hand. "Thank you for trying to save me. I love you like a sister, even if you do dumb things. Stela told me the lie you want me to tell. Why?"

"To protect the clan. The best lie is a story that's close to the truth and simple."

"Like your boyfriend in Scio?"

"Yes. I did it for a friend. You're doing it for your clan."

"You're scary. The Shadows made a big mistake letting you go, but I'm glad. Otherwise, I never would have had you…for a sister." She turned and hopped out of the wagon.

The second day I got up and walked around, answering the same questions repeatedly. I couldn't help but notice Alida's inquisitive looks as I retold my story. If she suspected it and the one with Ilka were lies, she didn't say.

Luckily, there were no acts the next day. I did little except sit and talk. In the afternoon, Yoan came and sat down next to me.

"I wonder whether the Wind Wizard attacked the Water Wizard because he attacked you, kidnapped Alida, or because of something between the two? In either case you were brave and stupid to try saving her." He frowned and shook his head.

"A knife in his back would have served him right." I laughed wryly. "They are harder to kill than they look."

"Hope you'll be well enough for our skit for Lady Roshan's party."

"Afraid I'm going to miss?" I gave him my best evil smile.

"It had crossed my mind." He gave a snort. "Ilka and I worry about you. You seem to be accident prone. We want you healthy for the wedding." He surprised me when he gave me a kiss on the cheek before walking away.

I didn't take part in our third performance. I would have been uncomfortable throwing knives. The pain in my side might have affected my aim. Only a few fingers' width off in the wrong direction could be disastrous.

As I stood and watched, an Earth Wizard wandered into the back of the crowd. Although he appeared to watch the performance with interest, he showed no emotion. At the end of the acts, I took my usual place in the fortuneteller tent. I was surprised when the Earth Wizard came in. I wasn't surprised that everyone stood aside to allow him to go to the head of the line. He didn't sit.

"I understand you can read the past as well as the future."

Word sure gets around fast.

"There are as more pasts than people in Ashtol. I can only give you the past I see."

"That will be sufficient." He placed a tora on the table and left. For a moment, I was confused. Then I realized I had been invited to the Earth Wizards' guild hall. The rest of the evening was quiet—no more

Wizards or assassins. I closed the tent and returned to the camp, where everyone had begun to gather to eat and share experiences.

"Well, Ryana. I see another Wizard wanted his fortune told. Pretty soon the king will be asking for a telling," Vali said, and the gathering turned quiet.

"The Wizards all seem to want to know the past, but they pay well." I flipped the gold tora to Stela.

"That seems more dangerous than the future. No one can challenge the future, as it hasn't happened yet. The past can be verified," Ilka said, frowning.

"What do you tell them about the future, Ilka?" I asked.

"Something that I can guess from the hints they give me, usually, nothing extravagant. A little hope that something good will happen to them."

"I tell them the future has many possibilities, and that I can only tell them the one I see. For the past, I reverse the logic. There are many pasts, I can only tell them the one I see." Everyone sat silent. Then Ilka and Alida began clapping, and soon everyone joined in.

"It gives them hope, not once but several times. The hope you give them and the possibility that another future could be even better," Alida said. "No wonder they flock to you."

After everyone had gone to bed, I wandered off into the trees and skirted the town. The Earth Wizards' lodge stood near the edge of the forest. Halfway there I changed into my blacks. When I arrived, a young Wizard stood outside the door.

"Shadow, you're welcome." He opened the door and led me into their meeting hall, where seven Wizards were gathered. An old Wizard with white hair and a pleasant round face spoke.

"Good evening, Shadow. We thank you for coming."

"I've answered your call, as will the Shadows as soon as I can get word to them." I looked around the room. Four women and three men sat in vine chairs. Most were middle aged or older.

"As we'll answer your call."

"Can you tell us the past you see with the death of the Water Wizard? We've heard a Wind Wizard killed him," an old, brown-haired woman with a wrinkled face said in a gentle water-like voice.

"A Shadow killed him…"

"You now know the weakness of the Fire, Wind, and Water Wizards. Soon the Shadows will also know. It's a very sobering fact that we Wizards are vulnerable to non-Wizards. Do you know our weakness, Shadow?"

"I would have to fight you to find out, which I've no reason to do."

"You've some opinion. What would be your approach?" the same woman asked. It was a dangerous question. Would they consider it a threat that could put them in jeopardy? I no longer felt time, only the moment.

"Since I've committed the Shadows to support you, I'll give you my conjecture. Right or wrong, I'll not share it with the Shadows." I paused to look around the room. "At any distance from you, I would lose, so I must cling to you or die."

"You're truly the Shadow of Death. We can hear it in your words and feel it in you now. Relax, Shadow. The earth has told us that you'll be true to your word. We mean you no harm." The old lady smiled. I felt like I had passed some test and relaxed.

"Let us tell you what we know…" The old man outlined a plot to overthrow the king and named guilds they knew or suspected were party to the plot. I had suspected as much, but now I had it confirmed. I had accomplished the task Morag had set for me and should return to Ahasha to report my findings. Logic required that I do just that. My intuition said to continue to Tarion, the center of the king's power. That had to be where the center of the plot lay. There was more to be learned. Besides, the Shadow Sisters had always supported the king; therefore, weren't we obligated to do what we could to warn him? I walked slowly back to my wagon.

* * *

Lady Roshan's castle was small compared to those of the more influential lords, and her reception hall seated fewer than a hundred. As we had before, we set up our props well before dinner and waited in an adjoining room while the nobles dined. Two hours later, we were summoned and put on an abbreviated version of our standard performance. I was still sore, so I watched from the side, waiting for our skit, which would be the last act.

Yoan and I put on the knife-throwing act because the other one required too much rolling on the ground during our mock fight. Our audience was boisterous and the skit a huge success. Lady Roshan waved Yoan and me over and gave each of us five toras. She stopped me as I turned to go.

"Aren't you the fortuneteller who tells fortunes for Wizards?'

It was a dangerous question. I couldn't lie because she already knew, and I couldn't refuse without putting the clan is danger.

"I've had one or two stop in for their amusement."

"So, you're a fake?"
Damn the woman.

I wished there were an answer other than yes or no. Both had potentially disastrous consequences.

"There are many futures, my lady. I can only tell the one I see."

"And the past?"

Double damn the woman.

"Again, there are as many pasts as there are people where the events existed. I can only tell you the one I see."

"An interesting answer. It would work for a fake as well as someone who had the ability to see into both. Come with me." She pushed her chair back and walked out of the room with me tailing behind. The hall buzzed like a swarm of bees. Two guards followed us into a book-lined study ten times the size of my wagon.

"Sit," she said and waved me to a chair. "Tell me about the past and the Water Wizard's death."

Triple damn the woman.

"Come closer." I pulled a small, polished table in front on me. She motioned to the guards, and they moved a chair close to the table for her. "Put your hands on the table."

When she did, I placed mine over hers. She tensed and so did her guards. I didn't know why I was doing this, but it felt right. I closed my eyes.

"The Wizard guilds are divided across Hesland—except one. Because of this, a guild can't rely on its brothers in another province. So, it's with guilds that are aligned in another province. I see other players in for the toras. One stands alone in the shadows. The Wind and the Fire Wizards are aligned in this province." I could feel her tense at times during my story. Intuitively, I knew she wasn't part of the conspiracy. When I opened my eyes, she sat staring at me.

"And my future?"

Damn, damn, and damn again.

I closed my eyes. I had a pounding headache.

"You're caught in two worlds that are being torn apart. Neither world is safe. As they separate, you must jump onto one or the other, or fall into the darkness. I see a shadow watching. One of many possible futures, but this is the one I see."

"If you see the future, which world do I jump to?"

"I can't tell. Your future's twisted with too many other futures for me to see one clearer than the other. Your eyes are on the world with the shadow."

She jerked her hands away, and her guards' hands went to their weapons.

"The Shadow of Death?" she whispered.

"I don't know, my lady. I see only the shadow. Nothing else."

She rose and walked to her desk. Unsure of her intention, I reached for the moment. She turned and stood starring at the wall.

"The question is whether you see the future or are a brilliant observer of what is around you…I guess it doesn't really matter. I should kill you for what you've…observed."

"What I see is for your ears only, my lady. I don't share what I see with the lowest commoner, my clan, or the mightiest Wizard. It would change what I see."

"Yes, it could." She placed ten toras on the table. "My guards will see you to your clan." She went back to her desk and sat as I followed the guards out the door.

* * *

Everyone was eager to hear what had happened with Lady Roshan.

"Okay, Ryana. What happened?" Alida asked. "We had equal money on you being whipped, thrown in her dungeon, or killed for being a fake, for telling her something she didn't like. We were unanimous in feeling sorry for you…for being stupid. No wonder you are always getting hurt."

When I looked around, no one was laughing. Roshan would have done one of those things if I had told her the truth.

"I told her she was the most beautiful woman in all the provinces and would be queen someday." I walked over to Stela and counted out the five toras Yoan and I had received for the skit and then the ten for telling Roshan's fortune. "She agreed."

"I'm beginning to believe you can tell the future. You've told commoners, assassins, Wizards, and lords their future and past, and you haven't been killed—yet. I would have to admit I tell people what they want to hear to make them feel better. I would bet you told her fortune."

"Anything else would have embarrassed the clan. I wouldn't do that." Realizing I wasn't going to tell them what I had said to her, they stopped asking. I had told her the truth, leaving out the messy details. Following my intuition, I walked a dangerous path for the Shadows, the clan, and myself.

CHAPTER EIGHTEEN

Ossic—Araby Province

We left Ashtol the next day and planned to be at the Araby border by nightfall. From there, Ossic was an easy three-day ride.

I looked forward to reaching there. I'd heard so much about it and had used many of the drugs made there. Some were beneficial, some were thought to have special properties, some were used in foods, and some were specialty items like berries and sausages. The city was also famous for good luck charms like hawk feathers and talons. Because of its unique goods, it was a prosperous community. Consequently, Marku planned to stay a sixday and put on three performances.

During our second day on the road, Marku rode up and stepped onto the wagon.

"Do you mind, Ryana?"

"Of course not."

"I didn't know what to expect when Mistress asked me to take you to Scio. I did know it could be dangerous because I had heard Shadows were being killed. It's been nerve-racking at times, but the Dorian clan would no longer exist if you hadn't been along. You not only saved Ilka and Alida's lives, you saved us from being forced into a vengeance that would have cost us our lives. Not to mention, you've earned us more money than we could have on a full circuit of Hesland." He looked away for a moment. "What do you plan to do when we reach Scio?"

"I've been considering that. I could leave at Scio, which everyone expects me to do. Thanks to you,

I've the knowledge and experience to travel on my own, but it would be harder to get past roadblocks on my way to Tarion. I must reach it."

"I can't make your mind up for you, but I wish you'd stay. I could make up an excuse…you could. You're better at stories than me." He shook his head. "I'm embarrassed to admit it."

* * *

The only unusual part about the trip was that there were no roadblocks. My enemies must still be trying to catch me on the road to Zeles or in the town or be busy trying to find the informant. I smiled at the thought. They were relying on logic—send the messages for "H" and catch the Shadows on the roads. I decided to wait and see what they did before deciding.

* * *

Our performance in Ossic went well. Afterward, I acted as a fortuneteller again. It seemed my exclusive duty since Kadal. I didn't mind, as I had always enjoyed making up stories, and the people were getting easier to read each day. Sometimes I felt I could see one possible future for someone. My musing was interrupted when a young man, impeccably dressed with a huge signet ring on one hand, stepped into the tent.

"Are you Ryana, the fortuneteller?"

There goes relax and enjoy myself.

"Yes. How may I help you, my lord?"

"First Lady wu'Lichak would like the Dorian clan to put on a performance the second night after you arrive."

"Why tell me, Lord? Marku's the clan leader."

"The first lady wants you there but doesn't want to invite you alone. If she must, she will but would rather not. You're to give her a telling. I'll meet you after you arrive to make arrangements."

"I'll talk to Marku, but I'm available at Lady wu'Lichak's pleasure." What choice did I have? *If I leave, the clan will suffer. If not, who knows?*

"Would you tell my future, Ryana?" the young man asked. So much for me not drawing attention to myself. Sister Rong would have told me to continue the game to the end.

"Put your hands on the table, please." When he did, I covered them with mine and closed my eyes.

I'm not sure whether I started putting my hands on theirs to prevent being killed when I closed my eyes or because people's emotions were somehow transmitted to their hands. I could often tell much just by when they tensed or jerked. "Over the next cycle, your life will see much change. A great responsibility will be thrust upon you. You'll accept, although it puts you in great danger. During that time, you'll walk in the shadows of your ancestors. And although you seek none, your loyalty will be rewarded. Further futures are too intermingled with others for me to pick out one clearer than another." I opened my eyes and found the young noble staring at me with his mouth open.

"Thank you, Mistress." He rose with a blank look, dropped a tora, and left. This fortunetelling had become scary. Nobles calling me Mistress, and worse, I had begun to believe what I said. I laughed.

* * *

At the evening meal, Vali gave me a poke in the ribs. "Ryana, you're earning more money in the fortuneteller tent than the rest of us working the other games, and now you've added another noble to your list of admirers."

"Marku, the noble told me First Lady wu'Lichak would like us to perform for her the night after we arrive. I told him he should be talking to you, but apparently the first lady instructed him to give the message to me."

"Maybe Ryana and Yoan can earn an extra twenty tora," Alida said.

"Even better, maybe the king will be next," Ilka said to general laughter.

Marku slowly shook his head. "Ryana, these are powerful people you're dealing with. You've convinced them your tellings are real. If they think for one moment they aren't, I fear for what will happen."

CHAPTER NINETEEN

Scio—Araby Province

Although the travel to Scio took three days, it seemed like three minutes. I drove my wagon during the day, attended the evening gatherings, and worked with Yoan on innovations to our skit. Every minute my mind churned with what would happen in Scio, and I dreaded our arrival.

Should I leave the clan in Scio? Would my leaving cause them problems? What does wu'Lichak want to know and why? How do I contact the senior Assassin/Spy in Scio? Is she loyal? Is our Intermediate plotting against the Shadows? My head spun with questions, which I couldn't or didn't want to come to grips with.

When we arrived, I realized why I couldn't answer the questions. I was trying to apply logic to them. That wouldn't work for me. I needed to let my intuition guide me.

"Ryana, are you going to see your parents and boyfriend tonight?" Alida gave me a conspiratorial wink. "Maybe they would like to see you perform. You're going to perform with us, aren't you?"

The lies rolled off my tongue easily. The days of worrying that had paralyzed me blew away on the wind.

"Yes, of course I'm going to perform with you while we're in Scio. I'm not going to tell my parents just yet. I think Lady wu'Lichak would be a little upset with me if she knew I'm not clan. It's best to wait until you leave."

"Won't someone recognize you?"

"Not likely. I'm so much older. Besides, they wouldn't believe I was the same obnoxious little girl who left to be a Shadow. People see what they want to believe." I laughed.

"We'll miss you, Ryana."

* * *

The next night found us setting up in First Lady wu'Lichak's great hall. It looked to seat close to two hundred people. Everyone in the clan snuck looks at me while we waited for the guests to finish eating. I didn't blame them. This fortunetelling session could land me in the dungeon—and them. But there was no option but to play the game to its conclusion. Winning or losing wouldn't be decided until the game ended.

The clan's acts were delivered with perfection. After a brief rest while our props were set up, Yoan and I entered our little stage. As usual, the audience gasped at times and at others laughed until tears ran down their faces. I received lots of helpful hints from them while throwing the knives. Afterward, wu'Lichak gave Yoan and me ten toras each. As we were getting ready to leave, the young noble I had met in Ossic beckoned to me.

"Mistress, the first lady would like to see you. The rest of the clan can leave. I'll see you safely back to the wagons."

Marku was about to protest, but I shook my head. He could do nothing but protest. It would annoy wu'Lichak and change nothing. The noble led me into a medium-sized room guarded by two soldiers, who stood at attention on each side of the door. The young noble ushered me into the room and closed the door. It looked like a private study with shelves of books, a large oak desk, and velvet-covered chairs with the Araby crest.

"Help yourself, mistress," the noble said, gesturing toward the table along the wall laden with food and drinks.

"A glass of water would be nice," I said giving him a small bow. He went to the table and filled a crystal glass worth several toras and handed it to me. I smiled. At Ahasha, most of the time, I drank water from my hands. I decided I wouldn't like this life. I preferred drinking from my hands.

Just then, the door opened, and a tall, thin woman entered the room accompanied by four guards. She had dark-red hair, a narrow face, slanted eyes, yellow-tinted skin, and thin lips. She looked dangerous. I bowed as she entered.

"Ryana of the Dorian clan?" It was more of a statement than a question. Her eyes seemed focused on my face, but she saw all of me as she evaluated me against some criteria. It was a technique Shadows used to evaluate an opponent's potential martial skills.

"Yes, First Lady."

"I see you haven't taken advantage of the food I've provided," she said while still evaluating me. The food had been a test of some kind. Just like at Ahasha when I had had trouble determining what the Shadows wanted. I had succeeded there because I never tried to use logic. It seemed right here, too.

"No, First Lady. It didn't appear right for the occasion."

"Don't you eat after a performance?"

"Yes, First Lady. I'll eat when I return to the clan."

"You don't like my food?"

"I'm certain it's far better than anything I've ever eaten in my life." That was true.

"And you don't want to get used to it?"

"I'm content to be what I am, First Lady wu'Lichak."

"Yes, I can see that. The question is, what are you?" She continued to evaluate me as I would an opponent for his strengths and weaknesses. "I've heard many tales. But then one must be careful when relying on tales. They can disguise many things."

This woman wasn't going to see what she wanted to see. She would see what existed. I didn't know what was coming and felt myself reaching for the moment. The game was about to begin.

"Sit. We've evaluated each other as much as we can for now." She waved me to a chair and began walking toward her desk. I looked around the room.

"First Lady, could I have that table moved in front of me and have you pull up a chair close to the table?" The game was in progress. She waved to a guard, who arranged the table and a chair for her to sit. She sat and nodded to me with a smile that said she knew this was an elaborate farce.

"Please put your hands on the table." She hesitated. I could feel her guards tense.

"Why?"

I was tired. It was a cat-and-mouse game, and we had yet to tell who the cat was. "Because I asked."

She looked at me hard, giving me an "I'm the cat" look. "Boyan, have the guards wait outside. You stay."

I almost smiled. I had guessed right about Boyan. She trusted him, and he would be by her side when the fighting began.

"Please place you hands on the table, palms down." When she did, I placed mine over hers. She flinched at my touch but didn't move hers. I closed my eyes. Time no longer existed, nor did logic. I would tell her the truth as I saw it but in abstract terms.

"The next two seasons will be a time of great danger and stress. Later you'll be at peace, although still a time of great danger. Two worlds are about to clash, and Hesland won't be the same afterward. In one world, guilds and nobles are divided among themselves and allegiances shift across provinces, except those who chase the toras. They will unite, but like the eyes that stare at you, all see different worlds.

"In the other world, one guild stands united and in the shadows. You'll decide which world will dominate, and your children's children will stand in your shadow.

"Two paths exist after the worlds collide. One looks to have few decisions. In the other, many decisions will be required, and you'll never be free. There are many futures, but that is the one I see."

Wu'Lichak jerked her hands free and jumped to her feet. She stumbled backward until her back pressed against the desk.

"Boyan, get the guards, now."

Boyan dashed to the door and waved the guards in. They came in, swords drawn. I turned to ice.

"Is the shadow the Shadow of Death?"

"I see only the shadow," I replied.

"Who are you, Ryana, of the Dorian clan?"

"The second that was is the past. The second that will be is the future. I exist between them." I didn't know or care what was about to happen. I existed only for the moment.

"Fortunetellers are supposed to tell you all the good things that are going to happen in the future. You've brought me nothing but bad news. Rulers don't like bad news. It makes them irritable."

"If you wish, I could pretend to see a happy future, First Lady."

"No, I already have enough people lying to me." She nodded to Boyan. "Boyan, take four guards and escort Ryana to the gypsies' camp. The guards are for you. I don't believe she needs them. Take twenty-five toras and give them to the clan's leader."

"Marku," Boyan added.

"Marku. Tell him it's for providing a glimpse into the future. Ryana doesn't want or need money. Let the soldiers know that the gypsies are to have my discrete protection while in Araby." She continued to look at me but said nothing more.

Boyan silently walked by my side on the way back, sneaking looks in my direction. I think he now realized the future I had told him was linked to wu'Lichak's.

After they marched away, everyone gathered around me. Marku continued to stare at the sack of toras.

"We thought you'd been arrested when we saw the guards, and maybe we were in trouble. Obviously, you're in one piece, for a change, aren't under arrest, and we've lived to see Marku speechless. What happened? What did you tell her?" Ilka said while shaking my shoulders. Alida stood at her side nodding.

"I told her she was a troublemaker and ugly. She agreed."

Everyone stood speechless.

"You never tell what really happened. If you would tell me your secrets, I could replace you when you leave and make lots of money for the clan," Alida whispered. Ilka leaned closer.

"The future has many possibilities. You can only tell them the one you see."

* * *

The next two performances got loud applause from the audience, and the skit continued to be a huge

188

success. I scanned the crowd when I wasn't performing. The usual number of thieves worked the audience, and I noticed two soldiers were always standing quietly off to the side. Wu'Lichak had been serious. I had sent Anil to spy on the Intermediate's house, but nothing unusual had happened.

Then an assassin strolled into the audience. He stood off to the side staring at three nobles. No weapons were visible, which meant a knife. Since there were three men, it meant he had an accomplice or two. I scanned the crowd and found one standing on the other side, also watching the three nobles. Amateurs. Then I thought I identified a third. This one wasn't sloppy. She was enjoying the acts, clapping and laughing at the right times, but inching sideways toward the assassin standing off to the side while keeping the nobles in sight. No doubt it was Fayza, the senior Assassin/Spy in Araby. The assassins' guild was about to lose two of its members. I sent Kasi to watch.

As the last act ran from the stage, waving to the clapping audience, the three nobles split up to wander the games. I suspected they were evaluating them. The Shadow slipped up behind the older assassin, grabbed him under the arms like they were both drunk, and staggered into the trees. The younger assassin raced to catch up to the pair. The Shadow strolled back alone, circulating with the crowd while watching the same games as the men. Later, Kasi followed her into the slums to a run-down shack.

* * *

The next day, Kasi followed Fayza as she went out to beg and scrounge for food. She was good. Since it was a rest day, I left after the midday meal to look over the town. The bar on the door of her shack was easily lifted. I entered and left a note:

SEE ME TONIGHT. HAVE FOOD AND
WORK FOR YOU. 100 BITS.

I hope she understood. See me tonight—an order. Have work for you—the Intermediate's house.
And—100 bits—100 paces away. I wanted anyone else
seeing the note to think it was work for bits. A hundred
bits was a lot for a beggar, but a Shadow could make
up a good story if necessary.

Since it was late, I stayed near the Intermediate's house, not knowing when she would arrive. I
changed and waited with Anil on guard and Kasi waiting at the shack for Fayza to return and see the note.
Several hours after dark, Kasi showed me Fayza and
her cat, Zara, leaving. She hurried into the forest well
to the north of the house, changed, and made her way
toward me.

I sat quietly, waiting as she ghosted toward me,
with Zara staying well to her left. When she was
twenty paces away, I could not have seen her without
Anil and Kasi. She was perfection.

"Welcome, Sister," I said quietly.

"You summoned me?"

"Yes. Please sit. What I have to say will take
some time."

She moved forward slowly, reminding me of
Sister Hajna. She moved like a cat, relaxed and easy,
yet ready to strike. She sat down a couple of hands'
widths from me.

She wants to be close enough to strike.

I existed only for the moment as I waited. She
looked at me for a long time.

"Interesting. That's a very good disguise. You
look and sound like a mature woman. You're not.
You're a girl…woman, who hasn't yet fully developed.
I know all the senior Assassins and Assassin/Spies, and
you're not one of them. You must, therefore, be either

190

a fake or an apprentice. But you're without a senior Sister. I would say fake except you sit ready to strike, as do I, and I see no fear of death, winning, or losing—only the moment. Now I must wonder how an apprentice orders a senior Assassin/Spy to do anything. Yet you're certain you can, and I'll obey."

"Give me your hand." I extended my left hand. She surprised me.

"You're the Shadow of Death, aren't you?"

She moved her right hand from near her body and weapon and turned it palm up to show she had no weapon in it. She reached out and I grasped her hand.

"Yes. Our senior sister has given you much responsibility, child."

I could feel her senior Assassin/Spy sigil.

"Why?" she asked.

"It started…" I detailed everything that had happened since I left Ahasha.

"You seem to have destroyed our nice, comfortable view of a Shadow. We're taught to use logic against our enemies, yet you use intuition. We're taught that we can't kill Wizards, yet you ignored your teachers and killed three. We're taught not to form close relationships, yet you separate personal relationships from your responsibilities. You live in two worlds. Ironically, against all logic, Morag also used intuition when she sent you. The two of you are much alike." Fayza paused as Zara joined her. "Our enemies have learned to fear you as you move through the provinces and have devoted more and more resources to find you. They're frustrated. You have them chasing ghosts. You've outmaneuvered an army desperate to catch and kill you. I know it hurts, Sister, but our enemies have named you well. Ironically, it makes them fear you more."

Fayza nodded. "I'll tell you what I have learned. What you do with it is up to you. A religious sect called the Eyes of God is trying to seize power from wu'Lichak. They have taken control of the assassins' guild. Those two I killed were priests sent to kill the three nobles."

"You were hired to protect them?" I had to wonder if this were part of my assignment or none of my business. "Who?"

"Boyan, the first lady's secretary. She trusts him when something needs doing in secret. Do you want my help, Sister?"

"No. I want you to go to Tarion. The king will need our support, and you need to get word back to our senior Sister. Send the Senior Spy and her apprentice back to Ahasha." Sanda was here mentoring Jelena.

"You don't believe you'll live to see Tarion, do you?"

"No. Our enemies are desperate to stop me and, unlike before, they know I'm going to Tarion and will be waiting. I can no longer send them off to chase ghosts." *Logic tells me I've accomplished everything Sister Morag asked and should return to Ahasha. But my intuition tells me there is more to learn, so I can't stop.* I hoped Fayza could make it there if I couldn't. "I expect you to be gone tomorrow."

"I'll leave tonight. May you walk in the shadow of our Sisters."

CHAPTER TWENTY

Scio—Araby Province

What were the priests to the Shadow Sisters or me? Were they part of my assignment? If not, should they be? Logically, they were the first lady's problem and not the Shadow Sisters', and therefore not mine. I wondered what Morag would expect me to do. I laughed. She had been extremely specific: "The only advice I can give you, although I'm loath to say it, is to trust no one. Place your trust in your intuition and don't linger on things you can't change. Stay focused. Don't look backward. What you should have or could have done can't be changed. You can affect the future not the past."

The priests of the Eyes of God threaten wu'Lichak and the future of Araby. She will support the king. The priest won't. They seek a province of their own to rule and will support our enemies to gain it. And Araby could decide whether the plot succeeds or fails. But if I stay in Araby, I'll lose my cover. Stay... Go? I had a splitting headache as I made my way back to the wagon.

As I neared, Marku and Stela sat talking, heads together, on a fallen tree trunk. I could easily avoid them, but something told me they were waiting for me. Besides, I had to let them know that I would be staying intuition had won.

"You two are out late," I said.

Stela jerked her head in my direction. Marku jumped up, knife in his hand. He lowered it when he saw me.

"Good evening, daughter," Stela said. "You walk like your feet never touch the ground."

"A necessary habit. My teachers would have told me that they could hear me a hundred paces away. That I would need bells to be any louder." I smiled at the thought of Sister Rong. I missed her.

"You need bells so we can hear you," Marku said as he put his knife away.

"I see you've no cuts or bruises. You must not have found any Wizards to fight today." Stela looked at me with sad eyes.

"We missed you. I wondered if you'd left," Marku said. "We had hoped you would share your plans with us."

"My plans have changed. I had intended to go with you to Tarion. A reasonable story why I had decided to stay with you would have been easy to make up. But I must stay in Scio for a while. A local cult is hatching a plot to take control of Araby. Hesland stands on the verge of chaos, and Araby could tip the balance of power."

"Make up a story and we'll stay. We gypsies have a stake in Hesland, too," Marku said. Stela nodded agreement. I leaned over and hugged her.

"You've helped the Shadows more than you can ever know. I'm no longer important. Go without me." It felt like I had nothing to look forward to.

Stela returned the hug, and I felt a tear against my cheek. "Don't say that, Ryana. You are clan whether you want to be or not—whether you stay with us or not."

"Give us one of your stories. I know you could make up ten on the spur of the moment. You've had enough practice this trip." Marku laughed.

I couldn't help the tears that my visual and traitorous shadow selves shed. I closed my eyes.

"You've been informed by First Lady wu'Lichak that the king has requested a performance but haven't been told when. The first lady's providing you with protection while you stay in Araby. You plan to stay to work up new routines while you wait. I'm staying with you until we meet the Tobar clan again. I want to see Luka to see if he and I still feel the same. If so, we may want to get married." My story surprised me. My life was complicated enough without Luka, yet I obviously had feelings I had repressed. Now they were out in the open.

"Wow!" Marku shook his head. "May I ask how you plan to get wu'Lichak's support and the king's invitation?"

Stela gave me a motherly smile for some reason I didn't understand.

"Didn't you see wu'Lichak's soldiers at the performance? If I'm not mistaken, we're under her protection. If the king isn't dead by then, I see it in your future."

"I believe you, my daughter. Judging by your recent clients, you seem to know the future. Is it something they teach you at Ahasha?"

"No. They teach us that only the present exists, neither the past nor the future."

* * *

Marku decided to give a performance every three nights to try out new acts and keep everyone busy. They couldn't stay forever, so I had to do something. I had Anil watching the Intermediate's house out of habit. That night, three men entered the house and quickly came out again. Anil followed them back to the cult's temple—three buildings in Slum Alley.

Everyone was excited that I planned on staying and the possibility that I might be interested in Luka, especially Alida and Ilka.

"He'll be waiting, Ryana. You've stolen his heart," Alida said.

"I'll bet he can't wait for us to meet up again. He'd be a fool not to marry you," Ilka said. "You're just right for him. He needs a strong woman like you to keep him in line." They both laughed. I wasn't sure why.

The next day the clan began unpacking and preparing for an extended stay. When the clan gathered each night, they excitedly planned which acts to use in the upcoming performance for the king. The days were filled with practicing and testing new acts. Yoan and I experimented with new ideas for our latest skit. If we were ever going to leave Scio, I needed time to myself to figure out how to get rid of the priests.

"Yoan, I need time each day while we're in Scio. I want to spend time with my parents to prepare them for me leaving again. Realistically, they won't see me again for a cycle or more, and they need time to get used to the idea I might marry a gypsy."

Yoan nodded agreement, but I knew he worried about the upcoming performance with the king. He would have liked to spend more time each day practicing and having me attend the evening gathering.

Using Fayza's idea, I dressed like a beggar for my visit to Slum Alley and the church of God's Eyes. The cult's priests and the houses they used were easy to pick out. They made no secret of their presence, but they masked the fact they were recruiting an army. They were having no difficulty in finding recruits. The slums and adjoining neighborhood provided fruitful ground for attracting the poor with the promise of power and wealth.

The next night, I attended their church service along with a crowd of shabbily dressed men and women. A priest in a yellow robe and gold mask preached about how the rich preyed on the poor. How that wasn't right in the eyes of God, who saw the injustice and would help the poor to get their share of the wealth… After the service, food and drinks were provided. On the side, collectors and junior priests were being recruited into the inner circle with the promise of money and power.

The senior priests were clearly local assassins. The junior priests were assassins in training, which I suspected was little more than a few weeks killing dummies. Perhaps the middle-level priests were practicing on real people such as those nobles Fayza had saved or merchants who refused to pay a tithe to the church for the priests' prayers of safety.

By the third night, I worked out the priests' rank system. Collectors took tithes from the merchants and general population for the priests' prayers. They wore headbands of white, yellow, and red. White was the lowest and red the highest rank. Junior priests, assassins in training, wore sashes colored to designate their rank. It seemed silly to identify yourself as an assassin and to wear something that could be seen from twenty paces away. The upper-level priests wore white, yellow, or red robes with a sword-like cross running down the middle. They appeared to be the instructors.

The next night I dressed in my blacks, deciding it was time to shake up their nice, comfortable world. Groups went out each night into a different district to collect money for the church. I picked a side alley that stank of rotting garbage and waited. Three hours later, a group of three collectors walked pass. Since they were feared and left unchallenged, they passed me without so much as a glance in my direction.

I had agonized for days over how to neutralize the Eyes of God's threat. The solution was easy;

rationalizing it wasn't. The priests were building an army, which would eventually attack wu'Lichak's forces, killing everyone that stood in their way. To stop them, it required an Assassin, not a Spy. It would leave scars I could never erase. But if I were right, the Eyes of God could destroy Hesland and the Sisterhood. I had said I would die for the Sisterhood. Perhaps there was more than one way to die.

Three rocktail-tipped darts took them without a sound. I dragged them into the alley, confiscated their night's collection, and made it look like several persons, using a variety of weapons, had killed them.

Avoiding people with my darlings' help, I made it to wu'Lichak's castle. Two guards stood outside the gates. When I stepped out of the shadows, the closest guard jumped and tried to draw his sword, but I caught his arm before he could. When he saw I was a Shadow, he relaxed. Shadows weren't only dangerous but worked for influential people. It could be disastrous to provoke one.

"Yess, Ssshadow," the young guard stuttered. The other guard stayed where he stood. I handed him a sack with the money I'd taken from the collectors.

"Give this to Lord Boyan." I turned and walked away.

The next night I killed another team with two collectors with yellow headbands and a junior priest with a yellow sash. When I reached the castle, Lord Boyan stood off to the side of the gate.

"Good evening, Shadow. Why the money?"

"For your safe keeping." I gave him the bag with my latest collection and left.

The next night there were two teams of five. Each consisted of two collectors accompanied by two yellow- and one red-belted priest. The junior priests were amateurs, the yellow-belts beginners with some training, and the red-belts supposedly trained assassins. Sister Hajna would have considered them more dangerous to themselves than to an opponent. I smiled at the thought. This time I followed one of the teams. At the second house they visited, they dragged a merchant and his young daughter into the street, shouting to get attention and make sure the neighbors knew what would happen if they chose to resist.

"Merchant Peadone no longer wishes to help the Eyes of God correct the injustices of the rich. Why? Because he's one of the rich who prey on the poor." The red belt had a rope around the man's neck and was dragging him around as he talked. "Look at his clothes and his daughter's. They wear silks while the poor wander the streets in rags."

While he talked, a yellow-belt man's hand roamed the child's body, his hands inside her shirt and up her flared skirt.

"I pity them if they lose the protection of the Eyes of God."

I sought the moment and waited. I wanted the leaders to think it was another gang, not a Shadow. I blended into the shadows and waited for them to reach the end of the row of houses. By then everyone had retreated into their homes for fear of antagonizing them. The collectors never knew what happened as two rock-tail darts took them in the neck. As the collectors fell, the priests spun around with knives in hand, scanning the area. They never saw the knives that killed them, although I stood less than five steps away.

I then made the bodies look like they had been attacked and robbed. I didn't bother looking for the other team and made my way back to the castle. My intention was not to kill all the followers of the Eyes of God, just to stop the threat to Araby.

"Evening, Shadow. Is there a reason for the money you've been giving the guards and me?" Boyan tested the two bags in his hands. "This is rather a lot of money."

"For your safe keeping, Lord Boyan." I smiled at his blank expression, although he couldn't see it because of my head wrap. He watched as I walked away.

The next night, I encountered a group of six. They were getting desperate. This group had two red-belts and two white-robed priests who lagged behind. Probably intending to surprise the attackers. With their white robes, Sister Rong would have told them the only way to be more conspicuous would be to carry candles and beat drums. I let the group go by and waited for the priests. I darted them and rearranged their bodies. When I caught up with the others, they were just leaving a merchant's doorway. I darted the two collectors. As they fell, the two red belts crouched, scanning the area. One saw me come out of the shadows.

"Thoma, a Shadow. There are rewards for her." He smiled and drew two knives. Thoma didn't look quite as happy but joined the other one.

"Garret, spread out. We'll trap her between us." They moved apart as they started toward me, swinging their knives back and forth. They weren't assassins. They were killers who thought in terms of face-to-face contests to determine the best man. Two knives took them while they were still ten paces away.

When I arrived at the castle, Boyan again waited for me.

"Shadow, please tell me why."

"It's a donation from the Eyes of God. Keep it safe. First Lady wu'Lichak can decide what to do with it." I turned and left.

The next night, one group of collectors went out. It consisted of one collector, four junior priests, and two yellow-robed priests. Except for the collector, they all carried swords. They were probably having trouble finding volunteer collectors and were determined to kill the priest killer.

I ignored the group and ghosted through the shadows to the side of the high priest's house, avoiding the two guards out front. I opened a poorly locked window and listened. Hearing nothing, I slipped in along with Kasi, leaving Anil outside to watch. Kasi found no one in the room. From the dim light and Kasi's echoes, the room looked like a small dining room. In the hallway, I carefully opened door after door and found each of the rooms empty, until the last door. A man sat in a chair sleeping. In the corner sat a steel box chained to the floor. I used a garrote as a weapon to keep the priests confused. The steel box was easy to open; I had spent a great deal of time at Ahasha learning how to steal. The locked box held several bags, totaling twenty-five toras. I assumed the money was used to pay daily operating expenses. I liberated the bags. The head priest would have more money stashed somewhere. But for now, I wanted to make them mad. Anger made men do foolish things. I left by the same window.

Boyan stood in his usual place. When he looked inside the bags, his mouth dropped open. I left before he could recover.

* * *

Even though I was gone a lot, Yoan and I were able to revise our knife-throwing skit. We decided to try it out on the clan. It was the original knife-throwing skit with some new variations.

"Stand still, Ander," I said to Yoan.

"I am. Have you been drinking?" My knife hit an arm's length from his head.

"Have not. Well, maybe a sip." The next knife was an arm's length away from his side. "My throat was dry."

"Lorea, stop now!" Yoan said to me. I wove a bit, the knife extended in front of me pointing at him.

"Coward, stand still and I won't hit you."

"I am!"

My knife flew right into the pants hanging below his crotch. Yoan screamed. Everyone watching gasped and several jumped up.

"Oops!" I ran up to Yoan and pulled out the knife, secretly wiping a red dye on the blade.

"Ow! Ow! Ow!" he cried as he crouched over holding his crotch. His pants had elastic at the waist. I pulled it open and looked.

"You shouldn't have moved. You were small before…you couldn't afford to lose that much. Serves you right for moving."

By now, everyone was in hysterics. By the end of the skit, most had tears running down their faces.

* * *

By now the priests were very unhappy with me, judging from the number of guards around the high priest's house and the size of the collector groups. I thought it would be a good time to drop in on the training area since no one was guarding it. They probably thought it safe because of the number and rank of the assassins in the building. I walked into a large dining room through a side door, which was conveniently unlocked. Three priests sat at a table eating, two yellow- and one red-belt. When they saw me, they jumped up empty handed just in time to meet knives in their chests and throats. If Sister Hajna had seen them, she would have given one of her disproving quips: The

202

only way you're going to win a fight is if your opponent trips and stabs himself in the heart.

In the yard outside, there were six wannabe beginners hacking at straw dummies, two red-belts practicing a technique, and a red-robed priest giving instruction. There were far too many to take on simultaneously, so I waited. After a while, the red-robed priest allowed the beginner group to go eat. I flattened myself against a wall in a corner and waited for all of them to enter the room. I caught the last two to enter with darts. If not for the sound of them falling, the other four would never have known. By the time they noticed, I had knives in two. The remaining two decided to rush me. I think they thought hacking at dummies made them real assassins. They drew their swords, forgetting they were wooden practice swords. If I hadn't dropped into killing mode, I would have laughed. Judging from the type of training they were getting, the priests were building an army. Two more knives stopped them. No sooner had I collected my knives when another red-belted priest came walking through the door. When he saw the men on the floor, he drew his knife while looking around. Too late. He dropped the knife as he fell to the floor. A moment later, the last red-belt and the red-robed priest entered the room.

"Get her!" the robed priest shouted. The red belt had moved fast and got a second's advantage because I had to dodge the knife the robed one threw. When the red belt reached me, he swung at my head. As he swung, I folded to a coiled snake-like position, and his sword passed safely over my head. I unraveled, putting my knife in his heart. The robed priest's second knife hit the red-belt in the back—not that it mattered to him. His third knife passed four hands to my right. These men were neither soldiers nor assassins. They were thugs. Only their numbers made them dangerous. I put a knife in his back as he turned to run. I doubted there was any money in the building, so I left after tidying up.

* * *

"Why, Sister?" Boyan asked as I approached.

"I trust you, Lord Boyan, to hold the money for First Lady wu'Lichak."

"Why? She doesn't need money, and what you've given me is a trivial amount to her."

"She will know what to do with it when the time comes. I need a favor."

"...if I can."

"I would like to borrow a good bow and about twenty arrows. Tomorrow two hours after sunset." I left before he could reply.

* * *

The next night when I showed myself, Boyan stood waiting with a good bow and a quiver of twenty arrows.

"I don't suppose you're going to tell me why you want these," Boyan said as he handed them to me.

"All in good time, Lord Boyan."

"Aren't you afraid I'll send troops to capture you for questioning?"

"You serve First Lady wu'Lichak, and she would not hinder a Shadow."

I worked my way to Slum Alley in my begging disguise. The streets were buzzing with priests and recruits, all in large groups. The collectors that returned were in groups of ten. There was no pretense of being unguarded. Well after midnight, the streets quieted down. Using the shadows from the buildings and my darlings, I checked all sides of the temple. Two guards were stationed in front and two in back. I suspected several more were on guard inside the house. Two darts and the front guards were down. The front now clear, I splashed alcohol over the walls and extra around the doors. I struck a flint and the building burst into flame.

I heard shouts of "Fire!" and dashed around to the back of the temple. Horses neighed and stamped in the nearby stable, but it was far enough away not to be in danger. Soon people began fighting to get out the back door, as there was no safe way to exit the front. Four yellow-robed priests came rushing out carrying heavy bags. Three head priests, judging by their red robes and masks, followed them. I'm not the best archer, but at twenty paces, I generally don't miss the bull's-eye. The first three arrows went to the red-robed priests. The ones carrying the bags got the next four. The rest scattered like frightened rabbits.

I borrowed one of the horses and loaded the sacks of money. They weighed too much to carry on my own. With that much money, the cult could have bought and outfitted a reasonable sized army.

In the square, I tossed a silver to a girl in scraps of a dress. She nodded when I told her to cover the town shouting for victims of the Eyes of God to let the authorities know their names. Three boys soon joined her. I promised each an extra five silvers if they worked hard. They were also to proclaim the priest's enemies of the Shadows.

At the castle, Boyan stood waiting. I handed him the reins to the horse with the sacks attached.

"First Lady wu'Lichak would like to talk to you."

"Lord Boyan," I said, ignoring wu'Lichak's request. "I promised five silvers each to four children in the slums. I'd appreciate you seeing they were paid. They're spreading the word to those coerced into giving money to the Eyes of God for protection, to make

themselves known. I believe the first lady would benefit if she would distribute the money I gave you to
those deserving it."

"Wait!" Boyan shouted as I walked away.

Back at the wagons, I told Marku the king
awaited us.

CHAPTER TWENTY-ONE

Udo—Araby Province

We left late in the morning, with everyone excited about visiting Tarion and a performance in front of the king. Later that morning, Marku joined me on my wagon.

"I understand the church of the Eyes of God and the Shadows have been having an argument. It appears the Shadows won." Marku stared at me for a minute. "I can't reconcile the girl I met in Sebec with the Shadow who's a match for Wizards, tells fortunes for First Lords, and destroyed the army of the Eyes of God."

"She was a different woman—one who looked forward to learning how to be a Spy, under the direction of a senior Shadow. She's dead." I grieved for that young woman.

"I can't imagine how it feels to kill someone, and you've been forced to kill many. I do know everyone in the clan loves you, and every kill protected those you love. Everyone benefits except you. The Dorian clan would accept you as a member any time you wanted." We lapsed into silence. I was thankful for Marku's thoughtful words, but it didn't change anything. We were headed toward Tarion, and my enemies hadn't stopped looking for me.

Someone shouted that there was a cloud of dust behind us. Soon afterward, a large column of Araby mounted soldiers came into sight, riding fast.

"What do you think they want?"

"Maybe Lady wu'Lichak didn't like the fortune I predicted." I couldn't imagine what she might want.

Perhaps it had something to do with the church. I did kill…murder a lot of people. It didn't matter, since there was no place to run, too many to fight, and the clan would suffer if I did. I relaxed. The past couldn't be changed. As we waited, two riders pulled ahead of the others, who had slowed to a walk.

"Good morning, master Marku, fortuneteller," Bolan said with a smile. "I'd like you to meet Captain Chelan."

"Good morn, Captain," Marku said. I nodded.

"We are headed to Udo. If you don't mind, we'll join you. It would be a nice diversion for the troops," the captain said. Of course, we couldn't really refuse. Chelan and Bolan were looking at Marku's horse, which trotted alongside the wagon.

"We would be delighted to have you. These are troubled times. Who knows what we'll meet on the road to Udo?"

With that, Bolan and the captain slowed to join the column.

"What do you think, Ryana?"

"Since they didn't arrest me, I think First Lady wu'Lichak has granted us her protection while we're in Araby, and no, I don't know why. I guess she didn't mind being called ugly and incompetent."

"You make us gypsies look like clowns." He shook his head as he mounted his horse and rode away.

If we rushed, it would take three days to reach Udo, but there was no reason to rush. Marku decided to stop early and to put on two acts and set up one tent for the soldiers each night. He reasoned it was worth the protection, and we could use the practice. The captain was delighted for the diversion from a long, boring ride. The first night we performed the tightrope and horse-riding acts. The mounted soldiers were fascinated with the riding tricks and afterward sat around debating whether any would be useful in battle. We ate in three large circles rather than one, with several gypsies joining each circle. It made for some interesting discussions on military and gypsy life. On the first night, Bolan came and sat next to me.

"The first lady was pleased that the Sisters intervened with the Eyes of God cult. She didn't realize the extent of their terror or real intent. The merchants and residents of the adjoining districts were afraid to report the extortion because of the threat to their businesses and families. In a time of chaos, the cult would have been a significant force." He stared at me for a moment. "They would certainly see a different world for Araby. She doesn't know your future but would see you safely into Dazel."

"When you see her again, give her my thanks. The gypsies are in great danger." I didn't add "because they carry me," but maybe she already knew. She was a shrewd woman who knew the bottles had narrow necks, the circles on the wooden balls were off center, and I knew more than I should.

* * *

On the second night, we performed our tumbling act and Stela's magic act. Afterward, I opened the fortuneteller tent. Captain Chelan was the first customer.

"I understand you tell fortunes for nobles, Wizards, and our first lady. Very impressive," he said as he sat. "I'm afraid this is going to be a long night, since all the troops will want a…telling."

"Put your hands on the table, Captain," I said, wondering what to say. I didn't know anything about military life—or did I? The Sisters and the gypsies were clans; perhaps the military were also a type of clan. And wu'Lichak would have sent someone she trusted along with Bolan. "Like Lord Bolan, First Lady wu'Lichak trusts you. There is a storm forming around Araby, and the first lady will need your support. You will give it gladly, willingly risking all for her…" Later that night, I noticed him talking with Bolan and sneaking looks in my direction. The tellings with the soldiers were lighter and easier. They tended to give hints or ask what they wanted to know. It was easy to weave in their loyalty to Chelan and the first lady.

* * *

The third night, Yoan demonstrated his skill with knives, and we put on our new skit. The soldiers roared with laughter. Afterward, I received all sorts of strange looks. When Bolan smiled, I knew wu'Lichak had discussed her suspicions with him. I guess it didn't matter any more. I felt my life as a Sister was over. I would have cried if I had had any feelings left.

We entered Udo late in the afternoon of the fourth day. I immediately sent Kasi to watch the Intermediate's house. That strategy had proved productive in the past. Ironically, my enemies' use of the Intermediates to locate Shadows had helped me locate them. Funny, I had begun to think of them as my opponents rather than the Shadows.

We rested that day and planned for a performance the next day. Marku didn't plan to stay in Udo long, since it was a mining town with a small population, although wagon trains loaded with workers did come in periodically to collect ore for processing. That meant I had a few days to find the Sister Spy who was operating in Udo for a Lord in Scio. I didn't know the reason, only that her last location had been here. Although nothing had happened early in the evening, I decided to hurry the process along with a visit. As everyone had come to expect, I wandered off into the night. Halfway there, I changed into my blacks and approached the house with caution. The Intermediates' houses had proved dangerous. After ensuring no one was watching the house, I entered through a side window into a storage area. The Intermediate, Angess, made and sold special breathing masks, gloves, and shoes for the miners. When I opened the door a crack, I saw her sitting at a table, writing. The room appeared empty, so I opened the door halfway.

"Don't turn around, Angess, your life depends on it." She froze. "What has been happening in Udo?"

"Lord Tenus is looking for a Shadow. He hired an Assassin to kill another lord who plotted against the first lady. Instead, she took money from Lord Tenus and intended to kill him. One of his men discovered the plot, and she was captured. He's holding her prisoner until he can find a senior Shadow to turn her over to. He believes she's an apprentice and willing to pay to get rid of her. Perhaps you could take her." She made no attempt to sneak a look in my direction. I guess she took my threat seriously; however, her story was the worst lie I had ever heard, even if I didn't know he captured a senior Spy. Apprentices are never by themselves—well, almost never—clients didn't hold Shadows to report them to another Shadow, and why pay when the Shadows would owe him for the broken contract?

"Tell Lord Tenus I've business in Windon, which I must finish first. I should be back in a sixday. When I return, I'll be glad to deal with the rogue Shadow. Send the following message to Ahasha:
        HAVE ROGUE SHADOW IN UDO.
        WILL PUNISH UNLESS TOLD OTHER-
WISE. Q."

I exited the way I entered. *Lord Tenus will probably set up a roadblock to Windon, but we've Bolan and his troops. Hopefully, the message to Ahasha will draw attention away from the gypsies.* The problem now was how to free Sister Morana. Maybe her familiar, Niki, a black monkey-like, tree-climbing animal, could help if I could find her. I changed back to gypsy clothes and sent Anil and Kasi to look for Niki. She wouldn't be far from Lord Tenus's compound. Closer to the wagon, I saw Bolan partially concealed behind a tree. I could have slipped by him but decided not to. I walked slowly, looking at the ground, staying some twenty paces from where he stood.

"Good evening, Ryana." He stepped out from behind the tree smiling. "You're out very late."

"I always wander around at night. I'm finding it hard to undo my training at Ahasha. The Sisters don't believe students need sleep. After a while, you can't sleep more than four to five hours a night."

"You trained at Ahasha?"

"Didn't you know? The Sisters decided I wasn't qualified and asked me to leave. They paid Marku to deliver me to Scio. I've decided I like being a gypsy. It's exciting." That seemed to deflate him. I suspect he thought he had proved me a Sister. My lie was close enough to the truth, as a good lie should be. If he questioned anyone, it was what he would be told.

* * *

We put on our first performance the next night. The audience was small, but the games were very profitable. A few thieves wandered through the crowd. The miners looked to be a rough bunch that few would want to antagonize—like by putting your hand in one of their pockets. I noticed one I thought could be an assassin. He walked around looking closely at the women. I guessed he hoped he would be the one who found the legendary Shadow of Death. Of course, I would bet he had never considered what would happen if he did. An Earth Wizard stood off to the side. He never showed any interest in me, but his presence let me know they were aware of me. As usual, I worked the fortuneteller tent. Most of my clients were women hoping to hear something good, even if they didn't believe it. Few men visited. Near closing, a young noble entered, sneering, and threw a tora on the table.

"Well, girly, you want to tell me how much I'm going to enjoy bedding you tonight?"

"No, young lord. I'm going to tell you how wonderful tomorrow is going to be because you didn't bed me tonight."

"You bitch, I've offered you ten times what you're worth. Maybe I'll just take it for free."

"Nothing's for free, young lord."

I put my left hand containing a knife on the table. He smiled. I smiled, knowing he planned to trap my hand with his and then grab me.

How had the idiot stayed alive so long?

Sure enough, his hand came down on mine. I made no attempt to move it. As his hand touched mine, my right hand came up with a knife at his throat.

"Now, doesn't the thought of waking up tomorrow seem good?"

He froze with the blade at his throat.

"If I cut your throat, I'd bet no one would care or miss you. I know right now you're planning to get even because you embarrassed yourself. I get a hundred men like you each cycle. I'm still here. They aren't." I slid my hand out from under his, and he backed up.

"I'll get even, bitch."

"Better to think about waking up tomorrow. I'm in a good mood today. Never can tell about tomorrow."

When he left, Yoan pulled back the flap.

"Trouble?" he asked, looking at the knives in my hands.

"Probably. Right now, he's forgotten I had a knife at his throat and is thinking how he's going to catch me alone."

"Be careful. Nobles are dangerous."

* * *

Niki, Morana's familiar, paced an area about a hundred paces from Tenus's compound. Judging from Anil's flight over and around his small castle, it looked to be a three-story building. The yard held a long, narrow barracks, stables, a workout area, and a small armory. A stone wall formed a battlement. Although the castle was small, it undoubtedly had a dungeon of sorts where Sister Morana was being held.

That evening, I went for my normal walk. When I had lost sight of the wagons and Anil and Kasi showed no one following, I changed into my blacks. When I reached Niki, she flinched away from me but didn't run. I hoped Morana could direct Niki to help. Although I could feel Niki's emotions as she could feel mine, it provided limited communication. I sat waiting for several hours until everyone should be asleep. Then I worked around to the back of the yard and waited until Kasi failed to detect activity. I took a running jump and caught the top of the wall with one hand. I struggled to grasp the top with the other hand but failed, sliding down the wall, scraping my hands and cheek. I stood there breathing hard and considered the wall. Suddenly, I felt pressure on my shoulder, and a moment later I saw Niki catch the top of the wall and pull herself up. She sat there with her arm hanging down toward me. I laughed. Niki would be a good familiar for a Spy. I moved back several steps and took another run at the wall. Again, I caught the top with one hand, but this time Niki caught my other hand and pulled it to the top. I dragged myself up and over onto the battlement.

Every hundred paces, stairs led to the ground, but I decided to jump down instead. I would be too visible on the battlement if someone were to walk by. When I looked up, Niki stood at the back wall of the castle. Narrow window ledges, corbels, irregular stones, and decorative features stuck out that would permit a climb to the roof, and that would be the safest way into the building. Niki started up when she saw me coming. I followed, keeping an eye on her for the best way up. As luck would have it, a guard wandered the roof. He wasn't particularly alert, but he could be a problem if I chose the wrong time to swing onto the roof. I hung there, my arms screaming with pain and my fingers cramping, while I waited for him to reach the other side. He strolled, looking out into the distance. Only my training saved me from falling. When he reached the other side, I slid over the wall and lay resting in the shadow created by a full moon low on the horizon.

I crept along. When I was in range, I used my longer blowtube to put a rockberry dart in his back. Why should he die for being a soldier and following orders? After kicking him in the head, I pressed against the wall, creeping down the stairs to a long hallway. It appeared to run along the side of the building. Another hallway ran perpendicular to it with several doors. The first room was a large study, the second empty. The third had two beds with small children soundly asleep. The fourth was another bedroom, three times as large as the last one. A man and woman lay there asleep. I pulled two sticks out, one rockberry and one rocktail. I tiptoed to the bed and dove between them. The woman got the rockberry. The man turned out to be Lord Tenus. He gave one last snort and was dead. Whether the woman was his wife or his mistress, she didn't deserve to die.

I retraced my steps back to the other hallway. The steps down to the next floor had two guards at the bottom. I darted each with rockberry. On this floor, there were ten or more doors, which probably belonged to minor nobles or high-ranking officers. I opened the first door and found one bed occupied by a man and woman. I darted both and dragged my two guards into the room. Someone wandering down the hallway would think the guards had roamed off. Out of curiosity, I walked over to the bed and found the noble who had been trouble earlier. I stabbed him with a rocktail stick and then broke his neck. The gypsies didn't need him causing trouble because of me. I didn't bother with the other doors and descended to the first floor. I could hear two guards talking from down the hallway. I couldn't ignore them, so I slipped down the hallway and peeked through the half-open doorway. It looked like a kitchen. I darted both then found a large pan and hit each several times in the head.

I had ten darts but needed to dip them again before I could reuse them. If that became necessary, I carried two containers with the poisons, but it would be time consuming. I could feel Niki's excitement as I neared the stairs leading down. I descended slowly, listening as I went. As I neared the bottom, Niki bared her fangs and extended her finger-length claws. Just then a man backed out from a narrow doorway.

"There, Shadow, now you know what a real man feels like."

Niki raced down the hallway and landed on his back. Blood sprayed across the walls as her claws ripped through his neck. As he collapsed, she shot through the open cell door. Morana lay on the floor, hands tied, her face bloody and her clothes torn into rags.

I knelt beside her, cut the ropes, and lifted her in my arms. She didn't cry out, but her arms tightened around me. She shuddered. After a moment, I leaned back and took out the extra blacks I had brought. She winced as I helped her strip out of the rags and dress. When finished, she eagerly grabbed the three throwing knives I handed her.

"We must hurry before it gets light. Think back to Ahasha and your training. We wouldn't want to embarrass Sisters Morag, Rong, or Hajna."

Morana smiled. "No, never."

She pulled herself up and staggered into the hallway. I couldn't support her and be ready to defend us at the same time. It was slow, but she made it up the stairs and to the front door by herself.

"Wait here until Niki lets you know it's safe to follow."

I used the shadows from the building and the wall to make my way unseen to the two guards at the gate. Although I needed to keep my identity, methods, and familiar a secret, I hated what I had to do, but… I knelt and tied my belt around Niki's face. Surprisingly, she let me. Two darts and the guards were unconscious. I pulled out my darts and cleaned up before urging Niki to get Morana. Seconds later she came stumbling across the yard looking like a drunk. We slipped out the gate door and into the night.

It took an hour to work our way to within two hundred paces of the camp. I left her and ghosted to Marku's wagon. The dim light of dawn had just begun to show, and the camp was quiet.

"Stela, I need help."

"Are you hurt?"

"No, but I've a Shadow who is. I'll need bandages, needle and thread, and salve." I whispered. She didn't say anything. A few minutes later, she came out with a bundle and followed me into the woods. We couldn't hide Morana's identity because she had to be stripped to treat her injuries. An hour later, Stela had finished.

"That's all I can do, R… She will need rest."

"No. Sister, you must go west. Go now." I gave her my hand. I could feel the mark of a senior Spy. She smiled and rose.

"I acknowledge your right. May you walk in the shadow of our Sisters." She limped off with Niki.

"She can't go. She's not fit to travel. If she must, why not go south? There is nothing west…yes, I see. You're using logic against them, like when you told us to stay when we wanted to run. What did she mean, I acknowledge your right?" Stela looked in the direction Morana and Niki walked.

"Spies are higher than anyone else except a senior Assassin/Spy, which I am. In addition, I've Mistress's seal. My words are Mistress's words. No one outranks me." *Yes, I speak for the senior Sister. I wonder if she would approve of my words now.* Stela remained quiet as we returned to the wagons.

"I pity you, Ryana. No one as young as you should have that responsibility, but I think Mistress has chosen wisely."

* * *

The town swarmed with mercenaries and the late Tenus's soldiers, who were under the directions of one of his nephews, Lord Phellen.

"We demand to search the wagons," Phellen shouted. He looked ridiculous with his twenty soldiers facing Bolan's forty.

"These wagons are under the protection of First Lady wu'Lichak. Do you presume to have the authority to question her?" Bolan asked as he put his horse next to Phellen's.

"My uncle was killed. We'll search these wagons."

"I doubt all your soldiers are willing to question First Lady wu'Lichak's word. Those who do will die."

As he spoke, his men drew their swords. Phellen paled.

"Marku, let them search under the same conditions you imposed on the mercenaries." I leaned toward him so as not to be heard by the others.

"Lord Bolan, I'm willing to let them search, if they will limit their search party to two men accompanied by one of mine. The death of Lord Tenus is a tragedy." Marku had ridden up to Phellen and Bolan. "We've nothing to hide."

"Under those conditions, you may search the wagons." Bolan waved to the captain, who pointed to his senior sergeant.

Phellen didn't like being refused. He obviously wanted to tear the gypsies' wagons apart, but he had no choice and waved to two of his soldiers.

The search took an hour. The sergeant had to caution the searchers several times not to damage anything. Phellen went away satisfied but annoyed.

"That was good of you, Marku," Bolan said after they had left.

"I appreciate your support. Without you, they would have torn the wagons apart. We owe First Lady wu'Lichak for her generous support."

The next day we left Udo.

CHAPTER TWENTY-TWO

Windon—Araby Province

As we rode out of town, Stela joined me on my wagon.

"You were right. The search never went west—that would have been illogical. We must remember the lessons you've taught us. We're getting closer to Tarion. Won't you be safe there?"

"My enemies haven't given up. By now, it has become personal. There are those in Tarion who want to supplant the king. It's the center of the plot. I've nowhere to go, so eventually they will find me; therefore, I intend to leave you in Tarion, if not before."

"Why do you say you've nowhere to go? You're a Shadow. You've a home in Ahasha."

"I've abused Mistress's authority. Even if I haven't, they won't want me back." I should have felt like my heart had been ripped from my chest, but I felt nothing. I had long ago reconciled myself to my fate. There was no sense pretending it could be otherwise.

"Then you can become a gypsy and stay with us. You'll heal in time." Stela put her arm around my shoulders. For a moment, I hoped it were true. My mere presence would endanger the clan, and I wouldn't do that. In a way, I wished Morag would send an Assassin to kill me. I smiled. I doubted she could succeed. I had become an instrument of death. Well, that was tomorrow, and this was today. Stela said no more as she stepped off onto Marku's horse. The trip to Windon was a one-day hard ride, but Marku planned to stop early and make it a leisurely two-day trip.

We had no Intermediate or Shadow in Windon according to the information Morag had given me, which meant I had little to do. Marku planned only two performances in the small town.

The audience at the first performance stomped and clapped, and the profit from the games good. I had lots of business in the fortuneteller tent. They were mainly women. A few men came wanting answers to business questions. I had little experience with business matters except for the theory I received at Ahasha, but if I listened hard, I could figure out what they were looking to hear. Stretching the result further into the future and adding: "there are many futures, but this is the one I see most clearly" seemed to satisfy them. Ironically, I learned a lot about business from those men.

On the second night, my first customer was Lord Phellen. I wondered why some lords seemed to be so vicious when they had such privileged lives.

"You've a reputation for being able to see into the future and that you did a reading for wu'Lichak." He grinned or it might've been a sneer. "What did you tell her?"

"I think you should ask her, Lord Phellen."

"I can make you tell me, and that would be very unpleasant. It would be easier to tell me now."

"When First Lady wu'Lichak finds you tortured me to discover what I told her, that will be very unpleasant."

"Who do you think you're talking to, gypsy? I can have you flogged, and no one can stop me," he shouted, his face twisted in hate and rage.

"That won't change what Lady wu'Lichak will do when she finds out, and word will get back to her one way or the other." He reached out and grabbed my arm and dragged me out of the tent. I let him.

"Sergeant, tie her to that wagon wheel. I'm going to teach these gypsies a lesson. Any commoner is better than them," he hollered loud enough for all the clan to hear. Yoan stepped out from behind the wagon. He had a knife in his hand and several in his belt. Lord Phellen didn't realize he stood seconds away from death, but if Yoan killed him, the soldiers would kill Yoan and probably destroy the wagons and most of the clan. If they did not, the mercenaries clustered behind the soldiers would. I shook my head.

The sergeant had just finished tying me to the wagon wheel when Lord Bolan appeared. The captain and his troop stood off to the side.

"What do you think you're doing?"

"She insulted me. I'm going to teach her how to talk to nobility."

"That is unforgivable. Ryana, what did you say?"

"I say she insulted me. Isn't that enough, Lord Bolan?" His face red and lips squeezed tight.

"It might be if you were in Udo. It might be if she weren't under the protection of Lady wu'Lichak. The first lady, who's your liege, in case you've forgotten. It might be if you weren't employing mercenaries. That's quite a few might be's. Of course, I would be willing to listen if you would like to clear them up." Bolan paused.

Meanwhile, the captain and his troops swung up onto their horses. Phellen stood silent, looking around for something.

"Ryana, what did you say to Lord Phellen?"

"I told him I wouldn't disclose the future that I told First Lady wu'Lichak."

"I would bet that would have been worth many toras."

222

"I'd rather be flogged." I wouldn't have wanted to be in Phellen's pretty leather boots at this minute.

"She's lying," Phellen shouted. His face had gone pale. He touched the hilt of his sword, and forty swords left their sheaths.

"Lord Phellen, I might've believed you if it hadn't been for all those other might be's. I'm sending you back to Scio to answer to your liege. Captain form a detail to escort Lord Phellen back to Scio. I'll give you a letter to give to the first lady."

"You can't do that. You've no authority." He looked around. "Soldiers of Udo, attack."

A couple drew their sabers, but no one moved.

"Ordering an attack on a representative of your liege. I guess we've another might be, Lord Phellen. Captain provide another detail to escort the Udo soldiers back to Udo. Any of them who would like to join the Araby army may accompany your escort back to Scio. I will send a letter authorizing their enlistment. Captain untie Ryana. She looks uncomfortable."

Bolan looked over to the mercenaries who had drawn their weapons, but none had moved.

"Mercenaries, you're not authorized to be in Araby and are unwanted. I would suggest you leave. If my men see you again, they have orders to kill you on sight."

The captain untied the ropes and I rubbed my wrists. Phellen hadn't intended to teach me a lesson. He had intended to whip me until I told him what he wanted to know, or I died. I didn't care. I would rather have died than have the clan hurt on my account. Otherwise, I would have killed the fool.

Bolan interrupted my musing.

"You wouldn't have told him, would you?"

"It was none of his business."

"He would have killed you to find out what you knew," he said, more of a question than a statement. I shrugged. He nodded and walked away.

* * *

Later, as I walked toward the fire and the scent of the savory stew cooking there, Marku stopped me.

"I'm not going to let you work the fortuneteller tent anymore. You've a tendency to antagonize our marks. What got Phellen so mad at you?" He smiled, but it didn't reach his eyes.

"He wanted me to tell him Lady wu'Lichak's fortune."

"We were lucky Bolan's here. We would have tried to help, but in the end, he would have killed you—and us." He looked at the ground, shaking his head.

"I should leave before you or someone else does something stupid just like that. I don't want anyone in the clan hurt trying to defend me. Marku, I could've killed Phellen any time I wanted. I chose not to. You must understand that if I choose not to defend myself, you must respect that decision. If not, I'll leave tonight." I stared at him, waiting for a response. My life had gotten far too complex. I could no longer decide whether staying with the clan helped or hurt them.

"You're right, of course. When trouble happens, we tend to react with our emotions. It's why you've been so successful. You use their emotions and logic against them." He took my hand in his. "You made a conscious decision to save the clan. I should have respected it. I would have gotten the clan and you killed. Stay. We will honor your decisions."

* * *

As I readied my wagon for the trip to Sandel, Bolan walked over to me.

"Good morning, Ryana."

"Good morning, Lord Bolan. I thank you for your help yesterday. Lord Phellen was in a very unpleasant mood," I said. "I'd appreciate it if you would thank the first lady for her protection."

"I'm curious. Did you submit because you saw the future or because you knew I would protect you?"

"I would have whether you were here or not." The clan was more important than me.

"To protect what you said to Lady wu'Lichak?" His eyes were wide and mouth partly open in disbelief.

"What I see is for that person alone."

"It's interesting that you told First Lady wu'Lichak that she would determine the fate of Hesland. She said the same about you. That's why she sent me to ensure your safe passage to Dazel. It appears that both of you can see the future. My liege apparently knows what you are. I don't. I do know that even with the earring, you are more than a gypsy and fortuneteller."

"Would you do me a favor, Lord Bolan?"

"If I can."

"I need a horse and an escort to take me to the border. They're to leave me there and return with the extra horse."

"Why?"

"To please your liege lady."

"When?"

"When we stop for the midday meal." I needed to be at the border by nighttime. The mercenaries weren't supporting Phellen. They were using him to find…the Shadow of Death.

"They will be waiting." He walked away shaking his head. He was a good man and faithful to wu'Lichak. She understood the machinations of the game the rulers played. He did not.

* * *

When we stopped, I pulled Stela aside.

"Stela, would you drive my wagon…sorry, the clan's wagon to the border for me? I need to do something." I need to do what I'd become adept at—killing.

"Why"

"The mercenaries are going to be waiting at the border for us. Everyone going to Dazel will get the same treatment, but gypsies will suffer more. If I can't stop them, the least I can do is stop you and ensure Lord Bolan will stay until we can figure something out."

"Can't you find another way?"

"Stela, the reason there's so much trouble is because of me."

"No, if you weren't with us, they would be searching for you and the result would have been the same. By now we would have been killed and other gypsies too. Never mind, I'll drive the wagon for you. What do I tell the others when they ask?"

"I'll be leaving with a couple of soldiers. Tell them it's to make sure I'll be safe until we reach Dazel."

"That's a good story, except I doubt it's any truer than the others. Go."

* * *

"Ryana, this is Sergeant Adler. The troopers are Dirk and Ebert. They will take you anywhere within Araby you want. May First Lady wu'Lichak's insights ride with you." He stood watching as we rode away.

"Sergeant, I want to go about a league south of the road leading to the Araby and Dazel border."

"Yes, Lady Ryana."

I laughed. "Lady?"

"Yes. Anyone First Lady wu'Lichak gives protection and Lord Bolan acquiesces to is a lady." He smiled.

What could I say? "Thank you for the honor."

After that, we rode in silence. We reached the border just as the sun began to disappear behind the mountains where I had been raised. I sat reflecting on my life from a worthless girl-child to a Shadow Sister and now to the Shadow of Death. I had gone full circle, from despair to joy and back to despair.

Enough, Shadow of Death.

I let myself slip into the moment between the past and future. I had turned to ice.

"Go now." My voice was flat, but I couldn't help it or care.

"May you walk in the shadows," Adler said before turning his horse, and the three rode away. Yes, it would be good if our dead Sisters would allow me to walk in their shadow. I crossed the small stream that defined the border and faded into the forest to the west. If they had soldiers, they might have spread them out as in Calion in case I tried to avoid the roadblock. With Anil and Kasi crisscrossing the area, I saw neither soldiers nor mercenaries.

On my hands and knees, I crept through the underbrush until I came to the hard-packed dirt road. Twenty steps off to each side of it, six men sat around a fire. They had whetstones out and passed a flask from one to another as the *whisk, whisk* of sharpening swords carried on the slight breeze. One stood in the middle of the road, looking toward Araby.

"God damn the Shadow bitch and se'Dubben. If we don't find her, he will run what's left of us out of Calion," one muttered, shoving his dark hair out of his eyes.

"She has to be moving toward Dazel. She's been collecting information for the king. That's why they want her killed," a tall, ugly man with a scarred face added. After that, the group lapsed into silence, although they continued drinking with an occasional "Damn her… She'll pay and pay when we catch her… Then we'll pass her around till she's dead…"

I lay in the shadows waiting, hearing the words without hate, revenge, life, or death. Frozen in the moment. After a few hours, they began passing out from too much drink or just needing sleep. I laid out my blow tubes, rocktail-laced darts, and knives.

One of them grunted and staggered toward the trees, unfastening his pants as he went. I darted him. Then I worked my way closer to the fire and began darting each man. Afterward, I lay there for some time lamenting the death of that young woman who only wanted to be a spy and wouldn't kill a rabbit when she was starving.

I picked up my things and slid into the shadows and across the road. Half of this group was also asleep. One paced by the fire while two sat playing with their weapons. They were on the other side of the fire from me. Those three would come last. I lay waiting. As their focus became directed in one direction or another, I darted one of those asleep. I had darted all three when one of them noticed the darts.

"She's here!" he shouted loud enough to alert the other two, who jumped to their feet and began scanning the area.

"There!" one said, pointing to where I lay several paces away. They charged, jumping over the men lying dead around the fire. I jumped to my feet and put a knife into the closest one, but his momentum carried him into me, knocking me down. He landed on my hand holding a rocktail stick. I jerked my arm free and rolled to my feet but not fast enough. Meaty arms grabbed me from behind, pinning my arms to my sides. I jerked my head backward, driving my head into his face, lifted my leg, and drove my foot down his leg

228

into his instep. Bones crunched. As he let go, cold steel sliced across my stomach. I felt wetness but no pain. If I lived, the pain would survive also.

I had my knife out as his knife came back for a slice across my neck. I stepped into him, blocking his arm with my knife and slashing his wrist. The blade cut deep, and blood sprayed over my face and chest. I rolled away from the man behind me but not soon enough. I felt skin and muscle tear as steel sliced across my back. I rolled to a standing position and turned to face him. He approached, tossing his knife from one hand to the other and smiling. Blood dripped from his nose as he limped toward me.

Big, burly men liked face-to-face fights where they had the advantage. I turned as if to run, spun, and threw my knife into his throat.

But I had forgotten about the man standing in the road until Anil and Kasi's echoes showed a man running toward me. He lunged with his knife aimed at my kidneys. I twisted, blocking with my arm a bit too late, and the blade tore through to the bone. He stumbled and fell as Anil and Kasi struck him. I threw a knife into his chest.

I retrieved my darts and knives, limped to the fire, and sat. My head spun and my vision blurred. I still had the pain somewhat under control, but I could feel blood running down my body from the many cuts. After several tries, I managed to retrieve a bottle of alcohol and poured it down my back, arm, and chest. Then I put a knife into the fire. When it turned red hot, I placed it on the cut on my stomach. It sizzled and the air stank of burning flesh. I bit down on a scream while holding it in place. It felt like I was being burned alive. The cut on my back took several tries before I thought I had sealed it. I passed out doing my arm. There is a limit to the pain one can tolerate—even an Ahasha-trained Shadow. When I woke, I slipped my blacks back on and sat there, controlling my pain and thoughts. I could not move even if I had wanted to. Strangely, I was content to die here—I was so tired of killing and of man's madness. Perhaps my dead Sisters would take pity on me and let me walk in their shadow.

* * *

The warmth of the morning sun felt soothing, and I slept for several hours. Still sitting in the same place, I considered my few options. I wouldn't be able to move, much less walk, for a while. My body needed time to recover. For that, I needed rest and food. But I couldn't summon the strength to move. It took all my energy just to sit up straight. The loss of blood, lack of food, and numbing pain had won.

Sometime later, the clatter of wheels and harnesses woke me. Soon they stopped. I wanted to laugh and cry at the horror on their faces.

The voices seemed a long way away. "A Shadow… She's dying… So many bodies… They meant to kill us. It must be the Shadow of Death."

Stela and Marku bent over me, their faces strangely wavy. Stela reached out and lifted the shredded material.

"My god, child. You cauterized yourself?" Stela whispered. A tear slid down her cheek.

"Her back, too," Marku said.

"They planned to kill you and more. Go now. I'll see you in Sandel if I can."

"We can't leave you," Marku said.

"You promised to abide by my decisions. It's for you to go. The shadow of my Sisters will determine my fate." I was so tired. I hoped my Sisters would not abandon me. I might've been hallucinating, but I heard, *No, you're our Sister.* "Leave me some food and go."

230

I sat in a haze as Stela laid food in front of me. Others approached. Some gave a small bow and others mumbled "thank you" or some other words of comfort.

At one point, Yoan knelt in front of me. "Once again you Shadows have saved us gypsies. We owe you so much. Come with us. We'll care for you—nurse you back to health."

I yearned to say yes, to feel the comfort of the clan. I touched Yoan's face. "No. Thank you, but that would undo everything I fought for. Go."

He returned to the wagons with the others.

Goodbye, friend.

CHAPTER TWENTY-THREE

Sandel—Dazel Province

I slept, woke, and ate throughout the day. By early evening, I had to move, or I never would. I collected my gypsy clothing and began a slow, unsteady walk in the general direction of Sandel. The town couldn't be more than a league or two. The mercenaries had picked a position a few leagues from the border to ensure the Araby detail wouldn't be able to see them but would have stayed well out of town.

The sky had just begun to lighten when I thought I saw an Earth Wizard walking toward me. But my vision was blurred and my mind too fuzzy to be sure. My body felt on fire.

"Shadow. May I help?" a deep bass voice asked. Another hallucination. A lovely one.

"Yes, pleeease. Take me into the shadows of my Sisters."

"That'll have to wait." Something lifted me, and I snuggled into its arms. When I woke, I lay in a soft bed supported by branches and vines with yellow and blue flowers. An Earth Wizard stood looking down at me.

"You had us worried. We reached you as fast as we could after we heard about the mercenaries. Many others are also looking. You're an exceedingly popular Shadow." He nodded. "I'm sorry we had to undress you, but we left your head wrap on. The Shadows trained you well. Your initial actions saved your life, but those wounds were too serious to go untreated."

I moistened my lips with my tongue and croaked out, "How bad?"

"You're still healing, but you can function if you must. You're at our guild house and may stay with us for as long as you wish."

"Do you know who's after me?" If I could avoid them...or kill them.

It seemed to be my first choice.

"We know some, but there are others. Your friends the Fire and Wind Wizards don't appear to like you. The assassins' guild will do anything for money and the senior noble of Sandel. Of course, some would like two hundred toras offered by se'Dubben. It's a very impressive list. We Earth Wizards remain committed to supporting the Shadows, in any way we can."

"Thank you...?"

"Baas."

"Thank you, Wizard Baas. I owe you for saving my life and supporting the Shadows."

Baas explained where the gypsies were located and that they intended to stay for a few more days. My bandaged right hand and arm would be an excuse for not participating in any of the acts. I certainly wasn't fit to do anything but creep about.

* * *

Later that day, when I limped into the circle of wagons, Yoan, Ilka, and Alida rushed at me and gave me a hug. I called on every bit of my training to stop from screaming.

"Ryana, are we glad to see you. We weren't sure if you were alive or if you had decided to leave," Alida said, speaking for the little group that surrounded me.

"After the guards left me inside the border, a mercenary tried to..." I shrugged. "I got away but was pretty banged up. An Earth Wizard found me, and they let me stay until I wasn't seeing double anymore. I heard you had some excitement, too."

"Yes," Ilka said in a rush. "A Shadow… She made us leave her. I hope she died peacefully. What do they say…in the shadow of their Sisters? She saved us from those mercenaries."

Later that day, Stela caught me alone.

"I'll leave as soon as I collect my things."

"Why?"

"You would let me stay after what you saw I did?"

"I saw a young woman, my adopted daughter, cut to pieces trying to save her clan. We left you to die. I hated myself and every one of those power-hungry maniacs on Hesland. How?"

"The Earth Wizards found and nursed me until I could walk. My arm is a good excuse not to take part in any of the acts. I can barely walk, mother."

"I'll come to your wagon after the evening meal and see if there is anything I can do to help."

* * *

I stood watching the audience as the acts went on. Wizard Baas was right about the assassins' guild. They were out in force, bumping into women to see their reaction. They obviously had heard I had been wounded. Ironically, they would ignore the gypsies because they had reported leaving the Shadow there. Logically, therefore, none of the gypsies were the Shadow. My enemies had let logic defeat them again and again across Hesland. A Fire Wizard stood at the back of the crowd. Right now, I would have a difficult time fighting some amateur assassin. There were no Intermediates or Shadows in Sandel, which was lucky. I needed to avoid everyone while I healed.

Normally, I liked telling fortunes, but tonight I dreaded it. I wasn't up for any confrontation. The night seemed to be going well with the usual numbers and types of customers. I was just ready to close the tent when one of the men I had spotted as an assassin pushed aside the flap of the tent. He looked to be middle aged, very few scars, thin build and face, wavy brown hair, and penetrating eyes. This assassin was far from an amateur, if not a professional in Shadow terms.

"Fake or real?"

"Yes," I replied. His laugh was genuine. He put down a silver and sat.

"It doesn't matter. It has been a boring evening, and I could use some entertainment."

"Entertainment it shall be. Put your hands on the table palms down." I mimicked the position with my hands. He hesitated and gave me a long, hard look. After a moment, he placed his hands on the table. Slowly, I placed mine over his. When I first touched his hands, he tensed but immediately relaxed. His reaction told me a lot about him. He was cautious, confident, and methodical in the way he had first positioned his hand on the table. He had no reason to suspect me of being anything but what I professed to be, yet he prepared himself for action.

I closed my eyes. I could almost see him smile at what he thought was an act.

"You live in a shadowy world…"

He tensed for a second.

"…that is fraught with danger, which you find exciting." Again, that slight tightening of the finger muscles. I walked a dangerous line but couldn't help it. I had become fascinated with reading people and projecting a reasonable future.

"For you, this world's a game where a cautious, well-prepared man excels. Sandel is a steppingstone to a bigger game—in Dazel. There too you'll do well, even though your enemies are better than those here. Be careful in Dazel; even fools with money can be dangerous." I opened my eyes to find him staring at me.

"Real?"

"The future has many paths since it's linked with others. This is the one I see most clearly."

"I think I've heard of you. If you are the one, you've quite a reputation. Wizards and rulers seek you out, yet you sit here telling fortunes for coppers."

"A fortune for you is the same as a fortune for a Wizard or ruler. All are interesting and vary only by money and power," I said and removed my hands from his.

"Yes, you do have an insight into the future. Real or fake, it was not boring. You don't happen to know where the Shadow of Death is, do you?

"I can only tell you what I see in your future."

He rose and dropped another silver on the table and left. I should have been more careful with my so-called reading of the future, but I couldn't help it. It had become a compulsion to tell what I…saw or was it what I deduced? I had no customers after him. When I left the tent, only a few stragglers milled around.

Ilka chuckled. "Well, Ryana, no Wizards or rulers or even a noble or two?"

Alida snickered. "Which means no toras tonight."

"No, it was a pretty boring night, although I predict Alida is going to marry a noble," I said, trying to look serious. Ilka and Alida stood there with their eyes wide and mouths open; then Alida stamped her foot.

"Don't do that, Ryana. Even us gypsies are beginning to believe you can tell the future. Anyway, I won't leave the clan for an old noble. He would want to teach me how to eat and talk and dress me up in silly clothes." She grinned.

"What about a young noble?" Ilka asked. We went to the evening gathering, arms linked and laughing.

Later, I ventured into the ubiquitous forest the towns almost always located us near, probably because they wanted us away from the town. I let Anil and Kasi go and watched as they flew in and out, catching bugs.

When I decided to return, I saw two men crouched low as they advanced on the wagons. Thieves? It would be interesting to see what they were after. Stealing from a gypsy camp didn't seem to be a good idea. Of course, Sandel was a modest-sized town and their thieves small-time amateurs. I had lots of options, some better than others. I could alert Marku and the others. The bats could disable them. Or I could just shout. They knelt, looking toward the wagons, and turned in the direction of the horses.

"Thieves, thieves!" I shouted as I came half running out of the forest. "The horses!" I yelled, walking in their direction.

The clan came alive. Men and women poured out of the wagons, knives in hand. I stopped screaming, content to watch the two men tripping, stumbling, and running into limbs and shrubs as they made a hasty retreat. They were better than our clown acts. I doubted they would ever try to steal from a gypsy camp again.

"Ryana, where?" I stood there with tears running down my cheeks from laughing. "Are you hurt? Talk to me," Yoan said, holding me at arm's length. By now, everyone was up.

"Two men were sneaking up to the horses. Probably Sandel's excuse for thieves. I shouted, and as I expected, they ran off like they were chased by hounds." That had been fun. I'd had little of that lately.

"You've done it again," Alida said, hugging me. "You're better than camp dogs... I didn't mean..." she turned red. I laughed again. Naturally, this was another excuse to sit around eating, talking, and dancing. I had to retell the story at least five more times. As the party broke up, Marku walked over to me.

"You couldn't see them from where you said you where."

"I may have left out a few annoying details." I laughed again as I walked toward my wagon, leaving Marku standing there shaking his head.

* * *

The next night I stood watching the acts and scanning the audience. My enemies knew I was in Dazel and seriously wounded. Because no one had found a body, they had to assume I lived. Halfway through the acts, the assassin who had been in the fortuneteller tent the previous night looked at me. I nodded.

After that, I lost sight of him. My tent was normal that night. After the evening meal, I wandered into the trees. By now, the clan expected it and was relieved I did. I sat a five-minute walk away from the camp, watching Kasi and Anil. Kasi alerted me to a man with a knife, coming from behind me. It was the assassin from the other night. I decided to wait to see what he wanted before I killed him. I hoped I didn't have to. I was sick of killing.

"Good evening, are you back for another telling?" I smiled when he stopped.

"Did you see into your future?"

"No, I can tell others' future but not my own. Funny, isn't it. Perhaps I'm too involved to see it clearly."

"How did you know I was behind you?"

"I've ears." I smiled.

And eyes in the back of my head.

238

His knife disappeared and he came around in front of me.

"How much does it cost to buy someone else's future?" he asked, frowning and playing with a tora.

"If I sold others' telling, I would be a fraud. Telling it to another would change the outcome and would, therefore, not be a true fortune. Not to mention, I'd soon be dead."

He stood silent for a moment, and then laughed.

"But what if you are a fake?"

"Then paying me to tell you something I made up wouldn't be of much value, would it?"

"I guess you wouldn't be surprised to find that someone might want to kill you for what you know." The assassin stood staring as he asked. He was debating whether to kill me or not. Little did he know his life depended on his decision.

"No, Lord Phellen had intended to flog me to death to find out what I had told First Lady wu'Lichak."

"Why didn't he?"

"Someone stopped him. What most of the fools don't realize is that although I see someone's future, it doesn't imply I understand what it means. Only the person hearing it knows that."

"You're a dangerous woman. You own too many people's secrets."

"If I were a fake, I would be rich."

"You knew exactly what I was when you told me my fortune, didn't you?"

"Yes, you're an assassin." I paused, lost in the moment and ready for an attack. When he relaxed, I continued. "Rich man, poor man, beggar man…assassin? What difference is it to me?"

"Good night. I enjoyed dancing with you. If you saw clearly, I'll see you in Dazel." He smiled a little and strolled away.

* * *

As we were packing to leave the next morning, Stela walked toward my wagon. She must have been well into her forties because she had a grown daughter, who had married a man from another clan, but she looked ten years younger with her smooth face and long auburn hair, which hung loose. Today she had on a bright skirt with shades of greens, reds, blues, and yellows that ran together like a rainbow, a white ruffled blouse with red trim, and red and yellow ribbons in her hair.

"Good morning, daughter." Her smile lit up her face and gave me a warm feeling. She had been calling me daughter more often lately, which made me feel wanted.

"Good morning, mother." I gave her a hug. The Shadows were fond of me, and I felt wanted by them. But I had never felt loved, and my mother hadn't shown me much.

"It appears you've had a boring couple of days. How are you feeling?"

"Boring but entertaining. I had an assassin visit me in the forest last night. I had told him his future, and he had decided he needed to kill me because I knew too much."

Stela's hand covered her mouth like she wanted to stop from saying something. "Did you kill…fight?"

"No, we had a long talk. In the end, he decided he liked and could trust me." I grinned at Stela. She shook her head in resignation.

"You call that entertaining. We should stop assigning you to the fortuneteller tent."

"Don't. I enjoy it. People are very interesting—rich and poor. To answer your other question, I am recovering. I think I'll be able to join the acts by the time we reach Dazel."

"How? You were close to death." She held me tight against her.

"I've had excellent care. Besides, the Shadows think pain is a lazy person's excuse to get out of doing something. You wouldn't want them to consider me lazy, would you?"

"It's little wonder the Shadows are viewed with awe and fear."

CHAPTER TWENTY-FOUR

Road to Tarlon—Dazel Province

By the time we left Sandel, the sun had baked the earth and the road dry. Deep in thought, I hardly noticed the bouncing and dust from the wagon in front of me. When I reached Dazel, what would I do? I had sent what I knew back with the Shadows I sent home. *I doubt the Shadow Sisters want me anymore, so I'll discard my blacks and...what? Will my enemies still chase me? If I stay with the gypsies, does that endanger them? Do I want to marry Luka, and does he still want to marry me? If he does, should I tell him the truth? Will that turn him away? Do I have a future?* My head ached with questions I couldn't or feared to answer. Yoan joined me on the wagon, to my relief.

"What are you going to do when we reach Tarlon?" he asked.

"I don't know. I'm confused and not sure what I should or can do."

"Stay with the clan. Become clan. Everyone loves you, including Luka." He smiled. I didn't.

"It's been a long time. He's probably found a girl or two better than me." I really felt sorry for myself. Yoan shook his head.

"No, you've stolen his heart. He won't be able to think about anything else until he sees you. No woman would ever dream of telling Luka he had to wait for her to consider his proposal. They would insist on a wedding before he had a chance to change his mind." He grinned. At the time, I hadn't been sure if I would live, if I wanted to get married, and if...

"For gypsy women, things are different. Their choices are limited to the clans' men and only to those who aren't closely related. Even after they meet the right man, they wait many seasons while he earns a wagon and everything they need. I can understand why they are in a rush and will accept any reasonable proposal. Not to mention, Luka's an exceptionally good catch," I said, concluding life was complicated for them as well as for me.

Yoan shook his head. "That's how it is. Making it worse, we need new blood. We love you and want you to stay, but that's in the back of our minds. You're at least going to stay for the king's performance?"

"I'll stay. By then I might have the answer."

"The Tobar clan should arrive while we're there. You'll have to give him an answer then, won't you?"

"Yes, I'll have to answer to many people then." I lapsed into silence. I think Yoan realized our talk had ended and left. We stopped early that night. Marku wanted everyone rested when we reached Tarlon. The mood was festive. I sat off to the side, trying to calm my emotions. I couldn't make any decision while my mind whirled in turmoil. Tonight, after our evening meal, I would go off by myself. I would seek to be blind, so that I could see clearly. That would require time and solitude.

"Daughter, you seem despondent," Stela said as she sat down next to me.

I wanted to be alone to think, and I wanted company, so I didn't have to. I had always known what I wanted: to be a Shadow, to find who was killing Shadows, and to walk in the shadow of my Sisters. Today I didn't know who I was, so how could I know what I wanted?

"Yes, mother." I didn't know what else to say.

"I wish I could help, but I can't. So much has happened to you. It has you doubting yourself." She wiped a tear from my cheek. "You're a Shadow. Use your training to find yourself."

After she had left, I wandered away from the wagons far enough so I couldn't see them or the evening fires. I sat there with my legs crossed, feet resting on my thighs, watching Anil and Kasi feeding on small bugs and occasionally the horses. Slowly, calm settled over my chaotic mind. I existed in the space between the past and the future, where nothing mattered but this moment.

I had sought this place many times to fight but never to find myself. The gray light of dawn brought me back to reality. I felt renewed, ready to face my fate without knowing why or how.

When I reached the wagons, an Earth Wizard stood some ten paces from Marku's wagon. Everyone was looking and watching him warily.

Marku jumped down. "What do you seek, Wizard?"

"I wish to speak to the fortuneteller."

Everyone turned and looked at me. Although I was still a hundred paces away, I somehow heard the Wizard's words.

"Why?" Marku looked back toward me.

"I wish a telling."

As I neared them, the Wizard turned and walked away. I shook my head at Marku and followed him. After a few minutes, he stopped.

"Shadow." He gave me a small bow of his head. I bowed back.

"How may I help you, Wizard?"

"There are two roadblocks ahead. Your enemies are desperate to stop you. Because they don't know what you look like, they are killing everyone in the hope that one will be you. A Fire and Wind Wizard support them, which gives them absolute power. They are raping the women, killing men, women, and children, and destroying anything they don't keep for themselves. They are a preview of what Hesland will be if the king's overthrown."

"Will you Earth Wizards help me?"

"We're in a difficult position. We cannot be seen as against the Fire and Wind Wizards as a guild. Wizards have, over the cycles, found that one on one, we are equal, and no one wins, but guild against guild we would destroy the country. We might create the chaos you fight to prevent. But if in the end it is necessary to save the kingdom; our guild will unite with you against the king's enemies."

"I'm alone, then?"

"No, Shadow. We have agreed to mutual support and will honor that pact. We've several Earth Wizards along the path who will give you their support. It must be seen as one Earth Wizard helping you and not the guild, just as the Fire and Wind Wizards pretend to be one Wizard aiding a roadblock."

"I thank you for warning me and what help you're able to give. How many mercenaries?"

"There are three or four at each roadblock along with a Wizard. They have another four to five spread out on either side to keep anyone from sneaking around them. That line is some hundred paces in front of the roadblock to ensure they can see anyone leaving the road. The killing has been bad, but it will get worse."

"I assume you're free to travel the road?'

"Of course. No one other than a Wizard, or the Shadow of Death, would threaten an Earth Wizard." His laugh was a deep bass sound like a drum.

"Then tell your brothers and sisters that the Shadow of Death is coming." I bowed and walked back to the wagons, where Marku and everyone had gathered. I realized that last night had helped focus me. I had resigned myself to being the Shadow of Death with a mission to complete—right or wrong in the eyes of the Shadows—and my visual-self, who was now a real person, committed to protecting my adopted clan. A conflict no longer existed. I would die for either.

"What happened, Ryana? He didn't want a telling, did he?" Marku asked as everyone awaited the answer. I had become the main attraction. I looked around at each of them. Yes, they were my clan.

"He wanted me to know that mercenaries and two Wizards have roadblocks up ahead. One is a half-day ride and the other a full day. They aren't just searching wagons. They are killing men, women, and children and taking what they have, which I suppose doesn't matter after they're dead."

"What did he suggest?" Yoan asked.

"He wanted me to see into the future," I said. In a way he had. He was asking what I would do, and what the Shadows would ask of the Earth Wizards.

"You're joking?" Alida asked.

"No, Alida. I'm serious. I see two options. Turn back, which is the safest option. They aren't looking for you. Or wait here while the Earth Wizard and I see if there is a way around them."

"No!" Stela screamed. Everyone turned in her direction. Some even stepped away from her. "Ryana, I forbid it."

"Mother, walk with me." I held out my hand. After a moment's pause, she grasped it. I gave a small tug, and we began walking away from the wagons.

"You'll be killed. They are waiting for you. I don't want you killed. You're like my daughter." Tears

246

ran down her face, but she made no attempt to wipe them away.

"I love you and feel you are my mother. Yesterday you reminded me that I'm a Shadow and that I should use my training. I did. I don't know what happened when I reached for the moment, but I resolved my conflicts. I'm clan and Shadow and willing to die for either. Those ahead are an evil that threaten the clans' way of life and the Shadow Sisters of Ahasha. They wish to find me, so I'll grant them their wish." The truth without twists and lies.

She choked a small laugh in between sobs. "I guess I got what I wished for too. What do you want us to do?"

"Run as fast as you can. There's no roadblock in Araby."

"All right. We'll wait here for you." She held up her hand. "You'll need a good doctor when you get back." She hugged me tight. "You and I both know either you'll win, or they will catch and kill you. In either case the roadblock will be lifted."

We walked back to the wagons in silence.

"Ryana, you're joking, right?" Ilka asked as we sat for a midday meal. Everyone watched us in silence, waiting for my answer.

"No. The Earth Wizard has agreed to go with me." The look Ilka, Alida, and Yoan gave me was priceless, as if I had said, "I'm going to die tomorrow, but don't worry, I'll see you the day after," which I guess is what I indirectly said.

Talk buzzed about the roadblock, the Earth Wizard, and me. Alida and Ilka sat on either side with Yoan in front of me.

"Ryana, what's the point of you going to see the roadblock? It's there and we should turn back. The Earth Wizard said they are killing everyone that passes," Yoan said, looking at Alida and Ilka for support.

"Yes. The clan should go back to Araby and Scio. You will be safe from the mercenaries. Maybe I can find another Shadow to help me," I joked but didn't get any laughs or even smiles.

"You're off to do something stupid—again, Alida said, stamping her foot for emphasis. "Why?"

A particularly good question if it were directed at my visual self. She could do nothing but urge a retreat to Araby. My shadow-self refused. The shadow-self screamed that I was a Shadow—wanted or not. Those mercenaries and Wizards had killed Shadow Sisters. They could not be allowed to triumph.

"Because they are evil. The Shadow Sisters insisted I leave because I didn't have the skill or commitment it would take to be a Shadow, not out of meanness. Maybe I feel I owe them. I hope I can sneak by them with the Wizard's help and get support from Tarlon." A weak story, but with all the stupid things I appeared to have done, it might be believable.

"Alida said you would do something stupid, but this tops the others." Ilka grabbed my arm and shook it.

"I'm pretty good at throwing knives, huh, Yoan?"

"Yes, Ryana. Are you going to kill them all?"

"What a good idea."

They lapsed into silence, until Alida stood.

"Ryana, become clan. Stay with us."

"I would like to be a member of the Dorian clan." I loved these people. Before I could blink, the mood went from sober to festive. After a while, Alida stood and waved.

"Quiet! If there is anyone here who wishes to speak against Ryana, stand and be heard." No one stood.

248

"She's already clan," someone shouted.

"I guess someone forgot to tell her," Ilka said with a smile.

"Sit," Marku said.

Yoan handed him a red-hot knife he had retrieved from the fire. If they branded clan members, I hadn't seen any I could remember, although that didn't mean anything. While I tried to imagine what would happen, a searing pain lanced though my ear.

"Ryana, you've been clan for a long time. Wearing our earring with our consent made you clan. Sealing it makes you a blood member, who will be recognized as family by every gypsy clan."

"You're going to return with us to Araby," Alida said.

I wiped tears from my face. "No. I said I wanted to be clan, not that I was going back to Araby."

"Last time you tried to save me and before that Alida. Who are you trying to save now?" Ilka asked.

"My clan."

I think they knew I was going no matter what they said. The talk shifted back to whether to stay here for a while or return to Araby. I hoped they could convince Marku to return.

* * *

I had just begun to pack when there was a knock at the door. I hesitated, as I had containers of poisons, blow tubes, darts, knives, and blacks lying on the floor.

"Ryana, it's Marku and Stela," a quiet voice said. It didn't matter if they saw. They already knew I was a Shadow. Only my bats were missing.

"Come in."

They climbed in and stared at the floor.

"I know we can't talk you out of or stop you from going, but is there anything we can do to help?" Stela said, taking my hand in hers.

"Yes, go back to Araby. Don't jeopardize the clan. You can't help me by staying, and it'll cause me to worry." It was true and not true. I would worry about nothing once I was committed to action, not life or death, clan or Shadows, only the moment. But the thought might help encourage them to retreat to Araby for my sake.

"You seemed so confused last night. You've changed overnight," Stela said.

Marku sat, staring at the floor.

"You helped me, mother. You told me to rely on my training. I did, and it resolved my confusion. I've been two persons: my visual-self, which I show to everyone, and shadow-self, which I keep hidden. Over time, they have become two distinct persons, one clan and one Shadow. Last night, they became one. The group supporting the roadblock will change Hesland. If they do, the clans and Shadows will be destroyed. Over the next few days, I fight for my clan and the Shadows."

"I understand. Marku and I would gladly give our lives for the clan. I can't ask you to do otherwise." She leaned over and kissed me on each cheek.

"What would you like us to do?" Marku asked, coming to life.

"Return to Windon. News should reach there quickly. If it's safe, I'll send word to join me. Now leave. I love you." A rock formed in my throat. I hoped everything worked out well for them. After the door had closed, Stela began speaking to someone.

"I know you love her, but she needs to be left alone. She's made her decision to leave. We also need to get ready. We're returning to Windon."

250

An hour later, I stepped out of the wagon. I wore my gypsy clothing over my blacks and carried a small bag with weapons. Although everyone was busy packing, they stopped when I exited the wagon. I blew them a kiss and began trotting toward a thin line of trees. There I stripped down to my blacks, distributed my weapons, and trotted into the night, hoping I walked in the shadow of my Sisters.

CHAPTER TWENTY-FIVE

Road to Tarlon—Dazel Province

I trotted at an easy pace as Anil and Kasi swept the terrain ahead of me. Sycorax, tonight a three-quarter moon, was low on the horizon, and Setebos, at half moon, was sinking below the horizon. The two moons made for a dimly lit landscape and eerie shadows—a perfect night for killing. I had resigned myself. If I just skirted the line, the roadblock would remain in place, and many more innocent men, women, and children would die. I was already scarred, so a few more didn't matter. As I neared the line of mercenaries, I sank into the moment.

About midnight judging by the position of Sycorax, I stopped while my darlings scouted the area to the road and back. As the Earth Wizard had said, five positions on each side and a hundred paces forward of the roadblock. With each man separated from the next by fifty paces, the line extended three hundred paces from the road. I lay flat. The land was open, with few mounds or shrubs to hide behind.

Shadow Rong would have thought it a good configuration in daylight but too far apart at night. Still too far away to be seen, I veered to my right, circling around the last man in the line. They would look forward, not behind them. An hour later, I lay several paces behind the last man in the line, listening for any communications between them. A faint crash like two rocks being hit together, repeated by two, three, four, and then five came from the man in front of me. Not a good system.

I darted the man in front of me, crept up and pulled out my dart, and began to circle behind the fourth man. I first moved well back before sliding forward, using the few bushes and growing shadows. The fourth man was fighting to stay awake. Every minute or so he would jerk up and shake his head. Two minutes later, his head would be resting on his arms. I waited, listening for the next signal. It came a few minutes later. The man jerked awake and hit his two rocks together four times. Just as he finished, I darted him, then rushed to pick up his rocks and knocked them together five times. I hit the rocks a bit softer to give the illusion of distance. They signaled on the half hour, so it gave me time.

I slid backward and worked my way toward the third man in the line. He seemed wide awake and scanning the area ahead of him. Each man had a sword and a bow. The last two had had them lying beside them. This one wore his sword in his belt and held his bow with an arrow nocked. An incredibly nervous man but not without reason, I conceded.

He gave the signal. I darted him and gave the fourth and fifth signals. So far, it had been simple with everyone staring forward. My teachers had trained me well. I ghosted across the land like a shadow, leaving no trail and making no noise. I reached the second man's position and lay five steps behind him waiting for him to give his signal, when a wild dog howled from somewhere behind me. The mercenary whirled. I lay too close to be missed. As he reached for his sword and prepared to shout, I put a knife in his throat. He stood gargling blood for a second and then collapsed. As he fell, his sword hit a rock, sending a clang reverberating through the quiet night.

"Charg, are you, all right?"

I could slide backward, hoping the number-one man would still have his attention forward even if he decided to check on Charg. Ignoring the logical response, I slid in close to Charg, propped him up, and waited. The signal came early. I assumed number one decided to check on Charg via the signaling system. I sent the signals for two through five, trying to give the illusion that each sound came from farther away. Apparently, it worked. The man in the number-one position said nothing more.

This time I backed up several paces and moved fast with little caution. By the time he noticed me, two knives were in the air. One hit him in the chest and one in the neck.

I kept going without bothering to collect my knives. Working my way well back and wide of the roadblock, I crossed the road well behind the line and kept going into the desert beyond. By the time the dim light of sunrise spread across the land, I was well out of their sight. If they used logic, they would think I was on the other side of the road, trying to avoid the roadblock and heading to Tarlon.

I sent Kasi and Anil ahead to scout the land of the Zunji. A nomad people, they survived with their small herds of cattle, drank milk mixed with blood, and occasionally found wildlife to eat. Few ventured into their land. The Zunji had a ferocious reputation and were masters at ambush. They guarded their land with fervor.

Exhausted from two days without sleep, I crawled into the shade of a thorny bush and curled up to sleep while I waited for night, when I intended to approach their camp. I woke as the sun was setting and Sycorax was rising. I lay waiting for a late hour when most would be in tents and the guards few. The guards would not be the problem, but the cattle would. Any movement would make them restless and alert the guards. I doubted I could keep the cattle quiet; I would have to quiet the guards. They weren't going to be happy when they woke with rockberry headaches.

I diluted the rockberry on four darts and began my approach to the camp. To my surprise, Kasi identified only one guard standing watch on a small mound. Unlike the mercenaries, he stood alert and scanned the entire area around the camp. Keeping to the shadows and the periodic cover the clouds provided, I stole forward as he turned to look in other directions. Then the clouds moved, and the moonlight exposed me. Luckily, I was only a few paces from him as he drew his spear back to throw. I blew a dart into him. The diluted rockberry took a bit longer to work, and he managed to throw the spear. I rolled as he did, but the spear still grazed my arm. Nothing moved. I stayed low until I was in front of the largest tent. I dove through the opening and rolled to a sitting position, my blowtube at my lips and ready to fire.

To my amazement, the chief was sitting up with a knife in hand. We sat facing each other. Neither of us moved as we sat evaluating the other. He amazed me again when he lowered his knife.

"Good morning, Shadow of Death. I hope you didn't injure my guard too much."

"He'll have a headache in the morning," I said, staring into his face, trying to understand his reaction.

"How can I help you, Shadow?" he asked just before someone opened the flap behind me. My eyes shifted to his wives. They would tell me more than him. He smiled and waved the person away.

"I'll have to remember that. My wives would give you more information than me."

"I would like to know which side you're taking."

"Interesting. I had planned to stay neutral. I'd be interested in knowing what you would have done if I had said with those against the king." A small smile touched his lips. Like me, he remained ready for action, although I think he knew I'd win.

"I didn't think you would, since neither position's in your best interest. I didn't take the Zunji leader for a fool."

"You have my attention." He seemed to relax. I stayed alert. He could afford to relax, since his people surrounded me. I would never leave alive if I killed him or he didn't want me to.

"Right now, three of the Wizards' guilds are divided across the provinces, but they will unite with those against the king. If they win, the Wizards will side with one of the contenders, probably the strongest but maybe not. In any case, the winners will have an unbeatable force. They will then consolidate their allies to create a loyal and powerful regime. Potential opposition will be destroyed. You will not submit to being controlled; therefore, you will be viewed as an opponent. You are strong, but you can't defeat Wizards. There is only one logical position that offers an acceptable solution." I smiled to myself at the irony of the statement. I used logic to argue my point, but I used intuition when making decisions.

"An interesting assessment and accurate. What do you want from me? My allegiance is to my people."

"I think with your help, I can end this war with little bloodshed and stop the coming chaos. If so, you might get the recognition the Zunji people deserve. Land that's recognized as your own province."

He laughed long and hard. "I see why your enemies want you dead. They have two roadblocks set up to stop you, each with a Wizard, yet here you sit. I'll wager even the Fire Wizard fears you. Do they have reason, Shadow?"

"Yes. I know how to kill them, as well as Wind and Water Wizards."

He clapped. "I'm impressed. Will you share that information?"

"With my allies."

"With the Earth Wizards who follow you?"

"I've told them, although it's of more value to the common man."

"Break fast with me and my sons, and we'll discuss your proposal. If for no other reason, I might support you just to know how to kill Wizards."

The meal was interesting. First a bitter-tasting soup, which was a mixture of berries, ground bark, and roots, and a milk-and-blood drink. Sizwe was the chief elder of the Zunji. His sons, Mosi, Kato, and Gero were the chief elders of tribes that occupied land extending from Tarlon east to the borders to Saxis, Tuska, and Calion. They numbered over two thousand but had never been recognized as a people.

"I think we should remain hidden and neutral. Many will die when the provinces clash," the oldest son, Gero, said. He resembled his father the closest with his long, narrow face, high cheekbones, and sharp chin. His hair had the thin braids of a warrior.

"If we choose the king's side and he loses we'll be hunted by the Wizards and destroyed," Kato, the youngest, said. He least resembled his father with his heavier build and wider face.

"If we support the king, we'll be recognized and given the land we occupy," Mosi said. Gero slapped the ground.

"No one else wants it."

"No one can remain neutral. You can call yourselves neutral, but will the warring parties recognize it?" I said. "No matter who wins, you will be seen as an enemy with no allies. If the king wins, he will appoint new rulers to include your land or make it a separate province under a new ruler. You can fight their armies but not the Wizards.

"You can fight the Wizards," Kato said, his face set in determination. "We could force you to tell us."

"Many will die, and the secret will be lost."

"I believe her." Sizwe nodded. "She isn't called the Shadow of Death without reason. She has somehow evaded the hundreds seeking her and killed many hands of them."

"You claim you can prevent the upcoming war. How?" Gero asked.

"If we break the roadblock, they will become desperate, and desperate people make mistakes. I believe they are massing forces here in Dazel. If we can discover their size and location, it will negate their advantage. Without the element of surprise, the king has the advantage. I'll see that the king gets that information and that the many who helped him are justly rewarded." I paused. When I received no comment, I continued. "I'm not asking the Zunji to rise up against the opposition, only that a small number support me."

The discussion went on for hours. Slowly, an agreement emerged with Sizwe's careful maneuvering.

"My son Gero will lead sixty warriors to aid you. More will be sent if he thinks it will benefit the Zunji people. I trust you to honor your commitment, Shadow. I would like to know how to kill Wizards."

"I'll try to give Gero a first-hand demonstration." An easy promise when life or death, winning or losing meant little. The outcome lay in the shadow of my Sisters.

CHAPTER TWENTY-SIX

Tarlon—Dazel Province

Two days later, Gero stood with his sixty warriors. It seemed to me the men he had assembled were looking forward to the coming sortie.

"Where to, Shadow?" Gero asked.

"I think we'll start back where the first roadblock had been set up." I hoped to find one of the Earth Wizards there and find out what had happened while I had been at the Zunji camp. As we trotted along at a ground-eating pace, Gero ran up beside me.

"You run well, Shadow. You've had good training."

"My teachers thought they were training Zunji warriors." In fact, the training to be a Shadow was as rigorous as that of a Zunji warrior, although Spies and Assassins weren't required to run miles in the scorching heat.

Gero laughed. "Sizwe's guard, Ayman, said you're a good warrior. He deserved headache because he didn't kill you." Gero looked serious.

Sizwe's guard should be happy all he got was a headache.

It took a half day to reach the old roadblock. The dead mercenaries lay where I had killed them, a feast for the vultures. The air burned with the stink and buzzed with swarms of flies. I stood waiting as the warriors searched the area. Shortly afterward, the Earth Wizard Wallia approached.

"Good day, Shadow. As you can see the Fire Wizard abandoned this area to chase after you. It appears he went in the wrong direction." His bass voice

259

rumbled, and the ground gently shook. Gero and the warriors looked a bit nervous. They didn't have any experience with Wizards and, like the Shadows, feared them.

"Wizard Wallia, these Zunji warriors are here to assist me in getting to Tarlon and the king."

"I didn't think you needed assistance. It seems you have your enemies running in fear of you. Not to mention confused."

"I'm tired of killing mercenaries and Wizards and thought to share with my Earth brothers and the Zunji."

"That's generous of you. A Wind Wizard waits up the road a league. The Fire Wizard has moved closer to Tarlon and set up another roadblock with twenty more mercenaries. Ten of the new ones are from the assassins' guild. The Wizards ridicule the mercenaries' fear of you. Little do they know that they should also fear. They still don't know you know how to kill them."

"How are they distributed?"

"There's a Wind Wizard at the roadblock with three mercenaries. Six men are on each side of the road. This time they are spread out even with the roadblock. I believe it's so that the Wind Wizard can support them. I don't know if it's because of the mercenaries' fear or the Wizards' arrogance."

"Gero, we'll swing well wide of both sides and be in position tonight. We'll strike them from behind two hours after midnight. They'll be facing forward and tired. Kill as quietly as possible and retreat two hundred paces back toward Tarlon. I intend to confront the Wind Wizard, with the Earth Wizard's help, when he retreats toward Tarlon in the morning." I looked toward Wallia, who nodded. Gero grinned and waved to his warriors. They split into two groups and began running on each side of the road. Gero and I followed the group on the east side, while Wallia ambled up the road toward Tarlon.

* * *

Gero and I lay curled up off to the side of the road to rest. I needed my strength for my contest with the Wind Wizard tomorrow. One of Gero's warriors stood guard over us while we slept, although with Kasi watching at the roadblock and Anil in the area where we slept, it wasn't necessary. As the sun broke the horizon, Anil's echoes told me that the warriors had returned. They were positioned well back on each side of the road. Kasi showed a commotion back at the roadblock and kept track of the Wizard's progress toward the Zunji and me. Wallia followed in his wake. An hour later, the Wind Wizard came into sight. He laughed when he saw me.

"Well, if it isn't the notorious Shadow of Death. Your title has gone to your head. Didn't they teach you that Shadows can't kill Wizards? Your Earth Wizard friend behind me can't help you. We're an even match."

As he talked, the wind began to increase in intensity. At first, it plastered my clothes to my body, then forced me to step backward to maintain my balance, and finally threw me on my ass. The Wizard laughed. The wind continued to get stronger and pushed me down the road, scraping over gravel and small rocks.

Suddenly the Earth trembled under me, and the wind lessened as the Wind Wizard redirected his main thrust toward Wallia. A Wind Wizard could maintain a high velocity of wind around him, but the most intense wind had to be focused in one direction. Right now, he had it focused on the Earth Wizard. Roots and vines thrust out of Wallia into the ground to hold him steady.

At the same time, he continued to shake the earth, disrupting the direction and intensity of the wind.

I jumped up and sent a knife at the whirling center, knowing it would be spun off course before it hit. He laughed and sent a gust of wind my way, knocking me off my feet and sliding me along the road. I'd feel the pain later. When his attention returned to the Earth Wizard, I leapt up, ran several steps toward him, and threw another knife. Again, a gust set me bouncing down the road, ripping the back of my blacks. If he could have focused all his attention on me, he would have killed me.

The trick was to make him think I wasn't a threat and that my throwing knives at him was pathetic. Anil and Kasi's echo-sight helped me tell the distance to his vortex. I rose more slowly this time and threw another knife at him. As he deflected it, I arched one after another high into the air. I imagined the vortex like the narrow bottles the gypsies used and my knives the balls.

The first was too short and swept away, the second, slightly to the left side and swept away. The third and fourth were sucked into the whirling vortex. The Wizard screamed as he fell to his knees. The wind died. I threw two more knives, one into his chest and the other his neck. He collapsed, seeming to disappear into his robe.

As I sat to rest, sixty Zunji warriors exploded out of the surrounding desert screaming, laughing, and jumping up and down around the dead Wizard.

"Well done, Shadow," Gero said, standing over me. "I thought for sure he would kill you. I see now that was a painful distraction."

"The spinning vortex is their weakness," I said somewhat unnecessarily. Just then, the Earth Wizard joined us. "Thank you for your help, Earth Brother. Without it, he could easily have killed me."

"I had heard how you did it, but it was more instructional to watch. If you had arched the knives immediately, he would have realized what you were doing and could have countered the attack. Very nicely done." Wallia nodded his head in approval. "You'll meet another Earth Wizard further up the road. She will update you on the next blockade. Good-bye, Shadow. I hope to see you in Tarlon." He wandered off into the desert.

"Gero, I know you and you warriors are ready for the next roadblock, but I'm not ready for the Fire Wizard. We'll rest here today and attack tomorrow night."

"That will disappoint my warriors, but I understand. After your performance today, they would follow you into the teeth of a sandstorm." He grinned.

We made camp well off the road. They started a fire to have cooked food now and cold food tonight when the fires could be seen for leagues. The talk was lively. They gathered in groups to discuss the attack on the mercenaries and my fight with the Wizard. Each took a turn elaborating on his kill that night. In the evening, the discussions switched to tomorrow's action. They talked well into the night.

In the morning, Gero produced a salve that helped ease the pain. I spent the time sewing up the bigger rips in my blacks while talking to the warriors about my trip across Hesland. I left out most of the details. In a small way, it helped ease my guilt for killing so many. Although I could have left some alive, I realized that I had not killed any innocent people. The warriors were fascinated with the story. They had trained to be warriors and to kill, but most had truly little opportunity. For better or worse, these sixty would. I still hoped none of them would die.

At midafternoon, the Earth Wizard stood waiting in the middle of the road. Gero and I went to meet her. She was a tall, thin woman with wrinkled skin. Although obviously old, she stood erect like a much younger woman.

"Good day, Shadow. I'm the Earth Wizard Egica."

"It's my honor to meet you, Wizard Egica."

"As it's mine to meet you. You've a good reputation among my brothers, and an unbelievably bad one among your enemies, or should I say *our* enemies." She smiled. "The next blockade is another league ahead. There is a Fire Wizard there. I'll be interested in watching you kill him."

"As will I," Gero said.

"I'll need your help, Sister. There is nothing to hide behind that I can use to deflect some of the fire balls."

"I'll be glad to help, where I can." With that, she began walking back along the road.

* * *

We left at dusk planning to use the same tactics. The warriors would swing well wide of the mercenaries' line and position themselves behind them. They would be in position around midnight and attack two hours later. Gero and I followed until they turned to get in position. We continued for another league.

"What can I do, Shadow?" Gero asked.

"Stay back as far as you can. A Fire Wizard can only throw his fireballs about forty to fifty steps. How are you at throwing a knife?" The Zunji had a reputation for being good with a knife. I didn't know if that included throwing.

264

"Good." He bowed slightly, swinging his arm to his chest.

"If you're feeling particularly bored of living, begin running when I do. Count to eight and throw for the center of the fire ring as many times as you can."

* * *

We rested and waited. At noon, the Fire Wizard came walking up the road. He stopped fifty steps from me.

"I wanted something to kill. Your Zunji friends killed all but three mercenaries. Those cowards are probably still running. Hopefully, you won't."

I threw my first knife. As I expected, he brought up the fire ring and the blade melted long before it reached him. He brought it down, and I rolled as a fireball roared toward me. Searing pain shot across the back of my legs, which I forced away—something for later. His ring was already coming up as I threw another knife. A sizzle and it disappeared. As he brought down the ring, the ground rippled and the ball went high to the right. He had anticipated me jumping to the right and the earth's ripple caused the ball to shoot upward. Instead, I had dropped to the ground where I stood. His shield went up as I threw another knife. Boring, but I had to convince him that I was stupid. A few seconds later, his shield came down and he threw the ball of fire at Egica. The ball smashed into a dirt screen. I started running.

One, two…seven, eight, I threw, and again and again, and then dove for the ground. My rocktail dart was ready just in case the knives weren't enough. He burst into flame.

Fire flashed in my face, and I bit back a scream. I'd been too close when he lost control, and my face felt burnt raw. As I lay panting, the Zunji came running from the sides screaming, laughing, and clapping. Gero stood over me looking down.

"That was fun, Shadow. Do you think we could find another one to practice on?" His eyes shifted to the burnt Wizard, half-melted hilts sticking out from his smoking body. Now the pain returned. When I looked, the backs of my pants legs were still smoldering. I considered myself lucky. Without the Earth Wizards, in the open terrain I would have lost both fights. I had fared much better than in my other two encounters. It helps when you know what you are doing and have help from a Wizard.

"That was nicely done, Shadow. You've discovered their weaknesses, which no one before has been able to do. You've shown us Wizards that we are as vulnerable as anyone else. The Wizards may not be as significant as they thought in the upcoming struggle," Egica said. "You should know there are armies gathering outside of the city. We'll help as we can." She turned and walked up the road toward Tarlon.

"Shadow, would you like the Zunji to do anything else? My warriors and I would be willing to help more. I think my warriors are in love with you." He grinned. "Me too."

"Can you scout the armies outside Tarlon? Where? How many?" Tarlon appeared to be the battleground. If so, why was it so important to stop me and the other Shadows? Logically, they want to keep the Shadows from knowing who was involved, when it would happen, or how it would happen.

That's it, HOW. Ironically, I don't know how— or do I? It must have something to do with the armies massing outside of Tarlon, but what?

"Gero, even more I need to know who."

"I'll send my warriors out tonight. Where will you be?"

266

"I'll be with your father."

CHAPTER TWENTY-SEVEN

Tarlon—Dazel Province

I sat just outside Sizwe's tent, enjoying an evening meal with him and his two wives, Nubia and Subira. Although I should have been anxious to hear what Gero and his warriors had been able to discover, I felt relaxed. Over the past few weeks, I had gained the ability to widen the moment between the second that was and the one to come, where neither past nor future existed.

"I hear that my warriors killed many mercenaries, and you two Wizards. Not a bad two days. A few more days like that and they will make you chief of the Zunji." He slapped his leg and laughed. Nubia leaned over and gave me several slices of goat meat on a stick and a bowl of hot soup. She was a small, delicate woman about my age. Subira was an older woman with a soft, mature figure who was probably the mother of Sizwe's three sons. Nubia's daughter, about three cycles old, clung to her skirt.

"Your people's warriors are feared by your enemies. I understand why no one dares enter the desert without your permission." I believed it to be true, and it turned attention from the past to the present.

"Yes. Like you Shadows, we train our young men to be warriors from a young age. They go through many rites of passage before they are considered adults. We haven't fought a war in my sons' lifetime, but we train as if we were at war. Perhaps we've been preparing for this day." He lapsed into silence as he ate. I looked around at the tents where groups of men, women, and children sat around small fires. I couldn't be sure, but there seemed to be a lot of excitement around the campfires. "Yes, they speak of war and the greatness of the Zunji warriors. If it comes to pass, they will talk about it for many cycles. The tales will be better than the war where real men, women, and children suffer and die."

They were the words of a chief who had seen war and its consequences, not of a young warrior's dream of glory.

Not too unlike the dreams of any young Shadow.

I shook myself mentally. The past had no place in the present.

Sometime during the day, Nubia had repaired my blacks. They had given me a robe and head wrap to wear while the blacks were being repaired. Sizwe understood my need to keep my identity secret. That night I lay in Sizwe's tent, watching Anil and Kasi feed on bugs and the Zunjis' cattle. Nothing moved beyond the camp except for a few small creatures. The tent and the blankets were welcome as the desert gave up its heat and the temperature plunged. I woke early when Kasi saw the warriors returning.

"You've good hearing, Shadow, or is it your familiar, which I understand all Shadows have?" Sizwe stood behind me looking in the direction of the coming warriors.

"Yes," I said and smiled. He nodded acknowledgment. Soon Gero and ten warriors neared. Gero knelt on one knee.

"Father." He rose and drank from a bowl his mother gave him. Then he turned to me. "Shadow, there are three armies amassed outside the city. The one in the center numbers sixty hands. The ones on each side each number fifty. My warriors believe the army on the right is from Tuska, the one in the center from Araby, and the one on the left from Calion."

"Gero, you and your warriors are as good as if not better than the Shadows," I said, giving the group a small nod. Gero's eyes gleamed at the compliment.

"Sizwe, please excuse me. I must think about what I've just learned."

He nodded and I walked into the desert where I could be alone. I called Anil and Kasi to me for comfort while I thought over what Gero and his warriors had discovered. Three armies numbering one hundred thirty hands versus the king's army of ninety. They out numbered the king's forces by forty, but he had a castle with massive walls to hide behind. The enemy had to have enough soldiers inside to hold the gates open or some way to draw the king's soldiers out. In either case, it would require deception.

I understood deception. My enemies were composed of many factions with conflicting interests and only tentative alliances. Like in the dart game, the bull's-eye was made to look like it was in the center when it was not. Of course, in this case the bull's-eye was in the center. I rushed back to Sizwe's tent.

"Sizwe, if you haven't chosen to remain neutral, I would like another two hundred warriors." I looked from Gero to Sizwe, who would, with input from his sons, make the decision.

"That's not enough if you plan to fight those armies," Sizwe said. Gero frowned.

"No. I plan to do what you do best, harass two of the armies. I can't promise no one will get killed, but it'll be ten to one or better." The game everyone was playing—gypsy darts.

"Will it stop the war or win it for the king?" Sizwe asked.

"That's my intention, but I can't guarantee it." I needed their help, but I wouldn't lie. These people were not my enemies.

"We'll help," Sizwe said after Gero nodded. "They will be ready by tomorrow night."

"I'll be back by then," I said as I began trotting toward the road.

* * *

I waited until late that night. In the camp, the cook fires had dimmed to embers. The only was sound a mournful song coming from one of the tents. Slipping into the camp would be easy. Negotiating the sleeping troops to get to wu'Lichak's tent would be more difficult, and then I would have her personal guards to contend with. Once there, wu'Lichak would decide whether I succeeded or failed.

The sentries were easy to avoid. They were positioned to detect large numbers of trespassers not a single invader. I waited until the one nearest me turned and began retracing his route. Once pass him, I used Kasi, Anil, and the shadows to avoid soldiers wandering the camp. I didn't want to dart anyone, as it could lead to a search of the area and me having to declare myself. It would get me to the first lady but might compromise her.

Two stood in front of her tent. I lay there considering my options. I needed to talk with her, but without anyone's notice. I chewed my lip. Lord Bolan's tent was next to hers with no guards. I crawled to the opening and slid inside. Inside, I stood and tiptoed to his bedroll, placed one hand over his mouth, and lay a knife at his throat.

"Lord Bolan, please don't move. The knife's sharp," I whispered.

His eyes flew open wide, and he choked back a shout to the nearby guards. Then he relaxed.

"Shadow, how may I help you?" he whispered.

I took that for a good sign. "I need to talk to the first lady without anyone seeing me. It could jeopardize her position, which, if I'm right, isn't good."

"Are you an assassin?" he asked.

"Yes, but it's a stupid question isn't it, Lord Bolan? You should know that the Shadows don't support opposition to the king. If you believe the first lady supports the overthrow of the king, shout for the guards when I let you go. If you aren't sure, let me talk to her. You can stay while I do." This was twice the risk. I would have to trust him now and wu'Lichak in the upcoming war. He nodded, threw on some clothes, and left the tent. I sat, dropping into the moment. I didn't know what to expect. I doubted I could make it out of the camp, but I would try if necessary. Several minutes later, wu'Lichak entered followed by Bolan. Two guards took up positions outside of the tent.

"Are you here to give me another telling?" she asked as she sat facing me, almost touching my legs with hers. Bolan's mouth dropped open, then he frowned. "You saw the future quite well. I thought I understood it at the time, but I did not see it as clearly as I should have. It appears I'll decide who will win and who will die."

"When did you and your friends arrive?"

"I arrived two days ago, the others early yesterday."

"You realize if the king feels you're the threat, he will attack you if he feels he has support of the armies on your flanks. When neither army supports you, your army and the king's will destroy each other. The throne and Araby will be up for grabs."

Wu'Lichak flinched. She realized she was in a no-win situation. If instead she attacked the other two, she would again lose, as they outnumbered her.

"What do you wish for, wu'Lichak?" When I left off her title, Bolan started to protest, but she waved him to silence.

"What I've always wanted: to have my people prosper and live in peace."

"I see a world where that is possible. It's not the only future but the one I see most clearly."

Bolan's mouth had been hanging open as we talked. "How?" Bolan blurted.

Again, wu'Lichak waved him to silence. She sat quiet for several minutes. "They have thrown their combined forces against you, and here you sit. They fear you more than the king and his forces. They believe you're the Shadow of their destruction." She tilted her head as she looked into my face. "I believe they maybe right, Shadow. I would like to think the future you see most clearly will be the future. What do you wish me to do?"

"Be prepared to move. If the king attacks the army north of you, attack the army on your south side. If he splits to attack both armies on your flanks, support him as you see fit. Otherwise, I'll send word with a Zunji warrior to Bolan."

"Bolan will see you out. It will save you an hour sneaking around. Good luck, Shadow."

* * *

I arrived at Sizwe's camp several hours before sunrise. He and his son sat around a small fire as if they had been waiting for me. Sizwe looked up as I neared. I assumed one of his guards had alerted him of my approach.

"The warriors are ready, Shadow." Sizwe resumed staring into the fire.

I squatted next to the fire and warmed my hands. "Gero, split your warriors into two groups. Each group is to do the same thing. One will take the army to the south and one the army on the north. Do what you did to the mercenaries. Sneak in and kill as many as you can then run. They will follow on horseback. Can you stop riders on horseback?"

"Yes, horses' eyes sensitive to sand like humans." Gero smiled. I knew why the Zunji remained unchallenged: the Zunji were good fighters, the desert an unforgiving land, and horses were useless.

"After that we attack again?"

"No. After that you return on their horses and taunt them from afar."

"Make them nervous?"

"Yes, and to make them watch you."

"And we hit them again from behind." He laughed. "And again."

"No, they'd be ready next time. After your second raid, keep your distance. Keep fires lit. Ride where they can see you. Keep them awake."

"You bad person, Shadow. Come join Zunji." This time Sizwe laughed.

* * *

I sat in the Earth Wizards' guild house in the middle of a circle.

The Wizard Egica spoke first. "Shadow, you have Tarlon in turmoil. Three armies sit outside the city and no one knows why. Everyone assumes they will attack soon. The Fire Wizards huddle in their guild house afraid. They now realize it was you who killed the Fire Wizard in Adak, and soon everyone will know their weakness. I don't believe they will support the attackers or anyone else now. They will be trying to overcome their vulnerability." Her chair slowly grew vines with delicate pink and purple flowers, giving off a fragrant aroma. "The Wind Wizards also hide for the same reason. You have neutralized both and made the Water Wizards question their vulnerability.

Only we are committed. We walk in your shadow, Shadow."

I felt stunned.

They walk in my shadow?

It felt wrong. If they walked in anyone's shadow, it was not mine. I had never longed for glory. I had never wanted to be anything but a Shadow Sister. Today more than ever, I longed just to be a Spy, whereas I was an out-of-control Assassin.

"Please, walk in your brothers' shadows, not mine. Mine's filled with blood."

"What would you want from us in the upcoming contest?" a tall thin man asked. He leaned back against a tree that seemed part of him. The ground rumbled as he spoke. I felt some mutual agreement with the question.

"Support the Araby army and the Zunji like you've supported me the past few days. I leave it to your judgment." That seemed to satisfy everyone. I couldn't be more specific because I couldn't predict everyone's actions. There were too many players and too many agendas.

"We hear the leader of the Tuska and Calion armies will seek an audience with the king tomorrow. The war is but a few days away."

I decided I needed an audience with the king.

CHAPTER TWENTY-EIGHT

Tarlon—Dazel Province

If I wanted to determine if any Sisters were in Tarion and, if so, who, my only option was to visit our Intermediate's house. She made candles for extra money, so I decided to enter dressed in a drab skirt and blouse like any other customer. Although it was still too early to be open for business, the front door of her house was ajar. I pushed it the rest of the way open. A woman lay sprawled on the floor, clothes torn and face bloody. Another woman stood next to her with a throwing knife in her hand. Although she was dressed in street clothes, I knew she was a Sister: the balanced stance, position of the knife, her deadly focus. Ignoring her and her knife, I closed the door.

"What happened?"

"Who are you, girl?" she asked, still poised to throw the knife. I said nothing. Instead, I held out my hand.

"I believe we met in Scio."

She paused for several seconds before she stepped forward and took my hand. Emotions flashed through her eyes: surprise, disbelief, and confusion.

"This poor woman and her customer were attacked. I found them both on the floor. She will live, but I am afraid her customer was killed. I've put her in the back room."

I helped her carry the Intermediate into her small bedroom and put her to bed. Only her nose appeared to be broken. Fayza reset it and together we bandaged the cuts. It would take her a couple of weeks

276

to heal, but she would recover. I closed the door on the way out.

"Who?" I asked.

"Assassins, looking for you...Shadows."

I detected no accusation, although she had a right.

"They must answer for the one they killed, who meant them no harm." I began changing into my blacks. Fayza looked at me like I was crazy, shrugged, and changed into her blacks.

"What now, Sister?"

"We'll need two bows, quivers, and a couple of bottles of alcohol."

Fayza frowned as we exited the house and began walking in the center of the street.

"Is this wise?" She looked around at the people staring. Many backed up against the buildings as we passed. They weren't used to Shadows out in public and especially not in daylight.

"I want everyone to know Shadows were responsible." Before Fayza could ask more, I stopped at a tavern. When I threw the door open, the room became deadly silent. I walked into the back room, collected three bottles of whisky, and threw a tora at the owner on the way out. We continued down the street. Several hundred paces later, Fayza pointed to a small shop displaying a variety of weapons. The owner stepped back against the wall when we walked in. He watched in shock while I collected two good bows and quivers full of arrows. I threw two toras on his table, at least a tora more than they were worth.

Our goal was on the other side of a densely wooded area. We ghosted through the trees to a small knoll overlooking a slum. Fayza pointed to a house on the end, which stood well separated from the others. The building looked old and worn like the others, but on closer inspection, the doors and shutters were strong and barred.

"What now?"

"When you see me coming around the building, shoot a fire arrow where I'm splashing this." I held up a bottle of brandy. "From here, you can see two sides of the building. Kill everyone leaving." I strode away before she could answer and made my way to an alley across the street from the house.

I stopped for a minute to lace the tips of my arrowheads with rocktail. Although I was good with a bow, I couldn't rely on hitting a moving target with a killing shot each time. Fayza could.

When I finished, I uncorked the bottles of brandy and began running around the building splashing it against the walls, doors, and windows. When I passed Fayza's corner, a flaming arrow arched into the air. By the time I reached the alley, the crackling fingers of fire had crawled around both sides of the building looking like snakes, met, and crept up the walls. I had just nocked my arrow when two men threw open the front door. I hit both. Another peered out and ducked back inside.

The door was engulfed in flames; choking smoke boiled out. After that, I had no thoughts but the moment, as arrow after arrow left my bow. The fire roared and crackled. My eyes watered, and I hacked between shots.

"Fire!" someone screamed. People came running out of their houses with buckets of water. They didn't try to put out the fire in the assassins' building but dashed the water over their own hovels. Children beat out sparks where they landed.

I left my bow and few remaining arrows and walked back to Fayza. She sat there frozen. At least ten bodies lay close to the building, several smoldering.

"I know why they are afraid of you," she said, choking on bile. "I could never have imagined..." She lapsed into silence, tears running down her face. I held her head and kissed each eye.

"I'm sorry I needed your help, Sister." The killing didn't matter to me anymore. I was dead inside. Everyone must know the consequence of killing Shadows. They needed a lesson no one would forget and to know the Shadows did it. I just hoped my dead Sisters would understand and allow me to join them in the shadows.

I left Fayza and made my way back to the Earth Wizards' lodge. A young Wizard held the door open for me. The Earth Wizards sat in their hall as if they had been waiting.

"Welcome. We understand you had an argument with the assassins' guild, and they lost," an old Wizard said. His hair was gray, and his face showed the wrinkles of age, but he looked to be trim and fit.

"Yes, my brothers. I'm already dead, so it seemed appropriate that I be the one to tell Hesland that it's not acceptable to hunt and kill Shadows like wild boar."

"I think your little demonstration will be noticed across Hesland. Since you've come to see us, I assume you've something you would like help with. Hopefully, we won't have to destroy the armies as another example of the Shadows' unhappiness with wars." The earth beneath me vibrated with what might be laughter.

"No, my brothers. Killing seems to be my destiny. I don't want to put that burden onto anyone else."

Although I've scarred Fayza for life with my obsession with death.

"I wish your help scaling the castle wall."
Again, the ground-laughter rumbled.

"Done, Shadow. One of us will help you. We hope you'll leave a few alive."

It was a joke, but I could no longer laugh at the thought of killing.

* * *

That night, the old Wizard, Wallia, and I lay on the bank of a moat, staring at the castle and its wall. Even in the daylight, it presented an impressive sight; at night it was overwhelming. I could just ask for entrance but identifying myself might have unintended consequences. I didn't want to spook my enemies into a knee-jerk reaction that could subvert my ability to stop them. I wanted them to use logic, not intuition. Logic would give me an advantage. The question was how to gain entrance without knocking at the front gate. There would be at least fifty castle guards between the king and me. Only the presence of the Earth Wizard made it possible.

I must have been tired because I was thinking logically. I wanted my enemies to think logically, not me. I sent Anil and Kasi out to explore the walls, barracks, grounds, and the main castle. I couldn't gain entrance from the ground level in less than a season, so it had to be from the top. Logically, no one would do that. An hour later, I found the weakness in the guards' security and the most advantageous place to make my climb.

A thin moonbeam peeked occasionally through the thick clouds as Wallia grew a thick vine up the rampart wall for me to climb. He could have grown vines up any of the castle buildings, but it would have been too noticeable to the sentries when they made their rounds.

When Kasi showed the guard furthest from my position, I climbed the vine and dropped onto the walkway. Quietly, I worked my way to the ground level and knelt in the deep shadows of the castle wall. The sentry wouldn't be looking at the castle but rather the grounds and outer wall. I began my climb. Fortunately, this wall was part of the original castle and the stones jagged rather than smooth like the newer buildings, which had been added over the cycles. I used rope and hooks, which allowed me to climb faster and reduced the risk of slipping. Even so, it took two hours to climb the eight stories to the roof. By the time I crawled over the edge, my fingers were raw and my shoulders screaming. Four two-story-high turrets jutted from the edge of the roof. I heard the mutter of guards' voices, but they couldn't see the castle walls without hanging over the side. Their job was to watch beyond the walls.

I lay on the roof in the shadows resting and waiting for the change of the guard. An hour later, twelve guards marched onto the roof. I waited in the shadows while they relieved the guards on duty and followed in their wake as they exited through a side door. It led down to the ground floor and out to the barracks. Ironically, the stairs were unguarded except, I imagined, at the entrance to the stairs at the bottom. I stopped at the third floor, where I sent Kasi out and watched her circle the hallway. It was late, and the hallways were empty except for two guards, who checked each door as they walked. Those probably led to offices that were off limits at night.

I ghosted along the hallway until I found a door leading to a small balcony overlooking the reception hall. As no stairs led to the balcony, it appeared to be a gallery for archers in case of trouble. I climbed over the rail and dropped to the floor.

The hall was a gigantic room with a vaulted ceiling that rose over four stories and floor space for a couple of hundred people. A golden chair sat on a

raised platform covered in a rug with the king's crest—
a blue background with five crossed swords on a gold
shield. The platform was large enough to hold ten,
enough space for the king's personal guards, his minister, and one or two advisors. A red carpet ran down the
four stairs twenty paces into the room. The walls had
the five flags, one for each of the provinces, and rugs
with scenes of the history of Hesland. Five columns
carved with ancient gods on each side supported two
balconies for royalty's use during special events. There
were no chairs.

The only light came from the twin moons of
Sycorax and Setebos. A side door gave the king a private entry to the platform. I sat down off to the side of
the throne in the shadows and waited frozen in the moment. Normal life didn't exist there: no emotions,
plans, or wishes, yet everything was crystal clear. I
smelled, heard, and saw everything. I sat relaxed but
ready to strike.

The dim light turned bright as the sun rose. As
the morning wore on, people passed, talking in the
hallway. An hour later, the side door opened, and the
king walked in accompanied by his minister, a captain
and two guards by his side and four trailing.

The king had just sat down when the captain
shouted, "Assassin." All six guards drew their swords.
Two rushed to stand in front of the king. The other
four advanced toward me, swords raised.

"If he moves, kill him," the captain shouted
from the platform.

"Stop!" The king said, pushing the two guards
in front of him aside, and stepped forward.

"Your majesty, please stand back until we dis-
arm him." The captain tried to step in front of him.

"Captain, have your men step back and stand
down. I have become fond of you. I'd hate to see you

killed." The king stepped back and sat, leaning on one arm of the throne.

"But your majesty."

"Captain, how many men do you have on guard?"

"Forty."

"Yet she sits in my reception hall. Don't you think she could've killed me if she wished?"

"She? Yes, your majesty," the captain conceded reluctantly. The king turned back to me.

"I would imagine that you're the infamous Shadow of Death. To what do I owe the pleasure of your company? You could have entered by the front door. My guards would never refuse a Shadow entrance."

"I didn't care to be seen until we'd talked."

"Someday, you should tell my captain how you entered the castle unseen. Although I've the utmost faith in him to protect me, it has to be embarrassing to have you sitting here unnoticed."

The captain didn't look happy.

"Shortly, two province rulers are going to play you for a fool –"

His minister stepped forward and pointed a finger at me.

"His Majesty is no fool –" The king waved him to silence.

"I'm sure the Shadow meant no disrespect. How, Shadow?" He leaned forward.

"You've three armies at your gates. They will tell you that Araby came here to overthrow you. They have hastily put two armies together and have come ready to support you, but they don't have the strength to defeat the army of Araby. They will beg that you attack while they attack from the flanks.

"In truth, Araby has been coerced into coming here for fear of an attack and will support you if given a chance. If you attack her, Lady wu'Lichak will have to defend her soldiers. Calion and Tuska will wait until you and the Araby armies heave weakened each other and attack you both."

The minister leaned over the king's shoulder. "Your majesty, you can't risk your throne on the word of a Shadow. The Calion and Tuska rulers are outside. I'll let them in."

I shook my head.

"Wait, Tomas, I would hate for the Shadow to kill you. I don't think she's in a particularly good mood." He nodded to me to continue.

"Your majesty, can sixty hands of soldiers breach your castle?"

"You've a point, Shadow. It would be foolish for Araby or anyone to attack the castle, but if they could get me out in the open… What would you suggest?"

"You could stay risk free in your castle. In that event, I suspect Calion and Tuska would eventually overthrow Araby and Saxis. That would effectively give them Hesland. Or you could take out only forty hands of soldiers and attack the army on Araby's north or south. Araby will take the opposite side. In either case, you should arrest the two rulers; unfortunately, that is not possible. They owe my Sisters and me their lives."

"You can't believe her, your majesty," Tomas said.

"I'll hear what they have to say. Captain, bring in a few more of your men, although the Shadow is undoubtedly enough. Tomas, give the captain a minute then admit the province rulers plus the four lords accompanying them."

A few minutes later, twenty soldiers filed into the room and spread along the walls on each side, giving me plenty of space. Tomas opened the doors and in walked se'Dubben and zo'Stanko. When they reached the beginning of the red rug, se'Dubben bowed and spoke.

"Your majesty… What's a Shadow doing here?"

"Sitting. What can I do for you, First Lord se'Dubben?

"Araby's here to attack you…" se'Dubben went on to outline the same story I said he would, leaving out his and zo'Stanko's part.

One of the lords with se'Dubben was staring at me, his face pale, mouth twisted.

"That's interesting. The Shadow told me the same thing just a few minutes ago. Of course, she added a few details you seem to have left out."

The lord, who had been staring at me, drew his sword and charged me. "Liar! Murderer!"

The security guards were slow to react. They had just drawn their swords when I had a knife in the air. The lord hit the white-granite floor with blood pooling where my blade stuck in his throat.

"The Shadow seems to disagree with the young foolish lord. She has suggested I remain in the castle and let you return home. Araby cannot breach the castle, so she will have to leave. That way no one gets killed."

"Sooner or later she will return with more soldiers." Se'Dubben's voice rose in anger. "The Shadow is obviously in league with Araby. We will attack Araby, your majesty, even though it'll destroy our armies. We came here to support you."

"Se'Dubben is right. I'm in league with Araby because she supports the king."

Se'Dubben ignored me.

"We've one hundred hands of soldiers; wu'Lichak has only sixty. If you will give us some support, we can destroy her," zo'Stanko said.

"Your majesty, there is a Zunji asking to see the Shadow," Tomas said after a whispered exchange at the door.

"Let him in, Tomas."

The Zunji knelt and bowed his head for a second, then ran over to me.

"Shadow, the north side is down by twenty hands and the south by twenty-five. The warriors in the north weren't as sneaky as those in the south. They need more training," he whispered with a big grin.

"Gero, the son of the Zunji chief Sizwe, informs me your count is a little off, Lord zo'Stanko. He puts your total strength at fifty-five hands. In addition, most of those will desert as soon as the Zunji give them permission to leave. I'm sure Araby and the Zunji could crush what would be left of your armies."

"Your majesty, the Shadow conspires with Araby to overthrow you!" zo'Stanko shouted.

"I've the solution. I will send out forty hands, twenty to the south and twenty to the north, to collect the weapons from your armies. If Araby attacks them, we will join with you to defeat them. If not…"

"If your majesty doesn't want our support, we'll leave."

I smiled. "Your armies may leave with his Majesty's permission, but for your killing of Shadows, you owe us your lives. I'm here to collect."

The remaining three lords stepped in front of se'Dubben and zo'Stanko. Two ran at me, swords raised as they came. This time the guards were faster. One hacked into one fool's belly. The other's sword clattered to the floor as he threw himself to his knees.

I threw a knife. It struck se'Dubben in the neck. I flicked a second at zo'Stanko. The room stank of blood. I sat back down facing the king.

"See, Captain. I told Tomas the Shadow wasn't in a good mood." He turned back to me. "What if I have you killed, Shadow, for killing two of my First Lords?"

"I'd die."

"That doesn't scare you?"

"No. Dying is easy. It's living that's difficult. It would be an act of mercy." I was so tired. As I talked, the soldiers had drawn their swords and circled the king.

"Put those away. The question was rhetorical. You have prevented a war and possibly saved my life and kingdom from chaos. How can I repay you— money to you or the Shadows?"

"I say for the Shadow Sisters you owe us nothing. I've taken payment. However, many risked their lives and all that they cherish to avoid this war and support your rule. I would ask a boon for them."

"Ask and I shall see."

"Declare the gypsies under your protection and let them each entertain you when they are in Tarlon." The king nodded.

"Declare the Earth Wizards the King's Wizards. They have been united in every province behind peace and your rule and supported me." He nodded again.

"Recognize the Zunji as a people and make the desert they inhabit a province with Sizwe the new First Lord." He hesitated, frowned, but eventually nodded.

"Araby has and will continue to support you. I doubt she wants anything more than to return home to her people. I'll leave it to you to decide what loyalty is worth."

"Tomas, prepare those declarations. Captain, the Shadow looks tired. Escort her wherever she wishes to go, and I think those men are ready to leave." He pointed to the dead bodies. "The other two to the dungeons until I can determine their part in this." He turned back to me.

"Shadow, you'll always be welcome here."

CHAPTER TWENTY-NINE

Tarlon—Dazel Province

Crossing the courtyard toward the gate, I would have like to lie down and never wake up again. The king didn't know how right he was. I was tired to my bones. I had avoided a war and lost myself in the process. I felt I had nowhere to go. Maybe the Zunji would take me in.

"Shadow, would you tell me how you got into the castle? The king's safety…"

"It's easy, Captain, I climbed to the roof and came down the stairs."

"You did what? You climbed to the roof?" He stopped to laugh. "Thank you, Shadow. I don't think I've much to worry about. Only a Shadow could do that. Anytime you want to see the king, ask for me and I'll save you the climb." He was still laughing as I walked through the castle gate. Out of habit, I stayed to the shadows, using Anil and Kasi to guide me to Sizwe's camp. Once in the desert, I made no attempt at secrecy. Sizwe sat at a small fire with his wives and sons waiting for me.

"Greetings, Shadow. Gero tells me I am to be a First Lord and that our land has become a province. I don't believe anyone could've taken this land away from the Zunji, but I thank you for gaining the Zunji respect as a people."

"You earned it for supporting the king." It had been amazing how they had devastated the two armies. Sizwe banged his leg and laughed along with everyone around the fire.

"We did it for you, Shadow. My warriors will sing of this fight and you for many generations. You've relieved the boredom and justified our training that some were beginning to question."

I spent the next sixday with the Zunji, resting and trying not to think, to remain in the present. Gero and his sons spent the days showing me the Zunji way of life. Except for the contrast in terrain, their life appeared not too different from that of the Shadows. The next day the gypsies arrived in Tarlon.

"I thank you for letting me rest here and for showing me your way of life. I must leave now. I've business to take care of." I felt a pang of sorrow leaving. I had enjoyed my time with them.

"You're welcome here any time, to visit or to stay. Maybe you could stop in now and then with another war." He almost looked serious.

I left at night because I only had my blacks and wanted to avoid notice. I made my way to the Earth Wizards' guild house and was ushered in immediately.

"Welcome, Shadow." They were all sitting in their audience room as if they had been expecting me, which they probably were. "We did little yet received much."

"Every little act helped avoid the war. You will now have an opportunity to do much, helping the king. I thank you for your help in fighting the other Wizards. Without you, I couldn't have won." I had had lots of help in living to see this day. I hoped the king's rewards helped pay for that help. I hoped Sister Morag wouldn't be too mad because I asked nothing for the Shadow Sisters. How could anyone pay for the death of a Sister? It would have been vulgar to ask. The deaths of se'Dubben and zo'Stanko seemed a just payment, although they hadn't acted alone.

I stayed until the next night. During the day, Wizard Egica gave me a tour of the guild house. It was an amazing collection of trees, plants, flowers, rocks, and water pulled right out of the earth—a garden in a building. The food—roots, berries, spices, and vegetables—tasted strange but was satisfying. I left at night and made my way to the gypsy camp.

I arrived late, hoping to collect my things and leave before anyone woke. Everyone seemed asleep as I slipped into my wagon quietly. When I closed the door, Stela lay curled up asleep on my bed. She had her arm around my traveling bag, so there was no way I was going to get it without waking her.

"Stela." I touched her arm and stepped back. She jerked awake with a knife in her hand, looking around until she saw me in the shadow.

"Daughter, you scared your mother to death. I knew you'd try to sneak away without saying goodbye. Where do you intend to go? Back to Ahasha?"

"No, mother, the Shadows won't want me there." Even if they did, I couldn't go back. "I didn't think you would want me to stay either now that your obligation to Mistress Morag was over. I might live with the Zunji for a while."

"My poor wild daughter. You're not thinking straight, and it's no wonder. You've been living in chaos for so long you've lost your way. I cannot speak for the Shadows, but I know all the Dorian clan loves you. Your clan and they would want you to stay."

"Not if they knew who I really was and what I've done."

"What? Save Alida and Ilka's lives, save our horses, and save us from losing everything we own, including our lives? The clan knows you risked your life for us. Nothing else matters to them. Stay with us for a while, at least until you can think straight again. Then decide what you want to do."

"I may never be able to think straight again."

"Then you'll stay with us all of your life. Sleep now. I'm going back to my wagon. This damn bag is uncomfortable to sleep with." She kissed me on both cheeks and left.

She was right, I couldn't think straight anymore. I was lost in the past. I loved my life with the clan and decided to stay for a while.

* * *

When I woke the next day, Alida, Ilka, and Yoan were sitting outside my wagon.

"You're back!" Alida and Ilka screamed at the same time, as they ran and wrapped their arms around me. "You did find a Shadow. She stopped the war, and the king has declared us under his protection, and we are going…" Ilka and Alida reiterated the events of the past sixdays while jumping up and down like kids at a party. "You're the craziest sister, and you do the stupidest things, but we love you anyway. Oh, Luka is arriving today."

Yoan gave me a hug. "It's good to have you back, safe and sound. You have got to stay. We must practice for the performance for the king in a sixday. I can't find anyone I can trust throwing knives at me."

Stela was right. This was my family, but the thought of facing Luka was terrifying.

* * *

I spent the morning telling a mixture of truths and lies about the past two sixdays. I said I had helped a little by scouting for her and got to watch what happened in the king's reception hall. I described everything as if I had been a bystander. In the afternoon, Yoan and I began practicing. It seemed like I had never been away.

292

That evening the Tobar clan arrived, and Luka jumped from his horse to run up to me.

"Ryana, you're here. I didn't see you in Scio. I thought you'd changed your mind." He touched my earring gently. "You're blood clan, that's wonderful. I hope that means you're going to marry me." His face lit with happiness. I dragged him away into the nearby trees.

"Luka, my love." I cupped his face with my hands. Tears scalded my eyes. "I can't marry you. I'm scarred beyond my ability to heal. I've no feeling left in me. I'd make a terrible wife and a worse mother."

"I don't understand. Scarred? How? You said, 'my love,' yet you say you can't or won't marry me. Is there someone else?" The questions poured out too quick to answer, and the answers were to complex for me to try. I no longer knew who I was or what I should do.

"If you knew, you wouldn't want me. I'm locked in the past and can't get out. I'm sorry, Luka." I turned and walked away, leaving him standing there. I didn't deserve him, and he wouldn't be happy with me. Tears slid down my cheeks as I climbed wearily into my wagon.

* * *

I woke, a rocktail stick in my hand and throwing knife in the other. The door was partially open, and a Shadow slid in, stopping just inside.

"Sister Ryana, I'm Sister Alina, if you remember."

"Are you here to kill me, Sister?" It seemed fair. I had abused Sister Morag's authority.

"Mistress said no one could kill you without your permission."

"You've my permission, Sister."

"Mistress wants to see you, tonight," Alina said with a sigh. I dressed quickly in blacks, probably for the last time. I would like to die a Shadow. We ghosted out of the camp past several people who were wandering around. Five minutes later, I stood in front of Sister Morag.

She put her hands on my shoulders.

"I'm sorry, Mistress. I've abused the authority you gave me. I killed without remorse or feeling. I killed without thought. I'm ashamed that I've soiled the Shadows' name." Tears shone in her eyes. I didn't understand.

"I've committed a grave sin that I hope our Sisters in the shadows will someday forgive, but I had no choice. I sent you off knowing you were too young, expecting you to die and knowing you would have to kill, although all you wanted to be was a Spy. You have done the impossible and stand before me broken because of what you had to do to achieve what I asked. Come home, Ryana."

"I can't. The Shadows wouldn't want me around. I'm out of control."

"Unfortunately, I think you're partially right. You would make some nervous, not because you are out of control but because you are too much in control. They would fear you. But you will remain a Shadow for so long as you live. You have given the Shadow untold glory by your actions, and your words were clearly mine. Although you cannot see it, the Shadows, gypsies, Zunji, Earth Wizards, and the king love you." She paused and took me in her arms. "Would you do something for me?"

"Yes, Senior Sister."

"You need to rest, but the Shadows need you. I've an idea that may achieve both. Travel with the gypsies. They love you and want you to stay." She touched my earring. "The senior Assassins/Spies and I want you to act in my name throughout the five…six provinces. You will have my authority to direct all the Shadows on assignment. They will contact you or you them through the Intermediates, who we are in the process of replacing. You will be available to give advice and direction when necessary. You've proven time and time again you've a sixth sense most of us lack."

"If you wish, Sister. All I've ever wanted was to be a Sister. I'll try."

"I can ask for nothing more. I give you permission to marry and to live your life separate from the Shadows."

"I don't think I would make a good wife. I'd have to tell the truth, and that would drive anyone away and expose my identity."

"Meet me back here tomorrow night, Sister Ryana."

* * *

I stood watching the Tobar clan practice. I shouldn't have, but I couldn't resist. I watched from afar as Sister Morag walked into the camp.

"I would like to speak to Luka."

Silence pervaded the area. She stood quietly, waiting. Luka reluctantly stepped forward, his face pale and set like a man going to his execution.

"I'm Luka."

"Good, come with me." She turned and walked away. I dressed and hurried to meet her as she had asked, curious as to what she wanted with Luka. Morag, Alina, and Luka sat quietly.

"Luka, what do you think of Ryana of the Dorian clan?" Morag asked as I sat down next to Alina. Luka stood there, mute for a moment, looking at each of us but mostly at Morag.

"I wanted to marry her, but she refused me. Said she was too scarred. I don't know what she meant, and she wouldn't say." He looked down at the ground. Morag took his chin in her hand and raised his head so that he looked directly at her.

"What I am going to tell you, you'll never repeat to anyone, ever. If you do, the Shadows will kill you. Do you understand?"

"Yes…Shadow."

"Ryana is a Shadow."

"What! I knew she was special. Is that why she won't marry me?" He gave a weak smile. "I thought she didn't love me."

"How much do you love her, Luka? She said she was scarred. The scarring is mental not physical, although I imagine she has her fair share of those, too. You'll have to have patience with her if you want her as a wife."

"I will. I haven't been able to think of anything else these past seasons."

"She is scarred because I sent her out to do the impossible, knowing if by some miracle she succeeded, she would suffer much. Ryana was never a killer. She wished only to be a Spy. But to free her Sisters, save those she loved, and evade the hundreds wanting her dead, she was forced to kill."

"She's the Shadow of Death?" Luka said in a whisper.

"Yes. Do understand now why she feels she wouldn't be a good wife?"

"Yes. I also understand she risked her life to save Alida and Ilka, stopped thieves from stealing the Dorians' horses, saved lives, and got us under the king's protection. She has done so much for us. No gypsy would care about the other things. If the Shadows are pleased with her, the rest doesn't matter."

296

"The Shadows are more than pleased. She's young but has taught us much. We are so pleased that we are asking her to direct the Shadows on assignment in the provinces. It will mean she may have to be gone some nights. Marrying her will be a great responsibility. That is why she said no, although she loves you."

"I'll go see her right now."

"No, I want you to wait a full day and think about what I've said before you talk to her. I do not want her hurt again. She has suffered enough for a lifetime."

"I will." He nodded. Morag waved him off. I stood there in tears. *I'll stay a Shadow, and they have given me permission to marry and have children. Even if Luka doesn't want me, I can stay with my second family.* I couldn't help but cry. *Maybe in time, I can leave the past where it belongs.*

* * *

The next day, Luka found me. He took me by the arm and walked me away from the wagons. I didn't know what to expect and willed myself to still my emotions, my wishes, and to exist only in the moment.

"Marry me, Ryana."

Made in the USA
Middletown, DE
22 March 2021